A Mortal Curiosity

Also by Ann Granger

A Mortal Curiosity

Ann Granger

 St. Martin's Minotaur   New York

A MORTAL CURIOSITY. Copyright © 2008 by Ann Granger. All rights reserved. Printed in the United States of America. For information, address St. Martin's Press, 175 Fifth Avenue, New York, N.Y. 10010.

www.minotaurbooks.com

Library of Congress Cataloging-in-Publication Data

Granger, Ann.
    A mortal curiosity / Ann Granger.—1st ed.
        p. cm.
    ISBN-13: 978-0-312-36352-9
    ISBN-10: 0-312-36352-4
    1. Teenage mothers—Fiction. 2. Maiden aunts—Fiction. 3. Rich people—Fiction. 4. England—Fiction. I. Title.

PR6057.R259 M67 2008
823'.914—dc22

                                                    2008011564

First published in Great Britain by Headline Publishing Group,
an Hachette Livre UK Publishing Group

First St. Martin's Minotaur Edition: August 2008

10 9 8 7 6 5 4 3 2 1

THANK YOU

to everyone who helped me with the research for this book; to
Alan Shotter for a description of the site and location of the
original Southampton Town railway station; to Graham Parkes
for information regarding the landing arrangements for the
Hythe (Hants) ferry before the building of the pier at Hythe;
and, as always, to fellow-writer Angela Arney who drove
me around the New Forest (and offered me her
ever-generous hospitality).

Thanks also to all those who regularly support me in my
labours: to my editor Clare Foss, my agent Carole Blake
and above all to my husband John.

Part One

Chapter One

Elizabeth Martin

THE MAN opposite in the first-class compartment wore a shiny black top hat draped from crown to brim in a large white silk handkerchief. It floated gracefully in the movement of the air and gave the impression his otherwise dignified form might levitate at any moment to disport itself above our heads, alongside the luggage racks.

The fancy made me hide a smile, because he was in all other ways a neat, even fastidious, figure. There were streaks of grey in his russet moustache and the luxuriant side-whiskers that followed his jaw line and joined forces beneath his chin in a forked beard. Still, I put his age at no more than forty-five or -six. His slim form was clad in a black frock coat; his linen – what could be seen of it – presented a snowy white contrast. His hands rested one upon the other on the carved ivory knob of a long malacca cane. The pose drew attention to his best quality braided kid gloves. The swell of my own skirts prevented my seeing his footwear but I was sure that, too, was immaculate. As for the hat, that had surely been an expensive purchase. Flying cinders from the engines entering and leaving Waterloo station might have damaged it. He'd prudently protected it with the silk scarf while on the concourse and had either forgotten to remove the covering, now we were underway, or still feared a flurry of hostile sparks might find its way into our compartment despite the tightly closed glazed windows.

Now then, Lizzie! That's enough of that! I chided myself as I realised I risked appearing rude in staring at him so critically. I hoped he hadn't noticed and hastily turned my gaze to the view outside, such as it was. We were rocking steadily out of the London and South Western Railway's Waterloo terminus and the sight was an unexciting one of soot-grimed buildings.

A sense of adventure was beginning to tingle through my veins together with just a little nervousness. The south coast of England was as unknown to me as London had been when I'd arrived there from the north, earlier that year, with my modest baggage. Now I was on the move again. Unpleasant and unforeseen events had cut short my stay in the capital. As things turned out, they'd also opened the door to new possibilities. Yet I might have been venturing into darkest Africa for all I knew of my present destination. It certainly didn't appear any less exotic in my imagination.

We rattled through Clapham and had reached the suburbs. Already the houses were smaller and clustered in brick terraces. Their carefully tended back gardens ran down to the railway embankment offering glimpses of modest domesticity. Linen flapped on lines and children's toys lay abandoned on lawns. Trees and open spaces suggested the countryside. The overpowering presence of commercial London with its thronged streets, dust, smoke and never-ending hubbub was fading.

I wasn't leaving it all without regret. One person in particular was very much in my mind.

'That young man of yours,' my Aunt Parry asked one day over the substantial midday meal she called a light luncheon. 'Is he intending to offer marriage?'

I'm not normally lost for a reply but this question, put without warning, left me floundering. Aunt Parry wasn't looking at me. Her eyes were fixed on her plate and she was apparently concentrating on one of her favourite occupations: eating. I watched as the spoon reached her mouth and her pouting lips parted. I thought how small her mouth was and how, with her snub nose and pink pouched cheeks, she resembled a middle-aged cherub. Auburn curls escaping from her lace cap enhanced it. Very auburn. I do believe, I thought, she's taken to using henna! Then my mind returned reluctantly to her question and how to answer it.

For the past three months I'd been officially 'walking out' with Ben Ross. In reality I saw very little of him. The truth was I had a rival and its name was police work. The criminal world took no holidays, I'd soon discovered. At all hours of the day and night, with a fine lack of consideration for the police officer and his private life, housebreakers relieved citizens of their valuables, fraudsters hatched their ingenious plots, while murder, that most ruthless of predators, prowled the alleys of the slums and slipped unseen into the dwellings of the better-off.

The continual foiling of any plans hatched by Ben and myself was embodied in the substantial form of Superintendent Dunn. He was a nice enough man, bluff and canny. But I'd quickly learned Dunn saw his junior officers as being at his beck and call, first, foremost and 'pretty well all the time', as I'd hotly declared to Ben.

So what on earth was I to reply to Aunt Parry? I could have told her that I thought Ben was probably working up to a proposal but, on the other hand, nothing specific had been said. What was more, if I would see as little of him as his wife as I was currently seeing of him as his 'young lady' I wasn't at all sure I wanted to be married to an inspector of the Metropolitan Police, plain clothes division.

My turmoil had been made worse by the note delivered only that morning by an impudently grinning urchin. In it, Ben begged my forgiveness and presented heartfelt apologies, but he would not be free to accompany me to the open-air concert in Hyde Park as planned that afternoon. When the outing had been decided upon Ben had assured me that, given the long hours he had been working and the not inconsiderable success of his efforts, it should be possible for him to claim a free Saturday afternoon. But no, again we were frustrated. I knew he was as disappointed as I was. But it didn't help, and the most annoying phrase in the whole carefully worded note, over which I knew poor Ben had sweated, was that in which he declared he was sure I 'would understand'.

Oh yes, I did understand very well. Superintendent Dunn had required Ben's services and the concert was pushed aside to make way probably for another gruesome murder.

So I replied at last to Aunt Parry's question with a brisk, 'I'm sure I have no idea.'

She looked up, startled. 'I am responsible for you, Elizabeth my dear!' she said as if to justify her curiosity.

She probably thought my brief frown meant I felt she was intruding on a delicate private matter. The question about Ben's intentions hadn't annoyed me but the declaration that she was 'responsible' for me did jar.

I wanted to tell her she wasn't responsible for me at all. She was only my aunt 'by marriage' being the widow of my late godfather, and currently my employer. I had been my widower father's housekeeper and general factotum until his death and looking after myself had always been very much my own responsibility. But it would not only have been imprudent of me to say any of this, it would also have been ungrateful. In her own way, she had been very kind to me. It was the fault of neither of us that we were quite incompatible.

When a child, if I had found myself faced with some difficult situation, I would run to the top of our ramshackle old house and hide in the attic until I had sorted things out in my own mind. I couldn't do that now. What I needed more than anything was to go away, be alone, and have time to consider my predicament undisturbed. Instead I spent most of my time (thanks to Superintendent Dunn) listening to Aunt Parry's chatter and playing whist with her and her friends.

'Dear Aunt Parry,' I said. 'I'm very grateful for all you've done for me. I know you worry about my future. I should of course be sorry to leave this house and the home here you've been so good as to give me, but I've been thinking that perhaps I should leave London altogether for a little while.'

'How about Hampshire?' asked Aunt Parry immediately.

I gaped, then pulled myself together. 'I don't know Hampshire. I've only ever been in my home town and here in London.'

'Oh, you'd like Hampshire,' said Aunt Parry confidently. 'Especially the area called the New Forest. It's very pretty and on the coast. You would benefit from the sea air.'

Was she proposing I take a holiday? I couldn't believe it. I was right to have my doubts. A holiday wasn't what Aunt Parry had in mind.

She pushed aside her dish of gooseberry fool – an action that told me how serious she was.

'I've been talking,' she said, 'to an old acquaintance of mine, Mr Charles Roche. Mr Roche was once in business with my poor Josiah; silks, you know. For a few years now he's added the import of tea from China to his interests. He owns, I understand, two fast clipper ships. Just fancy, from Canton to London in only nine weeks!'

Aunt Parry paused to smooth the fabric of her sleeve with her short podgy fingers. 'So clever of Charles,' she murmured, 'to combine silk and quality tea, two things no lady can do without.' She roused herself from whatever interesting byway this had led her into, and went on briskly, 'Now I've just learned that a little – private difficulty – has arisen in his family. It occurs to me you could be just the person to help out.'

I had to be intrigued. 'Yes?' I encouraged her.

Aunt Parry beamed approval. I wasn't going to be difficult.

'Well, dear, Mr Roche has a young married niece, Mrs Craven. She's called Lucy. Mrs Craven is not long since delivered of her first child but sadly the infant died after only two days.'

'I'm sorry to hear it,' I said sincerely.

'Her spirits have been very low ever since,' Aunt Parry went on. 'Her husband—' Here she paused and looked a little awkward.

'Mr Craven?' I suggested blandly.

Aunt Parry wasn't a fool. She blinked and said sharply, 'Quite so. Mr Craven is abroad on business. He and his young wife are by way of being cousins – once or twice removed, I fancy. At any rate, Mr Roche would like to see Mr Craven advance in the firm, and so he's sent him to China to learn about the tea trade.'

'Business is business, I suppose,' I said. 'But it seems very unkind to send the young man away when his wife is recovering from her lying-in and both of them in mourning for their child.'

'I gather he'd sailed before the child was born,' Aunt Parry admitted and held up her hand. 'The circumstances don't concern us, Elizabeth. The present situation is this: young Mrs Craven is living with Mr Roche's sisters, a pair of maiden ladies, at their home in Hampshire. I gather it's beautifully situated just where the New Forest looks out on the Solent. One may see right across to the Isle of Wight, where our dear Queen has that charming Osborne House.'

Aunt Parry paused to give a sigh. I thought it was in sympathy with Her Majesty in her widowhood. But I should have known Aunt Parry better.

'I often said to your godfather, "Mr Parry, you should buy a country retreat!" but he never did. "My dear," he would always reply, "here in Marylebone I am as near the countryside as I wish to be." He never liked to be far from his counting house.

'However, I was speaking of Shore House in the New Forest where the Roche ladies live. Although in an utterly delightful spot, it *is* quiet; there is no young company; the ladies are elderly and reclusive. As I said, Mrs Craven's spirits are very low. Charles Roche thinks having a female companion would cheer up his niece. It would also relieve his sisters of some of the burden of caring for her. He doesn't want someone *too* young, of course, and flibbertigibbet. He's seeking a person entering her more mature years but still considerably younger than his sisters. I thought of you at once.'

'I shan't be thirty until the end of the year,' I protested.

Aunt Parry made a brushing gesture to dismiss this trifling objection.

'You're a doctor's daughter, Elizabeth, and it seems to me that you're the very person to act as companion to Mrs Craven for a short period; until she improves. The situation would only be for a few months. After that you could return to London and this house – or perhaps to another place.'

It was clear which of these two options Aunt Parry preferred.

'I could look out for another situation for you while you're away,' she added, confirming it. 'Not, of course, that I have any desire to see you go, dear Elizabeth.'

Thus convention requires us to tell lies. I couldn't get out of this house fast enough and my employer was anxious to wave me goodbye. I told her I quite understood and let her make of that whatever she wanted.

I then fell silent thinking about it and Aunt Parry set about the rest of the gooseberry fool. She looked relieved at having got the matter off her chest.

I had to admit that, although there seemed to be a certain mystery about the whereabouts of Mr Craven, the suggestion had a lot to recommend it. My late father had treated many women in low spirits after a birth. I knew, without being a mother myself, that this wasn't uncommon, even with a squalling healthy infant. Poor young Lucy Craven had buried her baby. In supporting her, I would be doing something of worth and the short stay in Hampshire would give me time to review my future.

All that was very well – except in one respect: Ben Ross's likely reaction. But it wouldn't do to admit this to Aunt Parry. I also told myself that it would be silly to mention all this to Ben before I spoke to Mr Roche. After all, nothing might come of it.

'Perhaps I could meet Mr Charles Roche and discuss it,' I said.

'Of course, my dear. I anticipated you'd say that. Mr Roche would be pleased to see you at his house in Chelsea at eleven thirty on Monday morning.' She patted her chin with her napkin, picked up the little brass bell on the table and rang it. 'I think I could manage a little cheese. How about you, Elizabeth?'

★ ★ ★

I was very favourably impressed by Charles Roche. The Chelsea house, in an elegant terrace, was expensively furnished. The butler who opened the door gave the appearance of being in his sixties and I put his employer at about the same age. Charles Roche was a tall, large-framed man, a little stooped now. When younger, he must have topped six feet. He proved a gentleman 'of the old school': very polite and anxious that I should not be inconvenienced in any way. I would receive the same salary as I presently received from Aunt Parry. Living in the country, I wouldn't have the same expenses as in London. The Roche ladies didn't entertain, not only because of the current situation but because they preferred a quiet life. This meant I would be quite considerably better off. Mr Roche would provide a first-class railway ticket to Southampton. (Luxury indeed!) Miss Christina Roche, the elder of the sisters, would write to me before I left with instructions for my onward journey from there.

Mr Roche's concern for his young niece seemed so genuine, his worry as to how his sisters were coping with the difficult situation so frankly expressed, that before I knew it I'd agreed.

Aunt Parry was delighted. It only remained to break the news to Ben Ross.

'Have you taken leave of your senses, Lizzie? Who on earth is this Miss Roche at Shore House?'

Ben fired this salvo after I had, quite reasonably and gently, informed him of my intention.

'I don't think I have, Ben. I've given the matter considerable thought.'

I made my reply with as much dignity as I could muster. I'm the first to admit I'm inclined to be imprudent from time to time, especially in the matter of letting my tongue run ahead of my brain. But I've never been unable to make up my own mind.

Ben, standing before me with his hat in his hand, his face flushed and his mop of black hair rendered untidy by the hand he had just swept over it, positively glowered at me. We were in the room designated as the library in Aunt Parry's house. It certainly had some books in it but they were of the dry variety and nobody ever touched them.

'Josiah bought them at a house sale,' Aunt Parry let slip to me once. 'A job lot, as they call it.'

'Do you know, Lizzie?' Ben raised his hand to point at me, realised how rude it looked and hastily dropped his hand back by his side. 'Look here,' he went on with a poor attempt at calm, 'I'd have said you were the most sensible female of my acquaintance. You, if anyone, I should have thought had her head screwed on the right way. But you propose to go off to Hampshire, where you've never been in your life, and take up a post as companion to someone you never heard of until a week ago.'

His voice and manner were becoming agitated again and the tones of his native Derbyshire more marked. 'The whole thing sounds rum. Don't tell me I'm a policeman and have a suspicious mind. Well, yes, if you like, I *am* a policeman and I *do* have a suspicious mind and not without foundation. There is something decidedly fishy about this business, Lizzie, mark my words, there!'

He made a theatrical sweep of his hat towards the portrait of my godfather Josiah above the fireplace.

'Ben,' I said loudly and firmly since there was no other way to break into his tirade, 'if you'll let me explain?'

'Go ahead.'

'Only please do let me finish and then I'll listen to whatever you want to say.'

A snort in reply.

'In the first place I only continue to live in this house because I'm Aunt Parry's companion; although we'd both like to put an end to the arrangement. You and I know perfectly well why. While I remain here, she can't forget the murder of my predecessor that you investigated. I can't forget it, either.'

I drew a deep breath. 'Josiah Parry was my godfather and she can't put me out on the doorstep, bag and baggage, but she has gone to some trouble to find an alternative situation for me. I know that's the way of it. She doesn't care twopence for the Roche family or young Mrs Craven. But she does want me gone. I can only accept the arrangements she's taken such pains to set up.'

'Humph!' was the muttered response to this.

'The proposed situation is only for six months until Mrs Craven has fully recovered her spirits or Mr Craven returns to Britain.'

'If he exists!' snapped Ben.

'The thought did occur to me,' I admitted. 'But now I've spoken with Mr Roche that doubt's laid to rest. Mr Roche is a very respectable old gentleman. He explained to me that he hopes that young Craven will eventually run the tea side of the Roche family interests. So that's why he was sent abroad; to see how the crop is grown and shipped. He's in China somewhere.'

'Certainly!' was the cold comment. 'Why not on the moon?'

'That's unworthy of you, Ben.'

His jaw had set obstinately. 'See here, Lizzie, I know you're upset because I haven't had much time for us, but I do hope you aren't taking yourself off to Hampshire in revenge for my neglect of you. I'm the first to admit it and I know—'

'I'm not flouncing off in a huff!' I interrupted. 'Please don't think that, Ben. I don't deny I find Superintendent Dunn's constant demand on your attention very annoying. I also know it's not your fault and that whatever future we might have together, it would of necessity include Superintendent Dunn.' I managed a wry smile. 'My father was a family doctor and never knew when he might be called out. I do understand the situation.'

There was a silence. Ben came to take the wing chair next to mine. He cleared his throat and his face turned alarmingly red.

'Lizzie,' he began, 'you must know that my hope—'

The seriousness of his expression and the beads of perspiration that had broken out on his brow filled me with panic.

I burst out, 'Please, Ben! Forgive me if I'm presuming too much, but if you're going to ask what I think, then I really can't give any kind of answer just now. I'm very sensible of the honour,' I went on, sounding as stilted as he had done, but knowing no other way out of it. 'It isn't that I'm not – that I wouldn't like . . .' At this point I faltered to a halt, my face, I was sure, even redder than Ben's.

'In that case—' he began eagerly, but I interrupted him again.

'So much has happened in the last few months my world's turned fairly topsy-turvy. Some mornings I've woken up wondering what on earth will happen next. I need time to put my thoughts in order. Please try and see that.'

'Of course,' Ben said, looking so contrite that I felt a monster. 'I should have realised this isn't the moment. Take all the time you want. But I'd find it easier to be patient if I felt you weren't refusing me outright. Not,' he added hastily, 'that I have any right to presume you'd accept. And you certainly don't have to run away from London. I won't pester you for an answer.'

This was worse than being accused of taking myself off in pique. I assured him earnestly I never for one second thought he'd behave in any other way than utterly correctly. This at first seemed to cheer him up and then to cast him down.

'I'm pleased to hear it, I'm sure,' he said gloomily.

'I will give you an answer, Ben, but not at this moment. I do feel a need to be away from London. It *will* only be a short while.'

Ben looked even glummer. 'I don't like it. I'm not being selfish, Lizzie. The whole story is like a cracked cup. It just doesn't ring true.'

'Oh, Ben,' I said and took his hand. 'You mustn't worry about me. I am perfectly capable.'

'Perfectly capable of getting yourself into a pickle!' said Ben. He clasped my hand between his palms and begged, 'I know that once you've taken something into your head nothing will shift it. But promise you'll write to me every day, Lizzie, and tell me everything. All of it, agreed? I don't want yards of description of the scenery. I want to know what is going on.'

So did I, and the only way I would find out was by going to Hampshire. I promised I would write regularly and not devote more than one paragraph per letter to the scenery.

I knew his concern for me was genuine. But the journey to Hampshire was necessary to me; of this I was sure.

'Not more than six months,' I repeated.

Fate plays curious tricks. Ben did all in his power to be free to accompany me to Waterloo Station and personally install me in a first class ladies only compartment. But as usual the criminal world had other ideas on how he should spend his time that morning. So, in the end, Simms the butler had accompanied me to the station while Ben attended to 'police matters.'

Our cab was held up partly by the bustle of traffic and partly by Simms disputing the fare. At the station we had difficulty in finding the platform because of the higgledy-piggledy way these were numbered. The station had been built piecemeal and platforms added as required without any attempt to make sense of it all. Simms and I were not the only ones scurrying back and forth in increasing frustration. When we did locate the train, all the places in the ladies only compartment were taken. That is why I travelled in the company of the man in the veiled hat and two other people: a clerical gentleman absorbed in some book of devotions and an elderly lady whose nimble fingers produced a steadily lengthening strip of tatted lace. It was as well no one else had wanted to enter, as my crinoline-supported skirts and those of the old lady took up any remaining space.

I settled on the comfortable banquette; thrust all the arguments of the past weeks from my mind and concentrated on the possibilities of the future. As a start I opened my purse and took out the letter giving the directions for reaching my final destination, Shore House. I had unfolded it and begun reading it through when the gentleman in the veiled top hat took off his headwear and set it, still draped, on his knees. He then leaned forward and gave a discreet cough designed to engage my attention.

'Forgive my addressing you when we've not been introduced,' he said. He had a cultivated, reassuring kind of voice. Joined to a sober yet sympathetic mien it made me think at once he must be either a doctor or a solicitor. Also, to judge by his wardrobe, one with a profitable practice! 'But do I have the honour of travelling with Miss Elizabeth Martin?'

Chapter Two

Elizabeth Martin

I MUST have looked astonished. I certainly felt it and sat with my mouth open until I rallied and said, 'You do. But I'd very much like to learn how you know it.'

'I should explain,' he said quickly. He indicated the letter in my hand. 'This may help.' He delved into the side pocket of his frock coat and produced a letter very similar to my own and apparently written in the same hand. 'Your letter, as mine,' he said, 'is from Miss Roche of Shore House. We're both travelling to the same destination. Miss Roche told me about you. I understand you're to take up a position as companion to Miss Roche's niece. But I can see from your expression that she didn't warn you about me. Please allow me to introduce myself. My name is Lefebre, Dr Marius Lefebre.'

'So you *are* a medical man!' I exclaimed unwisely and hastened to add, 'My own father was a doctor in our town.'

'Really?' Dr Lefebre raised his eyebrows.

'And the police surgeon,' I added.

'Was he now?' Dr Lefebre looked thoughtful for a moment. 'I'm glad to have met you before our arrival,' he went at last.

'Perhaps we'll have the opportunity to discuss one or two things before we get there. Though now is obviously not the moment.'

His glance took in the clergyman and the tatting lady.

I found his words slightly sinister. Discuss what? I could hardly demand he clarify his statement immediately. Perhaps I shouldn't be surprised he knew why I travelled to the New Forest. If Miss Roche had taken the trouble to tell him about me, she would have added the reason I was on my way. But why hadn't she told me about him? That was annoying but, on the other hand, perhaps not strange. A companion like myself held a nebulous status, a little above a governess but not 'family'. It was a curious in-between world. Miss Roche had simply not thought it necessary to inform me I'd not be the only person arriving to stay at Shore House. It was none of my business.

Lefebre stayed silent for quite five minutes. Then, just as I was allowing myself to relax, he spoke again.

'Have you made this journey before, Miss Martin? Do you know the county of Hampshire?' He kept his eyes fixed on the passing scenery as he spoke.

'Not in the least, Dr Lefebre. I'm originally from Derbyshire and have never been south of London.'

'I think you'll like it. The air's very mild and the climate agreeable. The rail terminus at Waterloo has helped considerably to make it easy for travellers at the London end. Well, once they get the platforms sorted out! But the original terminus at Nine Elms was very awkward. So far out! Waterloo has proved a bless-ing. But when we reach the other end of our journey, Southampton, I'm afraid we may find things are rather different. In her letter, Miss Roche has no doubt explained to you what she advises on arrival?'

'She wrote informing me of a difficulty with their carriage,' I said. 'It can't be sent to meet me, as hoped. But there's a ferry-boat, I understand. It crosses from the city's port to Hythe on the New Forest side of Southampton Water. On the far side some other form of transport will be waiting for me – perhaps I should say for us. Something to replace the carriage, at any rate. I don't know what. Or how long it will take us to reach Shore House.'

'Believe me, it will be long enough for us to be severely jarred on a country track in whatever kind of substitute vehicle they've chosen to send,' said Dr Lefebre with some asperity. He turned a surprisingly direct look on me. 'Derbyshire, eh? Then you're a long way from home.'

'Well,' I said a little awkwardly, 'my father died and I had to make other arrangements.'

He held up a kid-gloved hand. 'I didn't wish to sound imperti-nent, Miss Martin. I was only about to remark that nowadays, given the excellence of the railway system, we all of us travel about the country with an ease and at a speed our forebears could hardly have imagined possible. Take my own grandfather, for example. When he made his annual journey to Bath to take the waters, he set out in his own carriage and it took him three days to get there! Now, armed with a copy of *Bradshaw*, we're able to cover half the country in that time. It's true he made frequent stops along the way; to call on acquaintances, to dine, rest the horses and so on. Also he travelled slowly because he carried with him his own sheets, to be spared fleas in the bedding of country inns. He took along his own tableware because he didn't trust the washing up – ah, and a supply of good quality tea, together with a bottle of embrocation and a flask of single malt to ease the discomforts of travel inside and out. You're smiling, Miss Martin.'

His sharp gaze softened to something like a twinkle.

'I beg your pardon,' I said.

'Not at all. It was my intention. You're burdened with some anxiety, I fancy. I only wished to relieve it. I am, after all, a doctor. I'm supposed to make you feel better!'

This was said gravely but with the same twinkle in the eye.

It struck me that he might be passing a long journey with a mild flirtation. I think the lady with the tatting thought the same. She'd cast a few interested glances our way. The gentleman with the book of devotions had a mind above all that. But perhaps my companion only had an idiosyncratic sense of humour. I wasn't sure I liked either explanation.

I think he guessed what was in my mind. He smiled benignly and gave a courteous nod towards the lady in the corner, who began tatting so furiously the little shuttle fairly flew. Lefebre turned his gaze towards the window.

He's being revenged, I thought. *I was examining him fixedly as we left Waterloo and now he's paying me back. I do believe it amuses him.*

I'd apparently be spending some time under the same roof as my disconcerting travelling companion. I hoped his visit to Shore House would be brief. He must have consulting rooms in London to attend to – and wealthy patients.

Lizzie! I told myself sternly, as our train gathered speed. *You must mind your manners and watch your tongue!*

In my head I seemed to hear an echo of Ben Ross's disbelieving snort.

As we grew nearer our destination our train became very full. Many of the passengers boarding had a great deal of baggage. Dr Lefebre began to look thoughtful, tapping his fingers on the shiny silk surface of his hat. Eventually he turned his attention to me again.

'Southampton's a busy port, Miss Martin. Many of these people will be travelling to the Town terminus with the intention of transferring to the docks to board the packets. The crush will be intolerable. I suggest that you wait on the platform. I'll find us a porter and a cab to carry us to the Hythe ferry mooring.'

I thought this sounded a good idea. The doctor was proving a practical travel companion. He was certainly right in his prediction. At the Town station the jostling through was as dense and lively as at any London terminus. That many people intended to take ship here was shown by the piles of luggage of every description quickly heaped about us. Porters appeared and their services immediately secured. Lefebre called to me to 'Stay where you are, Miss Martin!' and disappeared into the crowd. I was pleased to see him re-emerge from the smoke, steam and hubbub with a sturdy porter in tow. We were led quickly through the mob and found ourselves outside the station where our porter had commandeered a cab for us. In no time we were rattling away.

'It will be a short journey!' Lefebre's exertions had left him rather out of breath. 'You'll see some of the old city walls but not, I'm afraid, the great Bar Gate. That's a pity. Perhaps you'll find an opportunity to visit the city before you leave Hampshire.'

'I'd like that,' I agreed.

Lefebre leaned towards me. I expected he would continue his role as guide, but he had another purpose. He cleared his throat and said, 'I'm glad of this opportunity of a private, if brief, word with you before we reach Shore House. I mean, concerning Mrs Craven.'

I wasn't quite sure I liked the tone of this. 'Mr Charles Roche, Mrs Craven's uncle who engaged me, told me that his niece has been in low spirits since her recent confinement,' I said carefully. 'That's why he felt she needed a companion. Her husband, as I understand it, is abroad.'

Dr Lefebre gave a slightly irritated wave of his hand. I suspected he was unaccustomed to being interrupted. 'Mrs Craven is suffering from melancholia. It follows the loss of her child only days after the birth.'

There was a moment's pause. I didn't want to invite a second flick of the fingers. But this time he appeared to be waiting for me to make some sort of comment, so I asked, 'Are you to treat her, doctor?'

He hesitated. 'No, no, I'm only going to take stock of the situation on behalf of Mr Roche. He's unable to travel to Hampshire at the moment. I've known Roche for some years.' He smiled briefly. 'We French exiles stick together.'

I must have looked puzzled because he added, 'Both our families are of Huguenot descent.'

I digested this piece of information and wondered if he was trying to prove to me he really was a close friend of the man who'd employed me. Why? So that I'd chat more freely?

He cleared his throat again in that way he had of attracting my attention.

'You should be aware that Mrs Craven's melancholy takes a particular form of delusion.'

He paused again for my comment but I was learning to evade this sort of gambit. He was a doctor but I wasn't his patient. I wasn't here to confide my thoughts and fears to him. Quite the reverse!

My silence obliged him to go on.

'She cannot accept her child's dead.'

I'd meant to keep my own counsel, but the baldness of this shocking statement made me exclaim aloud. It also sent a prickle of alarm racing up my spine. The tragedy was apparently greater than had been indicated to me. For the first time I began to wonder quite why I was being despatched to Shore House. Was I to be a friend and confidant of the young woman simply to support her; or was I supposed to persuade her of the sad reality of her child's death? That would be a difficult and delicate task to undertake and a stranger like myself wasn't the person for it. And what, exactly, was her state of mind? I put the last question bluntly to my companion.

He shook his head. 'I know no more than you. I've not met Mrs Craven. I only know, as you do, what I've been told.'

'I have no nursing experience,' I said firmly.

'None, as I understand it, is required of you,' was his bland reply. 'Ah, we're at the docks.'

This brief conversation did leave me uneasy but it was swept from my mind as we descended from our cab at the quayside. Behind us towered the ancient grey city walls with a shoreside promenade beneath them leading away inland. About us we saw signs of recent building, some extension of the dock area, and before us – the sea! Or, at least, that wide inlet called Southampton Water. The stiff breeze blowing into our faces carried a salt tang. Gulls wheeled and swooped above us, alert to drive down and seize any scrap of food dropped from the hands of those waiting on the quayside. The sunlight glittered on the dancing waves. Across them on the far side, in a blue haze, I could see what appeared to be a tree-clad shoreline and a jumble of whitewashed buildings, presumably the small town of Hythe. I felt as excited as one of the many small children who raced shrieking through the crowd ignoring the despairing cries of their parents.

And what a motley throng surrounded us! Were all these people hoping to board the ferry? Noah must have faced a similar problem with a seething mob of animals all to be fitted into the Ark. There were country people with weather-beaten faces, the women wearing cotton sunbonnets, all laden with baskets and bundles; workmen pushing handcarts of baggage and cargo in the form of mysterious boxes. Dogs of all breeds (and some a fine mixture) tagged the heels of the children and barked wild enthusiasm for the chase. Here and there were one or two soberly clad and worthy figures, one a clergyman. To complete the mix were porters, crewmen from the packet ships which lay at anchor and, in among them all, idlers with nothing to do but watch the scene, hands in pockets. Some were members of that ragamuffin population which frequents all busy spots in hopes of profiting from the naivety of strangers. We were obviously both town-dwellers and newcomers. Some interest in us was being shown already.

'Mind your pockets, sir!' advised our cabbie as Dr Lefebre paid him. 'There is the ferry, right before you, and there is Albert. Hey, there!' he roared suddenly. 'Albert! Here's gentry for you wanting to take the ferry!'

I had never in my life been taken for 'gentry' but I supposed Dr Lefebre's distinguished appearance and authoritative manner was the reason.

Through the crowd towards us came a gangling form that revealed itself as a young man with a much-tanned face and limbs. He wore a peaked cap of nautical style, a knitted garment which was too short for his sinewy bronzed forearms which dangled bare, canvas trousers and stout boots. His most distinguishing feature, however, was that he had only one good eye. The other appeared to have met with some dreadful accident. The eyeball was a pale smoky blue and rolled upwards into the socket in an alarming manner, but the remaining good eye twinkled with humour.

'Albert,' our cabman introduced this newcomer, 'is crew of the ferry. I'll leave you with him. Good journey to you sir, and madam!' With that he clambered back on the perch of his cab and clattered away.

'Tickets?' enquired Albert, evidently a man of few words.

'Where do I purchase them?' asked Dr Lefebre.

Albert pointed to a small wooden hut with a window in it behind which a stout female form dispensed tickets to a waiting queue.

'Perhaps if you wait here, Miss Martin—' began Dr Lefebre.

'No need!' interrupted Albert. 'I'll take your bags and see the lady aboard. Follow me, ma'am!'

As he spoke he had gathered up our baggage with great efficiency and somehow managed to dispose it all about his person. He set off in a loping stride and I hurried after him.

We reached the jetty. Now I could see the tide was out and the water level many feet below high-tide mark, as shown by the crust of seaweed on the dock wall. The ferryboat bobbed several feet beneath us, secured by ropes fore and aft to a slippery-looking stone platform, in the shadow of the jetty above. It was a small iron paddle steamer with a tall funnel. Standing aloft by the funnel with one hand resting on the wheel, and positioned directly opposite us because of the trick of the two levels, was a maritime figure. His skin was weathered by exposure to the elements to the likeness of teak. Our skipper, I assumed. He was watching with a benevolent eye the confusion above and the mob streaming towards him down a wooden ramp. Immediately below his platform, a roofed structure appeared to be a saloon for the shelter of more fortunate passengers. Others were busy disposing them-selves about the deck in a well-practised manner.

The supporting piers of the jetty revealed by the low tide were, like the dock wall, smothered in curtains of black seaweed dotted with barnacles. The smell here was much stronger and not pleasant. There was a strong suggestion of sewage from the sea slapping at the supports. Rubbish of all kinds floated on it and collected around the piers.

So many passengers had already boarded I began to be afraid there would not be room for us and hastened to follow the crowd. Our baggage, in any case, was already aboard. I could see Albert stacking it tidily on the foredeck, which currently faced into the seawall. The ramp bounced and shook and I grasped at a nearby railing to steady myself. Eager would-be passengers behind me thrust me forward again. Nor were things any better at the bottom. Here a narrow gangway bridged the gap between the stone platform at the base of the ramp and the lurching ferry. At the jetty end of the gangplank a small boy relieved passengers of their tickets. They then launched themselves across the divide to arrive, shrieking and giggling, higgledy-piggledy on deck. I grasped my skirts and took an athletic leap, landing unsteadily on the first ship of any kind I'd been on in my life.

'Sit here, ma'am,' advised Albert, grabbing my arm and pointing with his free hand to a wooden bench by our baggage. 'Saloon's full.'

I sat down quickly before someone else claimed our seat and looked back anxiously for my travelling companion. Dr Lefebre was making his way down the ramp. He held on to his top hat with one hand and in the other I could see the small white paper tickets. On his arrival at the gangplank he held the tickets out to the boy who was so impressed by this well-dressed passenger that he gaped at him for a full two seconds before snatching the tickets. Dr Lefebre arrived, slightly breathless but imperturbable as ever, and took a seat on the wooden bench beside me.

'Well, Miss Martin. I wonder what other adventures await us before we arrive at Shore House?'

A bell was rung. Albert dragged in the gangplank and closed the metal access panel. The engine roared; the funnel above belched a cloud of white; the paddles began to turn and thrash the water. We pulled away from shore – backwards.

Almost at once, however, we began to describe a semicircle until we faced in the right direction, with the New Forest shore on the far side ahead of us. The doctor and I faced into the breeze and sun. I considered unstrapping my umbrella from my portmanteau to serve as parasol. But with so many people so close at hand, opening it would hardly have been possible.

The paddles made a tremendous racket, drowning out any conversation. The wind was stronger now as we moved out into the middle of the channel. Dr Lefebre produced his white silk handkerchief again and, folding it into a bandage shape, tied it over his top hat and under his chin. On any other it would have look ridiculous. On him, it simply looked practical. Or so it seemed to me. But others saw it differently. Opposite us two countrywomen were watching him with something akin to horror. One of them leant towards her friend and, following the line of her own plump chin with a forefinger, mouthed the words 'jaw tied up like a corpse!'

It took some half an hour to get us across and I thoroughly enjoyed my first sea voyage. The channel was busy with small craft. The larger ones, the passenger and mail packets and trade clippers, lay at anchor awaiting high tide. I was sorry when the paddles slowed, another bell rang and we began to drift towards our mooring. I was even sorrier when I saw what form it took.

At least, on the Southampton side, there had been a jetty. On the Hythe side I saw only a long gravel spit or hard reaching out across the pungent-smelling mud left by the retreating tide and the shallows, until it reached the channel deep enough to allow the draught of our vessel. On it stood another nautical figure waiting for us. There was nothing for it; we must clamber down somehow on to the uncertain surface and make our way to *terra firma*, laden with our bags. It looked hazardous and I must have let my dismay be seen, because an elderly red-faced countryman standing by me attempted to cheer me up.

'Tisn't so bad, ma'am. I never saw anyone fall off but twice, and one of them was full of liquor. See here, my boy will help you with your bags. Obadiah, take the lady's portmanteau!'

'We're obliged to you,' said Dr Lefebre.

Our informant leaned forward confidentially. 'We needs an act of parliament, sir.' He pronounced all the syllables: *parl-i-a-ment*.

Even Lefebre looked taken aback. 'Indeed?'

'Yes, sir, for us to have a proper pier like they have on the Southampton side. Then the ferry could tie up neat and tidy and we wouldn't need the hard. But although we've been asking for one for years, we must have an act of parliament to allow it. But they have promised we shall have it when the gentlemen in parliament's got time enough to think about us. We live in hopes, sir.'

Our skipper manoeuvred our doughty little vessel alongside the gravel hard. Albert appeared and wrestled out the gangplank, pushing it through the opened gate to be seized by the man on the hard and wedged into the gravel. The first experienced passengers were already scrambling down it. We followed and somehow got down on to the hard, one by one, bundled down the gangplank by

Albert into the arms of the man ashore. He caught us, steadied us and gave us a firm push in the direction of land. I grasped my fluttering skirts in both hands. Wet gravel crunched beneath my feet. Ahead of me tottered a stout woman carrying a wicker basket and behind me came Dr Lefebre uttering encouragement. In this way I stumbled inelegantly across the hard and with relief finally set foot on the stone quay.

Travellers from the Forest side to Southampton had been waiting their turn there. As soon as the hard was clear of incoming traffic, they began busily streaming down it with the intention of boarding our vessel. Soon she would steam away and become a dwindling black smudge until lost to sight. It suddenly struck me that although people of all sorts surrounded me, I'd been landed like poor Robinson Crusoe on an alien shore. I knew no one here, other than my curious travelling companion.

Our bags were deposited and Dr Lefebre presented Obadiah with sixpence. His father protested it wasn't necessary, but Obadiah had other ideas, seized the coin and made off with it.

Dr Lefebre untied the silk bandage from his hat, folded it neatly and tucked it away in his pocket.

'You are in good spirits, Miss Martin?'

'Oh, yes!' I replied breathlessly. I thrust aside my momentary qualms.

'Well done. Now then, where is our onward conveyance?'

There was to be no going back.

Chapter Three

Inspector Benjamin Ross

OF COURSE I wanted to conduct Lizzie south of the river to Waterloo station myself. I hoped that a last-minute appeal made there, with the reality of the hissing steam engines before her, might change her mind about going into Hampshire. Although, as I well know, once Lizzie's mind is made up, it would take something really extraordinary to shift it.

As things were, just about the time her train would be pulling out, I was sitting not far from another great London rail terminus, in King's Cross police station, face to face with an unprepossessing individual by the name of Jonas Watkins. He was a pasty-faced fellow with puffed eyes and a mean little mouth. He was dressed flashily in a suit of loud hound's-tooth check. I thought he was ill advised to draw attention to his spindly frame. He obviously thought otherwise. Despite lacking all charm, as far as I could see, he was a vain little peacock, repeatedly patting the top of his head where his thinning hair was plastered down with some pungent hair ointment.

'All right,' I said to him, 'don't waste my time. I can tell you that I'm not in a very good mood today and you'd be unwise to try it.'

'I'm sure I don't want to waste anyone's time,' said Mr Watkins. 'I don't want to waste my own, come to that. What am I doing here? That's what I want to know.'

What am *I* doing here? I thought with an inner groan. I ought be at Waterloo, dragging Lizzie out of that train compartment if need be.

I dallied briefly with the image presented and set it aside as impractical. Lizzie would be more than capable of putting up spirited resistance to being manhandled and I'd probably end up being arrested myself.

Why on earth must she set off for a place she knew nothing of, and people of whom she knew only what she'd heard from – to my mind – very unreliable sources? At least, when she originally left Derbyshire for London, it was for the home of a relative of sorts. She knew who Mrs Parry was. Even that turned out badly.

'Well?' demanded Watkins truculently, taking my momentary inattention for an inability to answer his question.

'You are here,' I told him, 'because of a complaint made to the police by a young woman by the name of Mary Harris. She says she left her at that time sixteen-month-old child in the care of you and your wife.'

'I don't know any Mary Harris,' he returned promptly. 'I told one of your fellows this already. He came to my house asking. Mrs Watkins was very upset. We're respectable. We can't have uniformed constables knocking on the door. Neighbours talk. I know a Mary Fletcher, mind you. She runs the King's Head pub. She ain't got no eighteen-month-old child. She's sixty if she's a day.'

'Jonas,' I said to him gently. 'I'm a busy man with no time to listen to nonsense.'

He looked alarmed at the quiet tone. He'd have preferred I shouted at him. He was ready for that.

'I don't know her,' he repeated sullenly.

'Very well, let me refresh your memory. Mary Harris is in service. She's a parlourmaid. Eighteen months ago, when she was employed as such in Chelsea, she gave birth to a male infant out of wedlock.'

'There you are, then,' said Watkins virtuously. 'You don't want to go believing anything she'll tell you.'

'But I do believe her. Despite being abandoned by the child's father, Miss Harris was devoted to her baby and, as she couldn't care for him herself, at first left him with her elderly mother in Kentish Town. Unfortunately, her mother passed away not long after that. Mary had no one else to leave her child with and was unwilling to put him into an orphanage. Then she heard about you and your wife. She was told you ran a business caring for infants who couldn't be cared for by their own parents. A baby farm, in other words.'

'Oh, well, we do that,' Watkins agreed. 'It's a lawful, respectable business and what you might call a public-spirited one. We help those in need, Mrs Watkins and I.'

'So,' I went on ruthlessly, 'that unfortunate young woman paid you out of her meagre wages to take care of her child. Unfortunately, she fell sick. She lost her place. She had to live on what little savings she had. She couldn't pay you the weekly fee for the care of her son and she came to tell you so and ask you to be patient. As soon as she found another place, she'd resume payment and make good the default.'

Watkins sighed. 'I've heard that story before. Not from Mary Harris, or whatever she may be called, because I don't know any Mary Harris. But I've heard it from others. First off, they swear they'll pay regular. But after a bit, it gets an inconvenience. So they disappear. Don't visit no more. Don't pay Mrs Watkins and me. We ain't a charity. We gotta live and feed all them other kids.'

'So,' I asked him, 'what do you do in such cases?'

'Take the child to the workhouse,' he said promptly.

'But you didn't take Mary Harris's child to the workhouse, did you?'

'Because I – we – never had him!' cried Watkins triumphantly, jabbing his bony forefinger at me.

'But Mary Harris *did* turn up again at your front door. She hadn't been able to find a place in London for quite some time and had to work in a country household. Eventually she did find a place back in London and the first opportunity she had, she set off to see her child and pay you what she owed. You told her you'd taken her child to the workhouse. She went to the workhouse in question and they knew nothing of your handing over a child during the period in which it was supposed to have happened.'

'Then they've lost him,' snapped Watkins. 'They've got more kids than they know what to do with and they can't keep track of them all. That's what's happened, they've lost him!'

'So now you are saying you did take him there? I thought you had never seen Mary Harris or her child? That's what you told me just now. Sergeant Morris here is witness to it.'

'That's right,' said Morris lugubriously from the corner.

'No, no, no, Inspector!' Watkins leaned across the table and addressed me in wheedling tones. 'You've got it all wrong! When I told you I took the children left on our hands to the workhouse, that was just telling you what we do in such cases. I didn't mean you to understand I was saying we took Peter there.'

'Oh? You know his name?'

'You told me it!' said Watkins immediately.

'No, I didn't. Sergeant?'

'No, sir,' said Morris. 'I've been sitting here writing it all down, like you told me to. Every word spoke is here in my notebook!' He brandished it.

Watkins glowered at it.

'Mary Harris went to the nearest police station to your house which happened to be here in King's Cross,' I went on. 'She told her story. She was believed. An officer went to your house and when you denied all knowledge of the young woman, he got suspicious at your manner. It was passed to Scotland Yard as a possible murder case.'

'Murder!' shrieked Watkins, leaping to his feet and flailing his arms in panic. 'I never killed the brat!'

Morris rose majestically and placed a hand on the wretched Jonas's shoulder. 'Sit down, Mr Watkins, why don't you?' he invited.

Watkins glanced at him and decided to comply. 'I never killed him,' he said sullenly.

'You don't deny he was in your care?'

'Well, all right, he was. But the girl, the mother, she took off somewhere out of London and we didn't expect to see her again. It's not the first time it's happened to us. People take advantage of our good nature,' snivelled Watkins. He wiped away a tear which might have been play-acting or, given he had seen an awful vision of the hangman's noose, might be genuine.

'You didn't take the child to the workhouse, though, did you?'

'No,' he admitted. 'I would've done but they'd been kicking up, been difficult, on the last few times I'd gone there. I thought it better if I stayed clear of them for a bit.'

'So what did you do with him?'

Watkins drew a deep breath. 'I took him to King's Cross station here and left him on a platform. He was as happy as anything looking at the engines. I just let go of his hand and slipped away in the crowd.'

Morris gave a half-repressed growl.

Watkins glanced nervously over his shoulder at the sergeant. 'I knew he'd be found. That's Gawd's truth. I knew he'd be found. I never did the little chap no harm, I swear. You've got to believe me!'

'No harm? What of his terror and bewilderment? What of whose hands he might have fallen into? What awful accident might have happened to him as he wandered unattended among the engines?' I thundered at him.

'They're mostly very respectable folk travelling out of King's Cross station,' Watkins objected feebly. 'And the station staff, they're very alert.'

'Yes, fortunately they are. They found him and called the police. He could hardly do more than to babble his own name, Peter, so you thought that you wouldn't be traced.

'He was placed temporarily in the care of a woman who fosters children on behalf of the parish. But, following Miss Harris's complaint to the police, a notice was placed in the evening press, asking for information to assist us in our enquiries. It was read by the husband of the foster mother in question. They feared they had the child in their care and contacted us. Miss Harris was taken to see the child and recognised him.'

Watkins now presented a dejected figure in his sporting attire. 'There ain't no justice,' he mumbled.

'On the contrary, there is. Think yourself lucky Peter Harris didn't disappear for good at King's Cross station because you'd be facing a murder charge right now, most likely. As it is, Peter has been reunited with his mother. She's found a new, permanent and much more reliable foster home for him. Her present employer, to whom she was obliged to confess the whole story because she'd taken time off to seek her child, was sympathetic and helped her in this.'

'All's well that ends well, then, ain't it?' declared Watkins, cheering up.

'Depends what you mean by "well" . . . and what we mean by it. Jonas Watkins, you are charged, under the Offences against the Person Act of 1861, with the abandonment of a child under two years of age in a manner likely to cause death, injury or other harm.'

His eyes filled with real tears. 'That's what happens,' he said, 'when you try and help someone.'

I left Morris to deal with the miserable creature and walked out into what is laughingly called fresh air in central London. A hubbub of voices, rattle of wheels, clip-clop of hooves, shrieks and cries of vendors and others, all assaulted my ears. My nose was filled with the familiar miasma of smells. Among the host of other odours I could distinguish the sulphur, coal and oil reek of the engine sheds at the nearby railway terminus. That brought my mind back to Lizzie and to Waterloo; not that it had ever been far away. I wondered if I should call at Mrs Parry's home and have a word with Simms, the butler. Just to make sure Lizzie got away safely on her journey to Hampshire. But if she hadn't I'd know soon enough. There was nothing I could do but wait.

Chapter Four

Elizabeth Martin

AS LEFEBRE and I looked about us at our new surroundings, we heard a shout. Hastening towards us was a middle-aged man in the corduroy breeches and leather leggings of a groom, with a bowler hat set square on his head. He raised this as he reached us and puffed, 'You'll be the party for Shore House?'

We told him we were.

'Ah,' he observed, eyeing our luggage and shaking his head to express his doubt. 'Then I don't know if I'll get both of you and all your bags in the trap. We can but try, however!' he concluded, cheering up. 'Lycurgus Greenaway, at your service, sir and miss.' He set the bowler hat back on his head and struck the roof of it a smart blow with the palm of his hand to make sure it was wedged there. As his head was itself very round and his form short and squat I was irresistibly reminded of a pepper pot.

'Lycurgus?' remarked Dr Lefebre. 'That's an unusual name.'

'Ah!' said Mr Greenaway again. 'My father was a teetotaller. Very against the demon drink, he was, all his life from a young 'un. He called me Lycurgus after another famous teetotaller, or so he reckoned.'

'Rather more than that,' Dr Lefebre told him, 'although I understand the logic in it. Lycurgus was a king in ancient times. He banned the riotous cult of the god Bacchus and ordered all the vines destroyed.'

Mr Greenaway looked much pleased to hear of this royal connection. 'Then my old father knew a thing or two. This way, if you please!'

We followed him round a corner into what appeared to be the main street where waiting before a public house patriotically named after the hero of Trafalgar was a trap with facing seats and a perch for the driver. It was harnessed to a dispirited-looking pony with a large head at the end of a ewe-neck. It certainly seemed a very modest vehicle to carry us all and our bags.

'Oh, dear . . .' murmured the doctor.

Lycurgus Greenaway looked mildly embarrassed. 'Miss Roche sends her apologies, sir, but an axle is broke on the landau and the smith has to fashion a new one.'

'Can't be helped, I suppose,' said Dr Lefebre philosophically.

'Ah, she's collapsed all of a heap on the ground,' said Greenaway, shaking his head mournfully.

We were both alarmed to hear this until we realised that Greenaway referred to the carriage as 'she', as sailors refer to a ship, and meant that it and not his employer had collapsed.

'Now then,' went on our driver, 'I'll pack your bags in first on the floor and then you hop in and take a seat either side. It will be fine if the lady doesn't mind resting her feet – begging your pardon, miss – on her portmanteau.'

'Will the pony be able to pull all our weight?' I asked. 'Is it very far?'

'We can go along the shore road or cut across,' replied Mr Greenaway. 'I prefer to cut across myself. That way it's about six mile, give or take a bit, by the shore road near twice that. The road's rough but I came that way this morning and it's not cut up. The trap didn't give hardly a bounce.'

I heard Dr Lefebre beside me give a faint groan. 'Let's go by the shorter route,' he said stoically, 'if Miss Martin agrees. We may be shaken about,' he added to me, 'but I fancy the shore road won't be much better travelling by that vehicle!' He gestured with his cane at the trap and the pony, catching sight of the movement, threw up its head and snorted, rolling a white eyeball at us.

'The shorter journey will be better for the pony,' I said.

'Don't worry about the pony, miss, it's stronger than it looks,' declared Greenaway.

It took some minutes to pack us all in during which several drinkers emerged from the *Lord Nelson* and stood, tankard and pipe in hand, to watch and offer advice. They all seemed to know Mr Greenaway well, addressing him in familiar fashion as 'Lye'. Mr Greenaway senior had perhaps not been so successful in inspiring his offspring to teetotal ways as he might have hoped.

At last, with a lurch, we were off. The party from the public house raised an encouraging cheer. Dr Lefebre removed his hat and saluted them gravely. They appreciated the courtesy and raised another, even louder, huzza.

We then turned a corner and were lost to sight leaving them to talk, probably, of nothing else for the rest of the day.

At first our road was level and followed the shoreline with the water to our left, but then it turned inland and became narrower between densely packed trees. I hoped we met no vehicle coming in the other direction as wayside bracken, dry and brown now in late summer, and brambles heavy with fruit encroached on the highway. It was cool under the branches, for which I was grateful. So we trotted on merrily until we came to the beginning of a fairly steep rise. Greenaway hauled on the reins and we rocked to a halt.

The groom turned on his seat to assess us with a practical eye and announced, 'I'm not sure, begging the company's pardon, that the mare can pull the load up the hill. The lady don't weigh much by the looks of her and can stay where she is, but if you don't mind, sir, perhaps you would just jump down and you and I will walk the hill.'

'I'll get down, too,' I said at once, not sorry to stretch my legs.

We scrambled from our perches and Greenaway from his. He took the mare's head and led her forward. The doctor and I fell in behind the trap side by side.

'Quite like a pair of mourners at a funeral!' observed Dr Lefebre unexpectedly.

I thought his humour in this instance tasteless, but he was an unpredictable man in all ways.

At the top of the hill we emerged into sunshine and I was surprised to see we had left the belt of trees behind us. Viewed from the water, the whole area had looked thickly forested. In reality the trees only lined the shore. We climbed back into the trap. It was an awkward task for me encumbered with my skirts, even though Dr Lefebre had mounted first in order to reach down his hand. Greenaway solved the problem.

'Beg pardon for the liberty, miss!' With that he gave me a hearty shove and I fairly catapulted into the trap and Dr Lefebre's arms. I found myself grasping his coat; my bonnet fell to the back of my head, saved by its ribbons round my throat, and his beard brushed my face.

We disentangled ourselves with mutual apologies and Greenaway, observing us with some concern, enquired if we were all right. Rather breathlessly we told him we were. I regained my seat and hastily secured my bonnet in its proper place.

'No harm done, then,' observed our driver as he clambered back on his perch.

Off we set again, the doctor and I avoiding looking at each other, which was awkward as we sat opposite. Or at least, I didn't look at him for some minutes, and when I did so, he wasn't looking at me but studiously at the scenery. At first we passed fields but then our way took us on to a wide expanse of flat heath. Mr Greenaway was keeping his promise to 'cut across'. I was surprised at the terrain, having assumed the name 'New Forest' meant the whole area would be wooded.

'No, no, miss!' shouted Mr Greenaway from his perch when the enquiry was relayed to him. 'Some of it is trees and some of it is heath, but forest is what we call all of it.'

The road now was a dirt one and although it was level enough, the trap rattled and subjected us to constant shaking. Dr Lefebre sat with his malacca cane planted firmly between his feet and his hands resting on the pommel as he had done on the train. The dusty earth was peaty and muffled the sound of the wheels. The pony's hooves echoed with a dull thud. But the air was clean and fresh and the drive would have been pleasant if it hadn't been so hot. I regretted the loss of the shady trees. Out here in this bare landscape the sun beat down relentlessly on parched soil. It was dotted with gorse bushes armed with wicked spikes. Earlier in the year, I thought, those unfriendly-looking growths must make a fine golden show. But now even the carpet of mauve heather couldn't prevent the whole area looking barren.

Winding across the heath I also glimpsed, as we bounced by, various narrow tracks, no wider than to allow a single person to pass along them between the heather. There was no indication where they might lead.

A number of unkempt ponies were grazing on the clumps of

sparse grass, some singly or in pairs, occasionally in larger bands. There was no shelter for them and I saw no sign of water. I couldn't think the owners chose to turn their stock out on such poor pasture and wondered if the animals were wild. I gathered breath and bellowed my question to Greenaway.

'Not exactly, miss,' he shouted over his shoulder, waving his whip at the nearest group. 'There's folk have the right to graze livestock on the forest. Commoners, we call 'em, and all the ponies belong to a commoner. Pretty soon now they will be rounding them up, what we call the "drift". They sort them out, and auction some of them off. They are hardy little beasts. You'll see other animals, if you keep your eyes open, pigs maybe, or a donkey or two. There's deer in the trees, o' course.' He pointed with the whip again, this time to the horizon on our right where woodland began once more.

'What's happened here?' asked Dr Lefebre, as we were passing by a sizeable area of blackened burnt vegetation.

'Summer fire, sir, we get a few of those, especially when the weather's been as dry as it has this year. There's been precious little rain to dampen things down. The gorse and heather go up like a lot of fireworks. It's a fair old job to beat it out. By the way, if you want to go walking up here, keep an eye open for adders. See that path there?'

He waved his whip at one of the narrow tracks I'd noticed. 'The ponies make those. They always pass the same way to where they know they can find water. Year after year they've been doing it, why, going back hundreds of years I don't doubt, all plodding along the same trail made by those that have gone before 'em. Now then, on a nice warm day like this, the adders take a fancy to lie out in the middle of those paths and you can tread on 'em easy. If you find yourself about to step on one, and can't stop yourself, then try to tread on the head. Tail can't harm you but the fangs give you a nasty bite.'

After this daunting advice we carried on in silence and reasonable comfort, seeing nothing but the occasional grazing pony. We met no other traffic than a gaily painted gypsy caravan drawn by a piebald horse, with barefoot children running behind it. The sight of their merry, impudent faces made me laugh and brought a smile to Lefebre's features. We exchanged glances and briefly grinned at one another, as two people sharing a joke, but what the joke might be, I wasn't sure.

Lefebre unexpectedly called out to me above the rattle of the trap, 'Freedom, do we ever know it again, once childhood is left behind? What do you say, Miss Martin?'

'Not all children enjoy freedom as they ought. The lucky ones do, I suppose,' was my reply.

He raised his bushy eyebrows. 'Do you count yourself among the lucky or the unlucky?'

'I enjoyed considerable freedom! But that was because I was motherless, my father was a busy man, and there was no one to worry what I did.'

'Then you were unlucky,' he observed.

I contradicted him vigorously. 'By no means! The children I'd count unlucky are those who must work for their livings from a tender age, even in the coalmines around my home town.'

'The poor live by harsh rules, it's true,' returned Lefebre calmly, 'but to have money brings its own constraints.'

'One can't expect to be given everything and nothing be required in return.' I didn't really know what he was talking about and it seemed a totally unsuitable conversation to be conducting as we were shaken about in that jolting trap.

My tone must have told him I disliked the exchange so he

said no more on the subject, but gave me a thoughtful look.

Perhaps he thinks me strange? I thought. Well, if so, it can't be helped. 'I speak as I find!' people used to say in my home town. Mind you, it was generally said by those who knew they'd just 'put their foot in it', to borrow another expression. But the thought niggled at my mind that perhaps he'd been trying to tell me something.

After that we carried on for a little way in silence. Eventually we saw two figures ahead of us on the road walking in single file. A woman plodded behind a man who strode out jauntily with his hands in his pockets and his hat at a rakish angle. It had started out as a top hat, but one side had been punched in deliberately so that instead of standing up straight, it bent to one side. I'd seen this fashion on louts in the London streets.

'Ah!' exclaimed Greenaway, slowing the trap and pulling up as we reached the two. I saw then they were accompanied by a pair of small terrier dogs, which scampered from the heather where they had been foraging and watched us with bright, malicious eyes.

Greenaway leaned from his perch and hailed the man.

'Well, then, Jed Brennan, you're back in these parts! I was remarking only the other day it was about time we saw you again.'

The man approached the trap and the woman fell back and stood waiting, head bowed. She was a poor drab creature indeed. Although the weather was so warm she wore a plaid shawl crossed over her chest and fastened at the small of her back. Dank greasy locks of hair drooped from beneath a wide-brimmed felt hat. She had secured the hat as Dr Lefebre had done his on the ferry, by tying a scarf over it and knotting it under her chin, so that the sides of the brim were flattened against her ears. Her skirt had been turned up some inches at the hem and pinned there in an attempt to protect it from the dust and mud of the road. It allowed me to see she wore a man's boots, which hadn't been so protected and were caked in dried mud. It was she who carried the couple's possessions in a large and heavy-looking wicker basket strapped to her back. She may or may not have been aware of my scrutiny. She kept her face down. This made me the more curious and suspicious so that I attempted to get a better look. I fancied I saw some bruising but could not be sure. What did strike me was the weariness in her whole demeanour. It was that kind of exhaustion that leaves the sufferer afraid to sit down, for fear it will be impossible to drag himself to his feet again.

The terriers came a little too close to our pony and barked. The pony snorted and threw up its head. Our trap rocked.

The man called roughly to the dogs and they fell back. It drew my attention to him.

He was a bold-looking fellow about forty years of age with a skin burnished by sun and wind and abundant black curls. He wore a workman's strong boots but was otherwise much better dressed than his poor wife, something of a 'masher' in a suit of brown corduroy with a waistcoat of moleskin. Unfortunately the result of this attire was to make him resemble some kind of large, upright, short-furred animal. A bright scarlet handkerchief was knotted at his throat. He was handsome in a coarse way. The woman, if ever she had any looks, had lost them.

Brennan turned to the doctor and myself and raised his crooked hat with a flourish. 'Good day to you, gentlefolk!'

I was getting a little annoyed at being taken for gentry, which I am not, being a respectable doctor's daughter and no more; but I disliked even more being greeted by Brennan, whose manner verged on the insolent. His bright dark eyes mocked us and when they rested on me seemed to gleam with unwished-for appreciation.

Both Lefebre and I nodded silently in acknowledgement of his greeting. He replaced his hat and turned his attention to Greenaway again.

'I'll be calling on your ladies to see if they have any need of me,' he said.

'I'll tell 'em,' replied Greenaway curtly. Perhaps he too had noticed the mockery in Brennan's gaze. He shook the reins and we moved off, leaving Brennan and his wife behind us.

'Who on earth was that fellow?' called Dr Lefebre.

Greenaway twisted on his perch. 'Jed Brennan, sir, a travelling rat-catcher by way of trade. He makes a circuit as regular as a judge and appears always at about the same time, though I do believe he's from London by way of permanent dwelling. I fancy he is of tinker descent and likes it better on the road than in the city.'

'Is he honest?'

'Why, yes, sir, if you mean, does he pilfer? No, or he's never been known to. He's well paid for his work. There are always rats and a rat-catcher never goes short of business.'

I had a question of my own. 'Does that poor woman always travel with him?'

'Yes, miss. She always comes along, even when she's carrying. The pair of them strikes a little camp wherever they stop for the night, put up a rough sort of tent. They cause no trouble as I've heard.'

I said no more but pressed my lips together angrily. I realised that when Greenaway spoke of the woman 'carrying' he meant not the wicker basket on her back but any child she might have in her womb. I wondered who cared for the couple's children while they tramped the countryside.

I thought of Brennan's sharp shiny dark eyes, so like those of the vermin that gave him his living, and shivered.

We continued, passing through isolated clumps of trees and across more heath until unexpectedly our dirt track joined a better one. I could smell the salt tang of the sea again. I thought of the yellowed atlas I'd discovered in Josiah Parry's library and calculated we had cut diagonally across the heath and now reached the shoreline again, not on the inlet but 'around the corner'. We were at some point where the sea formed that channel of water between the mainland and the Isle of Wight that is called the Solent. The land hereabouts was farmed. We again passed through hedged fields.

Greenaway raised his whip and pointed. 'Shore House,' he said.

Chapter Five

Elizabeth Martin

I WAS surprised to hear Greenaway tell us we'd arrived because we hadn't yet reached any village or even a cluster of dwellings. In fact, owing to Greenaway's 'cutting across', we'd seen little sign of any habitation at all.

Shore House stood in apparent isolation, although a bend in the road ahead might conceal more buildings. A tall hedge of glossy-leaved laurel surrounded it but once we had trotted through the open gates we saw a pleasant garden, the lawns broken by islands of rhododendrons and trees clipped into ornate topiary shapes. The house looming up before us was built of unpleasing yellow brick and didn't appear particularly old, possibly no more than fifty years or so. It must have been built when fashion was turning to the Gothic rather than the Palladian style. All the windows had pointed arches above, like church windows, and there were incongruous turrets stuck at the roof corners. In a further flight of architectural fancy a band of red and black brick ran all round it at first-floor level. It was an ugly house, but somehow confident in its ugliness. It seemed an odd retreat for a pair of maiden ladies. Weren't they lonely here?

Nevertheless, I rather liked Shore House's eccentric appearance, but Dr Lefebre didn't.

'What a monstrosity!' he murmured more to himself than to me.

Greenaway drew up before a large solid square porch jutting from the façade where we were decanted, together with our baggage, and abandoned. The trap was driven off at once, presumably in the direction of the stables. The pony, sensing its stall and a feed ahead of it, broke into a canter and Greenaway, with the human equivalent no doubt awaiting him, did not slow it.

'Dear me,' murmured the doctor, again to himself.

But our arrival had been heard or seen within. A severe, capable-looking woman in black bombazine with a fob watch pinned to her bosom opened the door. She could only be a housekeeper.

'Welcome, Doctor,' she said stiffly, 'the ladies are waiting for you.' She glanced at me and added, 'And for Miss Martin.'

She was already slotting me neatly into the order of things within the household she ran – and letting me know it. Dr Lefebre was a guest. I was there by way of employment, although living as one of the family. The staff would be suspicious that I might 'give myself airs'. This dragon was already drawing an invisible line over which I might not step. Someone more easily wounded than myself might have been overawed. I'm of tougher material.

'Yes!' I agreed cheerfully. 'I'm to be companion to Mrs Craven.'

'Indeed, miss' replied the housekeeper dourly. She stood aside to allow us to enter. 'Your hat and cane, sir?'

The doctor meekly handed over both articles. They were placed on a large well-polished hall table already covered with objects including a box for outgoing letters, a silver letter tray and an ornate oriental letter knife with a curious wavy-edged blade.

'If you would be pleased to follow me, I'll conduct you to the ladies.' The housekeeper was not permitting us to linger.

There was only the faintest emphasis on the last word. I was not a 'lady' and should remember it. On the way there we had twice been taken for travelling gentlefolk, and I found the sudden fall in my status amusing. Glancing at Dr Lefebre I saw a faint smile on his face and I guessed he'd noticed it, too. Nothing, it seemed, got by the doctor without his taking note of it.

A strange man, I thought; what, I wonder, is he really doing here?

We followed the housekeeper, leaving our bags on the doorstep.

She showed us into a spacious drawing room. The furniture was of first quality but mostly half a century or more old. It showed the elegant lines and fine workmanship of the beginning of the century when old King George was still alive and talking to the trees in Windsor Great Park, while his plump son waited impatiently to succeed him. Everything had that mellow patina of pieces lovingly cared for, and all harmonised, as if the items had been bought together and always stood in the same rooms, grouped together like old friends. From this I deduced it was inherited furniture. The Roche ladies had no reason for or interest in buying newly fashionable. Their parents had done so more than half a century before and the ladies preserved the choice of their forebears in pious memory, or possibly simply through thrift.

The Gothic windows looked out on to a smooth lawn, dotted with more topiary work and bordered by shiny bright green leaves of laurel hedges. The far ones had been trimmed low enough to allow a glimpse of shingle beach. Beyond that – and I couldn't repress a gasp of delight – was the sea, sparkling like tinsel in the sunlight. Now I understood the choice of this lonely place to build a country retreat. What a view! I had to tear my gaze away from it to concentrate on meeting the residents of the house.

You can imagine how curious I was for my first sight of Mrs Craven, but she wasn't in the room. Present were a pair of ladies who could only have been sisters. Like the furniture, they belonged, and had always been, together. Though they had adopted the modern fashion for the crinoline, they were, like the furniture, somehow of another period.

I thought them both younger than their brother, Mr Roche, but not unlike him in build, having large-boned but spare figures. At first glance they might even have passed for twins, as they wore gowns of identical material, a tartan pattern in muted browns and greens. Both wore their greying hair parted centrally and crowned by confections of ribbons and lace pretending to be caps. But one woman appeared a year or two older than the other and on second look I noted a definite difference in their features.

The elder lady had rounded cheeks, a receding chin and straight jutting nose that somehow contrived to give her the look of a ship's figurehead. As the billows part before the ship's wooden prow, so one instinctively felt all opposition would step aside before the will of this middle-aged woman. She sat perfectly still with her hands resting in her lap. Her gaze watched us and assessed us, but not a muscle of her face moved. Yet despite the controlled composure of her manner, a gleam entered her eyes when they rested on me as if she were already anticipating that we'd clash.

The younger-looking one possessed a larger squarer jaw and sported a couple of false ringlets over each ear, perhaps to soften or draw attention away from this unfeminine feature. She also wore a cameo brooch at her throat whereas her sister had a ruffle of lace at the neck of her gown. The younger woman's expression was gentle and even timid in comparison with the very direct, assertive look of her sibling.

They had surely spent their entire lives together. There had been such a pair of sisters in my hometown, grown into each other's ways so completely that it was hard to imagine one without the other. As for the identical material of their gowns, perhaps their brother had sent them a bolt of cloth from his warehouse? At any rate, it clearly didn't seem strange to them to dress alike. It might have heightened their feeling of togetherness. But it wouldn't do for me to be turned out in exactly the same way as another lady in the same room.

They had been playing chess immediately prior to our appearance. A little table with a marquetry chessboard inlaid in the surface still stood between them. Now the formidable housekeeper came forward unbidden, lifted table and chess pieces together and set them to one side against a wall in a smooth movement. Not a single piece slid out of its station.

The elder sister broke her silence at last to say, 'Thank you, Williams. We'll take tea now. Ask Mrs Craven if she would join us, would you?'

'I'm Miss Roche,' she informed us as the housekeeper withdrew, confirming her senior status by this old-fashioned manner of referring to herself. 'This is my sister, Phoebe. Do sit down.'

'I'm very pleased to meet you both, ladies,' said Dr Lefebre with a courtly bow. If he thought it odd or discourteous to have been kept waiting in this way while he – and I – were so obviously sized up, he didn't show it.

'How do you do?' I added, determined to add my response to this cool welcome.

'Your journey was comfortable?' Miss Roche asked now in the same rather perfunctory way.

'Very tolerable, ma'am,' returned Dr Lefebre, 'and not without interest.'

'No, indeed,' I put in. If they thought I would prove a mouse-like creature who barely uttered a squeak, they might as well find out at once I wasn't. 'I enjoyed the ferry journey very much indeed. I'd never been in any kind of boat before.'

'Really?' returned Miss Roche with a faint flicker of an eyebrow.

'And your countryside hereabouts,' the doctor added quickly, distracting Miss Roche's attention away from me, 'it's really most attractive. Wild and perhaps not all of it conventionally beautiful, but very interesting. We had a curious encounter, not far from here, on the heath. The trap overtook a fellow with his wife following him, who your man Greenaway told us was a travelling rat-catcher by trade.'

'Brennan?' demanded Miss Roche immediately in a sharp voice. 'Is he back in the district?'

'I don't like that man,' said Miss Phoebe nervously, entering the conversation. 'He frightens me.'

'Nonsense, Phoebe,' said her sister, without looking in her direction, 'he is always perfectly civil.'

'So you always say, Christina. But he brings bad luck with him.'

'Don't be foolish, Phoebe,' Miss Roche advised briskly. She turned her head towards her sister at last but it was to deliver a reproof. 'You've been listening to village gossip.'

Phoebe persisted, supporting her argument with, 'Last time he was here, one of his horrid little dogs killed the kitchen cat.'

'Then Cook should have kept the animal shut up until Brennan left. Anyway, we've need of him again. I must tell Greenaway to ask him to call. There is a rat around here somewhere. I've seen it twice recently.' She indicated the room about us with a general gesture.

'I haven't seen it,' protested Miss Phoebe anxiously.

'Because you usually have your nose in a book. The last time it appeared, in the middle of the afternoon, it was just over there.' Christina Roche pointed an imperious finger to a far corner.

We all looked in the direction with some apprehension. What was that under a chair? Did it move?

'It ran out into the hall,' said Miss Roche. 'But it's certainly still here. Brennan will flush it out.'

'Couldn't Cook just put down arsenic as usual?' asked Miss Phoebe, waving her hands despairingly. 'Must Brennan be involved?'

'No, no, the creature has its nest nearby somewhere, probably behind some skirting board. I cannot have dishes of arsenic set about the drawing or dining rooms. If you don't want to see the man when he comes, you don't have to, Phoebe.'

It was fortunate that the tea arrived at that moment and the topic of the rat dropped. The tea-things were brought in not by Williams, the housekeeper, but by a middle-aged parlour-maid. She had not left us for more than a minute when the door opened again. Dr Lefebre rose to his feet. Lucy Craven had joined us.

I already knew that she was young but I hadn't realised just how young and I must confess it shocked me. This child could not long have passed her seventeenth birthday. She was very pretty, or would have been with some liveliness in her face. It was still babyish, with a rounded chin, full lips and snub nose. Her most striking feature was a pair of large blue eyes, fringed with dark lashes. Their colour was tinged with purple and reminded me of bluebells. The shade was reflected in the simple lilac striped gown she wore. Her fair hair had been braided into a long plait curled into a knot at the back of her head. She was very pale and wore no jewellery other than her wedding band, no lace or ribbons. The effect was of a porcelain doll.

Why, she is no more than a schoolgirl and looks it! I thought, shocked.

'Your servant, ma'am,' said Dr Lefebre, bowing to her.

Animation entered her face then, or rather, entered the blue eyes. Suddenly they blazed with such hostility directed fully at him that I was even more taken aback. But it was only for an instant and then the expression was veiled, the striking eyes returning to their previous doll-like lack of any expression. Lucy merely nodded acknowledgment of his greeting.

Knowing the doctor already as I did, I was sure he wouldn't have missed the brief enmity shown him. Lucy had probably had enough of doctors. But even so, such a real hatred and towards a total stranger?

'And Miss Martin,' said Miss Roche, gesturing towards me.

'I'm very happy to meet you,' I said as sincerely as I could.

The girl stared at me for a moment and I wondered if I, too, was to be treated to such a look of dislike. But she only nodded, as she'd done to Dr Lefebre.

We took tea in an atmosphere of such awkwardness I couldn't wait for it to be over. Fortunately Dr Lefebre proved skilled at light conversation and conducted most of it with Miss Roche. Miss Phoebe said little and sat frowning at the tea-things, perhaps still worrying about the rat. I didn't say much more. Lucy Craven said nothing at all except to decline a slice of cake in a subdued and light, childish voice.

I was relieved when Miss Roche set down her cup and said to

me, 'I dare say you'd like to see your room, Miss Martin. Your baggage will have been taken up there by now. Lucy, perhaps you'd show Miss Martin where we've put her?'

Lucy got up silently. I followed her out of the room and up a wide staircase. At the top we followed a corridor, still without a word spoken, until we reached a room at the far end. Lucy opened the door and we both entered.

The room was small and square but very well appointed. I'd be comfortable here in this respect, if in no other. Best of all, it looked over the sea.

Unable to wait, I ran to the window and threw it open to gaze out over the expanse of bobbing waves. A pair of white-sailed yachts played a game of chase in the distance and beyond them I could see the purple outline of the Isle of Wight. The light had a wonderful luminous quality to it. The warm sea breeze caressed my face. After the smells of London it tingled so cleanly in my nostrils I had to fill my lungs.

I turned to Lucy and exclaimed: 'You can't imagine how exciting this is to me! You live by the sea and I dare say think little of it, but I come from a Derbyshire mining town where the air is filled with coal dust, and have only otherwise lived in London which is a place of fog and smoke.'

She had been standing in the middle of the room watching me. Perhaps my enthusiasm had the effect of allaying some of her reserve. She spoke at last and her tone seemed to challenge me to contradict her.

'They've sent us both out of the drawing room so that they may discuss me with that doctor.'

'Dr Lefebre and I travelled together,' I said. 'I didn't know him before today.'

I don't know quite why I said that. I think I sensed that she saw the doctor and me as a joint force. I wanted her to understand from the first that I was quite independent.

She shrugged her slight shoulders. 'He's come to watch me – as have you, Miss Martin.' She fixed me with a knowing, mocking look and her full lips twisted into an unbecoming cynical smile.

For a moment she looked older than her years and the effect was unpleasant. She reminded me of those ragged children I'd seen roaming the streets of London, their years belied by their sharp little faces; or worse, decked out in tawdry finery, lining the pavements of an evening offering their immature bodies, their eyes mirroring the loss of all innocence, of all hope.

I had to take charge of this situation immediately or we should never get anywhere. 'In the first place,' I said, 'please call me Elizabeth, or Lizzie, if you like. I'd like to call you Lucy, if you agree. Secondly, I've certainly not come to "watch" you.' I drew a deep breath, 'Lucy, I know, of course, you've suffered a sad loss—'

At this her expression altered again. She looked so fierce, I hurried on, 'I'm truly very sorry for – for your present unhappiness. I hope we can be *friends* and I'll be able to offer at least some comfort and support. I've come to be a companion, that's all. I haven't the skills to be a nurse or the inclination to be a gaoler! So, that's not my purpose in being here. Please, do believe me.'

I found myself wondering, as I spoke these words, if Lucy had ever had a real friend, if the notion of friendship was itself strange to her. At any rate, my words seemed to make little impression.

'*He*'s come to watch me,' she repeated impatiently as if I were being particularly dense.

'Not you, Lucy, just the general situation on behalf of your uncle,' I protested. 'He told me. Your uncle can't come himself. He just wants Lefebre to tell him how you are all getting along here and, probably, to report back on how suitable I'm proving. The doctor told me particularly that he hasn't come to treat you.'

I tried to sound confident but a pang of doubt had struck me. She was so sure of my complicity. Could Ben be right? I was beginning to have a horrid feeling I'd been tricked in some way.

She hissed in annoyance and shook her head violently to dismiss my argument. 'He's telling lies,' she said, as if this were a statement beyond any doubt.

'I am not!' I retorted, rather sharply.

Perhaps the sharpness reached her in a way my reasoned earlier speech hadn't. 'How do I know *you* are telling the truth and you really aren't his assistant?' She searched my face.

That annoyed me. I felt it would do her no harm to see that it had. 'That's an insult. I'm not untruthful and I've not come here with any secret purpose. You'll find that I speak my mind, perhaps sometimes when I ought not to. The one thing I most certainly am not is devious!'

She seemed confused. A faint pink flush entered her pale cheeks. 'I'm sorry,' she mumbled. 'But if you really haven't met the man before today . . .' She paused for reassurance but her eyes were not antagonistic now, only anxious.

'Never,' I said stoutly. 'I didn't even know he existed, much less that he was to be a houseguest and on his way here. I got into the same compartment on the train only because the ladies only compartment was full. I was reading Miss Roche's letter and he saw it and recognised the handwriting. He introduced himself. I was very surprised.'

'Well, then,' said Lucy, 'you perhaps won't know what kind of doctor he is.'

A tremor ran over me as if a cold breath had touched the nape of my neck. Perhaps it was only the draught from the opened window. 'No,' I confessed, 'he didn't say. I told him my late father was a doctor but he didn't tell me anything of his own practice. He appears to be successful.'

She gave a bitter bark of laughter. 'Indeed, very successful! Our family's interests are in silk and in tea. Dr Lefebre's interest, his *business*, is insanity. He is an alienist.'

I gasped. 'Are you sure?'

'Oh, yes. He has come here to judge whether or not I am mad.'

The Roche ladies dined at seven. I'd been deeply shaken by what Lucy had told me. But I'd no time to think it over now and none to begin a letter to Ben Ross letting him know of my safe arrival. I knew I mustn't be late joining the company downstairs. It wouldn't be well viewed. I chose to wear the grey silk I'd bought when in half-mourning for my father. That wouldn't give rise to a twitch of Miss Roche's eyebrow which, I'd already realised, indicated I'd said or done the wrong thing. I fancied I'd see that twitch often during my stay at Shore House.

The Roche sisters had also changed for dinner. Their gowns, like their day attire, were again apparently cut from the same cloth: in this case very expensive dark blue watered taffeta. Phoebe, the more adventurous in dress I decided, had ruffles at the hem of her skirt and smaller ruffles down the middle of the bodice. Christina inclined towards a plain style with a row of little buttons of the same material down the bodice. The saddest thing was that these beautiful gowns were quite wasted on such a plain pair of wearers and in this sober setting. Or had the presence of a gentleman at the table led them to bring out their finery? I didn't imagine it was because of me.

The dinner was also very plain but well cooked. Conversation was polite and uncontroversial. Lucy, looking very pretty but subdued in pale pink, took no part in it. I noticed that she watched the doctor surreptitiously but if he turned to speak to her, immediately looked down at her plate and only mumbled the minimum reply. More than ever she struck me as a child: one who had been thrust into a hostile adult world with little preparation and did not know, finding herself there, how she should fight off its slings and arrows. I wondered about her upbringing, whether her aunts Roche had had charge of it or whether she'd been sent away to school. What of her parents? There'd been no mention of them. All these things I meant to find out, if possible from Lucy herself, but it would require considerable tact. Tact was not always my strongest point, alas, and like poor Lucy, I felt myself adrift in unknown waters.

After dinner we ladies retired to the drawing room leaving Dr Lefebre to sit in solitary splendour in the dining room with the port decanter. Miss Roche led the way out, followed by her sister (both with much rustling of taffeta), and then by Lucy and me.

Lucy murmured resentfully, 'I am a married lady and I ought to go first!'

But she seemed to make the observation more to herself than to me so I didn't feel I had to reply. It would be a brave person who undertook to debate this nice point of etiquette with the formidable Miss Roche. Looking at the sisters walking ahead of me, I realised that both of them were a good head taller than I was. I wondered briefly what they'd been like as girls of Lucy's age. Nothing like their young niece, I decided.

'Tell me, Miss Martin,' asked Miss Roche unexpectedly, once we were settled in the drawing room, 'what were your duties with regard to your previous employer?'

'I read to her sometimes, I wrote letters for her, I made up a four at whist,' I told her. 'I accompanied her sometimes when she went out.'

'Whist?' said Miss Roche and her eyebrows twitched. 'My sister and I do not play cards. It's an occupation that leads to unfortunate habits.'

I glanced at the chess table still with the abandoned game in place on its squares. 'I am sorry I don't know how to play chess,' I said meekly.

'No matter,' said Miss Roche, 'Lucy doesn't play. Our doctor, Dr Barton, has advised Lucy to take exercise and fresh air. Perhaps you could walk with her tomorrow morning.'

As this was said in Lucy's presence without even a glance at her, I almost blushed in embarrassment. Was it normal in this household to talk of Lucy as if she were deaf and dumb or just incapable of expressing any opinion?

'If that is what Mrs Craven would like,' I said and turned to Lucy in as deliberate a manner as I could without causing offence to Miss Roche. 'Would you care to walk tomorrow, Mrs Craven? I long to explore the neighbourhood. Perhaps you'd be kind enough to be my guide?'

'Of course,' said Lucy. Her voice held no expression but she threw me a quick little glance and in it I fancied I saw a flicker of gratitude.

Miss Phoebe spoke unexpectedly. 'It will be so nice for dear Lucy to have younger company.' She smiled at us.

Miss Roche pursed her lips and fixed me with a very direct gaze. 'This is a respectable household, Miss Martin. Our family is an old one. Our forebears came from France when the French King Lewis so cruelly persecuted the Protestants there. Before that they had been persons of importance in La Rochelle. Sobriety and diligence have always been our watchwords.'

Miss Roche raised her hand and pointed to a smoke-darkened oil painting hanging above the fireplace. It showed a man in full-bottomed wig and lace collar although, owing to it needing a good clean, nothing could be made out of the background.

'That gentleman is John Roche, the first of our family to settle in this country, painted by Sir Peter Lely.' Her voice rang with pride.

'Indeed, ma'am,' I said politely.

I have no great knowledge of art but it seemed to me that the picture suggested a less skilled hand than that of a great portraitist. Perhaps the dirt obscured its finer points. It didn't quite obscure the rakish look in the sitter's eye, which hardly indicated to me an industrious, God-fearing silk merchant. I managed to conjure up a suitable expression of awe since it was clearly expected.

'So,' continued Miss Roche, satisfied that I was impressed, 'I don't want you and my niece to waste time in idle chatter. Perhaps you could study some instructive book together.'

I almost shouted out that I'd not come to be a governess. But Lucy was so young. Marriage and motherhood had probably curtailed her education. Perhaps her aunt felt this was part of the problem and if Lucy could find new interests, her spirits might improve. This was putting the best possible interpretation on Miss Roche's words. I was however beginning to understand why Mr Charles Roche had sent me here. Whatever was wrong with Lucy, the Roche ladies were not the ones to deal with it.

Dr Lefebre rejoined us and I was heartily pleased to see him. He had a knack of talking to the ladies without ever saying much of real interest but keeping them chatting. The portrait by Sir Peter Lely was duly pointed out to him. He passed a hand over his mouth and observed: 'You're very fortunate to have it, ma'am.'

We were then subjected to a history of the Roche family, generation by generation. They were all, we were told, of the utmost probity and piety. They valued their Protestant faith, their family honour and good name and the successful running of their business. It didn't surprise me that such a line of humourless if efficient dullards had produced Miss Christina and Miss Phoebe. I looked again at the gentleman in the lace collar. Perhaps it was because I was so very tired that his rakish gaze appeared to wink at me. Take all that with a good pinch of salt! he seemed to be saying.

At nine thirty sharp Miss Roche rose to her feet, followed almost at once by her sister.

'We retire early. That does not apply, of course, to you, Dr Lefebre.'

But, by implication, it did apply to Lucy and to me.

'I'll take a turn in the garden, I think, before I retire,' said the doctor. 'I might even go a little way along the shore, mm?'

'As you wish,' said Miss Roche tersely.

In fact I was not sorry to go up to bed. It had been a long and busy day and I was feeling sleepy. Williams came in, as if part of a set routine, with a tray of candlesticks. There was no gas at remote Shore House and downstairs the failing light had been supplemented with oil lamps. But upstairs it seemed candles were the usual thing. We were provided with a candlestick apiece. At the head of the stairs the corridor ran to left and to right. The sisters turned to the left. Lucy and I turned to the right and bid one another goodnight before her door, next to mine. I wished I didn't have the annoying sensation of having been despatched to the nursery wing. I didn't know where Dr Lefebre would be lodged but I was sure that it would be in the left-hand wing, where Miss Roche could monitor his coming and going. He appeared to be a single gentleman and in such a respectable household would not be allowed a bedchamber anywhere near an unmarried woman such as I was, or a pretty young matron with a husband in China.

On a table in the corner of my room stood a rosewood writing slope inlaid with ivory. It reminded me of my promise to write to Ben as soon as I arrived. Weary as I was, I opened it up and took out a sheet of the fine quality paper contained inside. Close by I found a supply of pens and ink in a glass inkwell with silver lid. This is indeed a wealthy household! I thought. Even in a spare bedroom there's an expensive item of furniture like this, in case a guest wishes to write a private letter.

By the light of my candle I settled down to describe my journey, the surprising meeting with Lefebre on the train and the ferry crossing. Then, fearing Ben would count this as description of the scenery and become impatient, I hastened to write that I'd met the Roche ladies and found them rather formal and stiff. I'd also met Mrs Craven, I told him, but had little time to talk to her. I'd been struck by her extreme youth.

I decided not to tell Ben of Lucy's claim that Lefebre was a 'mad-doctor'. I would like to hear that confirmed by someone else, preferably the man himself.

Reading it all through, it struck me that Dr Lefebre played rather a large role in my narrative. But that couldn't be helped. The candle flame guttered and drew my attention to how low it had burned. I couldn't write on for much longer and in any case my eyes were tired. I saw ruefully that my handwriting was beginning to sprawl all over the page. I promised to write more as soon as I could, signed my letter, found a little bar of sealing wax in the box and, using my candle, sealed it up. As I replaced the bar of wax I saw that it was decorated with a sinuous Chinese dragon. I wondered if the writing slope originated in the Far East, as did so much of the Roche fortune. I propped my letter on my dressing table. I'd take it downstairs in the morning and put it in the box for outgoing post in the hall.

The act of writing had thoroughly tired me out. I struggled out of my clothes and into my nightgown. It was very warm and stuffy in the room. When I'd undressed, I blew out the candle stub and went to the window to draw back the heavy curtains and open the casement. The cool night air would help me sleep more easily, I thought, and the morning sun awaken me.

The same gentle sea breeze brushed my face, much cooler now, and I could hear the distant lapping of the waves on the beach. The garden below was a pattern of dark and silver, shadows thrown by the moonlight and strange shapes formed by the topiary trees, rhododendron bushes and laurel hedges. As I looked out my eye caught a movement and a small red point glowed in the shadows. As I watched the red point moved back and forth and eventually described an arc through the air, fell to earth and was extinguished. Dr Lefebre had concluded his evening stroll with a cigarette. He'd been out there some time. I wondered how far he'd gone on his moonlit walk and if it had taken in the shingle beach.

I left the window and placed my stout balmoral boots on the carpet by the head of my bed in case the rat should dare to show his whiskers and I needed something to throw at him. Then I fairly fell into bed and went straight to sleep.

It is an odd thing but when one falls asleep like that, dead to the world, one can awaken just as suddenly and for no obvious cause. I awoke in such a way and sat bolt upright in bed. I was filled with an unreasoning alarm, my heart throbbing in my breast and my skin fairly prickling with awareness of something being wrong. I told myself at once this was only because I was in a strange place. *Come, come, Lizzie, pull yourself together, you are not a child to be afraid of the dark!* I admonished myself. Yet the feeling of unease did not leave me, even though my eyes adjusted slowly to the gloom. The shapes of the furniture identified them as harmless constructions of wood. My petticoat thrown over a chair back glowed palely in a sinister fashion, but showed no inclination to rise and flap towards me.

I threw back the covers and slipped out of bed. I hadn't the means to relight the candle stub, so I padded barefoot to the window and leaned out to take advantage of the moonlight.

The noise of the waves seemed louder and nearer to hand; the tide had come in. Perhaps it was only that, then, which had disturbed my slumber? Then, as I leaned on the sill, I heard a different noise: a whispering followed by a low bass murmur. I frowned and leaned further out, the air currents catching at my unpinned hair and blowing it across my face.

The garden still showed the pattern of silver and black. Nothing moved except the tips of the trees in the light wind. Perhaps I had only imagined the strange noise; it must be the waves. I was unaccustomed to the variety of sounds they could produce.

But there it was again: a whispering followed by something louder, definitely a human voice, quite high in pitch but too muted to assign to a sex. It was echoed by the bass murmur, more expressive and forceful. There were at least two people in conversation in the garden.

Was Dr Lefebre still there? I held my unruly locks away from my eyes and peered more intently. I wished I knew what time it was. As if in answer to my wish, the long-case clock downstairs in the hall struck two. No, Dr Lefebre would not still be there in the early hours, unless he suffered from insomnia. Were that so, as a doctor he should surely be able to prescribe himself some opiate? Should I rouse the household? Were thieves plotting together to force an entry?

But even as I wondered, the conversation below came to an end. A figure slipped out of the shadows and came towards the house, disappearing again before I could see whether it came indoors or made its way round the outer walls. It was impossible to say of which sex it had been, so well enveloped in draperies was it.

The second speaker was still down there; I caught just the barest movement and instinctively drew back so that if he or she should look up I would not be seen. Whoever it was kept in the shadows and did not come towards the house. I sensed, rather than saw, the presence pass by my room and quit the scene.

Then, just as I was about to leave my station at the window, yet another movement below caught my eye and a small white shape, almost luminous in the moonlight, pattered by in the wake of the visitor right beneath my window.

I was almost sure it was one of the rat-catcher's little terrier dogs.

Chapter Six

Elizabeth Martin

I CAME down the following morning and dropped my letter to Ben in the postbox on the hall table before making my way to the dining room. I found Dr Lefebre alone and just finishing his breakfast.

'Good morning, Miss Martin, did you sleep well?'

'Thank you, very well,' I replied.

'You weren't worried about a visit from our fur-coated intruder?'

'You mean the rat,' I said. 'Not a sign of it.'

'So, no disturbances, then?'

I was surprised at his persistence and wondered if I ought to mention the scene I'd witnessed in the early hours of the morning. But, truth to tell, I'd seen hardly anything, only heard voices and fancied I recognised the dog. It would be more prudent to keep it to myself.

'No, none at all,' I repeated firmly.

'Good!' He seemed unduly pleased that I had not had any kind of a restless night.

'And you?' I asked politely. 'Did you enjoy your walk yesterday evening?'

'Thank you, it was very pleasant. I strolled through the garden and down to the sea. I recommend it to you. I couldn't see much, of course, by moonlight, though it created quite a romantic scene shining on the water. Sadly I'm neither a painter nor a poet! But if you walk that way today you should get a good view across the Solent to the Isle of Wight. I believe it's possible to make out individual buildings over there.'

I told him I would certainly explore later and asked if he had seen any of the ladies of the house that morning.

'Miss Roche has breakfasted and gone to confer with Mrs Williams. I understand the fellow Brennan has arrived and awaits his instructions.' The doctor mopped his mouth and tossed his crumpled napkin on to the table.

'And Miss Phoebe?' I asked.

'Miss Phoebe, it seems, takes only coffee and a slice of toast in the morning in her room. I've not seen Mrs Craven.'

'Perhaps she's keeping away from you,' I said calmly, seating myself and reaching for the coffee pot.

Lefebre leaned back in his chair and observed me. 'Why should she do that?'

'You were not entirely frank with me yesterday,' I charged him. 'Mrs Craven tells me you're a doctor who treats the mad.'

'And what is madness, Miss Martin, eh?' He stared at me benevolently and, when I hesitated, smiled. 'Let me tell you that the illnesses of the mind take many forms. Say the word "mad" and to most people it still means a gibbering idiot, poor Tom o'Bedlam.' He shook his head. 'But I've treated patients quite severely mentally ill who've appeared as sane as you or I, Miss Martin, always supposing that you and I *are* sane. That raises not so much the question: what is madness? But rather, what is sanity?'

He paused only briefly to mark my discomfiture and then, dropping his bantering tone, leaned forward and added seriously, 'If I achieve nothing else on this earth, I hope I shall advance the day when people will cast off the superstitious attitude towards illness of the mind which clings so obstinately even among the educated. That, and the ridiculous notion that such an illness is somehow not respectable. People still hide their mentally afflicted or simply refuse to believe there is anything wrong. I've been brought so many patients far too late for anything to be done, yet I might have helped those same sufferers if only I'd been called on in time.'

I was struck by the sincerity with which he spoke and which glowed in his eyes. Yet his words prompted me to say, 'Mrs Craven believes you've come to judge *her* state of mind. Is that true? You told me yesterday you hadn't come to treat her.'

He frowned and drummed his fingers on the cloth before replying. 'Nor have I. I'm here only to assess the general situation. Charles Roche is very worried about his niece. He's head of the family and responsible for her while her husband's away. For his sisters, too.'

'She's very young,' I said, 'so much younger than her uncle and aunts. Do you know anything of her parents?'

'I know only that her father was a younger brother to the Roche ladies and Charles; I fancy his name was Stephen. Lucy was his only child. Both Stephen and his wife died when Lucy was an infant; I don't know in what circumstances.'

'I see,' I said. 'Well, I've come here to be companion to Lucy and not to be your spy, Dr Lefebre, nor that of Charles Roche. I wish to make that clear.'

'I wouldn't dream of asking you to spy on my behalf,' he returned calmly. 'That would be unpardonable behaviour on my part. Nor, in order to form an opinion, would I seek the help of someone so recently arrived on the scene.'

So that was me, put in my place.

I set down my cup. 'You're very direct,' I said. 'But I'm glad the matter is clear.'

He smiled. 'So are you very direct, Miss Martin. But I'm glad of it, truly. The people with whom I so often have to deal tend to prevaricate. I appreciate your plain speaking. Nor did I wish to suggest I thought your opinions of no value. I would always take anything you said very seriously, believe me. But in medical matters I have to make my own decisions and before I can do that, I have to dig out the details of the business in my own way.' He leaned forward. 'I am a teaser out of secrets, Miss Martin!'

With that, he pushed back his chair, bowed to me and walked out.

He had not been gone five minutes when the door opened a crack. I looked up and saw Lucy peeping into the room.

'He's gone!' I called.

The door opened more widely and she came in. 'I didn't want to meet him,' Lucy said truculently, staring at me as if I would reprove her for her lateness.

'I think he knows that,' I said.

Lucy shrugged and went to the sideboard to help herself to a single slice of cold beef. She put her plate on the table opposite to where I sat and took a chair. She was wearing a blue gown today. I'd decided to dress soberly in brown. I was, after all, the companion and Miss Roche would be watching details like dress with an eagle eye. I didn't intend to give her any occasion to criticise me. But I had added crocheted collar and cuffs.

'I heard you talking with him,' Lucy told me. 'I was in the small parlour next door.'

'Did you hear what we said?'

She shook her head. 'No, though I tried and I'm usually good at catching what people are saying. Your voices were too low. But I suppose you talked about me. In this house people do discuss me when I'm not there. Even when I am there they talk about me sometimes as if I weren't. You saw that yourself yesterday after dinner.'

'I told Lefebre I wouldn't be his spy,' I said.

Lucy, cutting into her beef, looked up at me and for the first time smiled. The change in her was remarkable. She was so pretty and had seen such tragedy already at so young an age. If nothing else, before I left here, I'd like to see that smile often dimpling her cheeks. But I mustn't hide things from her or she'd never trust me.

'I did ask him if he knew anything of your parents and he told me you're an orphan,' I confessed.

I was sorry immediately I'd said it because the smile faded from her face and eyes. The sullen look returned.

'Oh yes,' she said. 'They drowned.'

'But what a terrible thing!' I exclaimed. 'A tragedy!'

She shrugged. 'I've no memory of them. They were returning from the East. My father had gone out there to set up the office to deal in tea. Until then, the family were all of them in the silk trade and had been since the first Roche arrived in London and set up his shop in Spitalfields. Naughty old John Roche that Aunt Christina was telling you about yesterday. They made the cloth themselves then, or rather the weavers did. The weavers worked in the attics of the merchants' houses in those days using handlooms, whole families of them, even their children as soon as they were big enough.

'But the firm of Roche has always moved with the times. As

soon as the new factories opened in the north of England, where silk thread's woven into cloth using the power looms, Uncle Charles bought shares in factories in Macclesfield and Derby. The London looms were closed. Of course, that put the home weavers out of work. Many found themselves in the workhouse because of it and there they were put to such rough tasks that their hands were ruined for handling silk forever. But, as every Roche is taught, there is no place for sentimentality in business . . . and precious little room for it anywhere else!'

Lucy paused to sip her tea.

'When I was only twelve Uncle Charles took me north with him to visit one of the factories, because he believed I should see the progress of our modern age. It was quite terrifying, Lizzie. You should have seen the great waterwheels turning with such a roar and splashing. We were led into a huge shed full of machinery making an even more deafening noise. The heat was such I thought I'd faint. And, do you know? Some of the workers were children, just like me then. Some were younger than me, some my own age, a few a little older. I was very distressed and asked my uncle why they weren't in school. He told me they must work because their parents were poor, and they were fortunate to have such an employer offering many jobs. He said the very small ones were only supposed to work six and a half hours a day, and that too was "progress". Before the government brought in some new laws, they could work much longer. Now older children and women work only ten and a half hours a day. That still sounded a great deal to *me*, although Uncle Charles said it was a great improvement and "a sign of the enlightenment of our times". I still thought it very sad, the children looked so pale and ill. While I was there I saw one little boy fall asleep where he stood at the loom. He would have been caught in the machinery but Uncle

Charles ran forward and pulled him clear. Then the foreman came, a great bully of a man, and beat the poor little boy for falling asleep. After that Uncle Charles hurried me outside. He said I'd seen enough. I think he'd seen rather more than he wanted to.'

'What led him to add the import of tea to his interests?' I remarked, curious.

She hunched her shoulders. 'Uncle Charles believes in diversifying.' Suddenly she adopted a deep sonorous voice in imitation of her uncle. 'Don't put all your eggs in one basket in business!'

I thought wryly that my late godfather had been of similar mind when he diversified his business interests out of cloth and became such a notable slum landlord. I wondered what other pies Charles Roche had his thumb in? Lucy had a kind heart and was sorry for the young workers toiling among the noise, heat and dust of the factories to produce luxury cloth for wealthy women to wear; and the impression I'd received of Charles Roche was of a kindly man. I believed his genuine concern for his niece's welfare. But no doubt in business he saw only profit and loss instead of human beings. It reminded me of the people who stoked up their fires to a cheerful blaze with coal produced in such dangerous conditions underground, so often at the cost of lives.

'You know a great deal about your family's business interests, Lucy,' I remarked.

As had happened on the evening before, her childish features suddenly took on such a look of cynical resignation that I was again shocked. It seemed so out of place. Then it faded and was replaced with an almost equally abhorrent levity.

'I was born a Roche. Business, business, the talk is of nothing else in my Uncle Charles's house,' she said carelessly. 'It would have been the same in my father's had he lived. Perhaps it was to escape the talk and my aunts' company my mother accompanied my father on his journey to China. It must have seemed a great adventure and I don't blame her. They left me with servants and in the guardianship of Uncle Charles. The ship sank in a typhoon, as I told you. As soon as I was old enough, Uncle Charles sent me away to school.'

She swallowed another mouthful of beef before adding with that same unreal and misplaced cheerfulness, 'So, you see, I have always been an inconvenience to everyone.'

'I'm sure that's not how they see you!' I protested.

She shook her head and leaned across the table in a dramatic manner. 'Oh, but you don't know them yet. The Roche family is most respectable, Lizzie, as my Aunt Christina was at great pains to tell you last night. Even though we know from John Roche's diaries what a rascal our ancestor was. I found the diaries when I was twelve, hidden away in a drawer in Uncle Charles's house. Nobody knows I've seen them, only you. Seventeen illegitimate children, only fancy! In the end, even the other Huguenots would have nothing to do with him. Except in business, of course: they put their scruples aside for that.

'Aunt Christina, naturally, has chosen to "forget" all that old scandal. If she knew the diaries existed and Uncle Charles has them, I'm sure she'd seek them out to burn them. But Uncle Charles has quite a collection of books nobody knows about but me. He keeps them all in that desk.'

Her eyes met mine. There was a challenging gleam in them. She wanted to see if I was shocked and waited in anticipation for my protest.

She looked disappointed when I received her confession calmly. But I could well remember hiding myself away with my father's anatomy textbooks and poring over the curious illustrations. I, too, must have been about twelve years old at the time. But my early study of the human body appeared innocent compared with whatever Lucy had found in Charles Roche's secret cache of what he probably called 'erotica' and, where I came from, they called 'dirty books'.

'I'm surprised your Uncle Charles doesn't keep his collection locked away, not just lying there where a child could find them.'

'Oh, he does,' Lucy assured me. 'I saw him hiding the key. He put it in a blue and white vase on the mantelshelf in his study. So I waited until he was out and got it down and opened the drawer.'

I couldn't help but laugh although for a twelve-year-old to have found her uncle's collection was hardly desirable. 'And did you read the other books too, Lucy? Not only the diaries?'.

'Yes, of course I did. Or looked at the pictures mostly. Some of the books were in French. But the sort of French they taught us at school didn't have the right words in it.'

The image of prosperous, respectable Charles Roche floated before my inner vision. He probably locked his study door before he took his private reading from its drawer, to avoid being caught by a servant, or, indeed, his niece wandering in. 'It's a – a sort of hobby some gentlemen have,' I said. 'He would be embarrassed to know you'd seen them.'

'He shouldn't have locked the drawer,' retorted Lucy with simple logic. 'If he hadn't locked the drawer, I wouldn't have bothered to open it. Anyway, Aunt Christina will remind you again and again of the high standards of behaviour expected from all the family members and anyone associated with us. Respectability means no awkward loose ends. "A place for everything and everything in its place." That's Aunt Christina's favourite motto. My sin, Lizzie, is that there is not – nor has there ever been – any place for me. I litter the place like an unfinished piece of embroidery left on a chair. I should be tidied away. That's what your Dr Lefebre is here to do, tidy me away into the expensive private asylum he runs. I'm to be locked up where no one can see me, like John Roche's diaries.'

'He's not my Dr Lefebre!' I said sharply.

Lucy's response was to look mulish in a way already familiar. My one-time governess, Madame Leblanc, would have said firmly that pulling such a face was not *comme il faut*. What a strange little thing Lucy was, a doll in appearance, but on closer acquaintance a damaged doll.

I couldn't say I liked the idea that Lefebre, besides being a specialist in his field, also ran his own asylum. It did lend colour to Lucy's misgivings where he was concerned. But there again, as the doctor had pointed out, I knew nothing about the situation. If Lucy were deluded enough to believe her baby was not dead, she could also easily fancy Dr Lefebre had come to take her away with him to his private madhouse. I knew young people could cling to an idea against all argument. Lucy, having once seized on the notion, wouldn't easily relinquish it. It struck me that in all her chatter she had made no mention of her husband – and none of her child. The last, given her reported delusion, was odd.

This wasn't the moment to talk of them. In any case, the housekeeper, Mrs Williams, interrupted us.

'I'm sorry to disturb you, Mrs Craven – and Miss Martin, too – but Brennan is anxious to begin. He's waiting in the kitchen with one of his dogs and wants to let the animal loose here to see if it can sniff out the rat Miss Roche saw.'

Lucy shivered and pushed away her plate unfinished.

'You won't want to be here, ladies, so I suggest you go out for a walk,' went on Mrs Williams briskly.

I leaned across the table to Lucy who sat with downcast eyes and reminded her that she had promised to show me some of the countryside.

'Oh yes!' She looked up with quite an eager expression. 'We can leave now, if you're ready. I only need to fetch my hat.' Scrambling to her feet she hurried from the room.

I made to follow but Williams, who'd remained, touched my arm delaying me.

'You won't bring her back until you're sure the rat-catcher's gone?' the housekeeper asked in a low voice, her eyes searching my face. 'She has a sensitive nature. To watch Brennan at work wouldn't be helpful.'

'I'll make sure, trust me,' I returned.

The housekeeper's dour expression softened. 'Thank you, miss.'

I was surprised at her concern and thought that here at least was someone who cared for Lucy. I went to fetch my outdoor things.

Although it was still quite early the sun was up and the air fresh and warm. We walked out through the gates into the road and turned to the left.

'This is the way to the village,' said Lucy, 'although there's nothing much to be seen there. We have no society here to speak of. My aunts would play no part in it even if there were, so it makes no difference.'

She said this almost cheerfully as if she, too, were glad of the absence of the usual country social round: the calls, the card parties, the croquet matches, the subscription balls, all passed in the same limited company. But how often did she leave Shore House? Probably never without the company of one of her aunts.

Now I was here to relieve them of that chore. I glanced at her again. Her broad-brimmed hat was tied with blue satin ribbons matching her gown and both mirrored the colour of her eyes. In the shadow cast by the hat-brim her face had gained a liveliness that enhanced her prettiness. I ventured to congratulate myself on suggesting the walk and thought perhaps bringing Lucy out of her melancholia might not be so difficult, after all.

'Couldn't you visit your Uncle Charles in London?' I asked, suddenly struck by what seemed to me a very good idea. Surely a lively city with its varied distractions of a more sophisticated nature would be preferable to nun-like seclusion here.

'I'm not well enough to travel.' The vivacity had vanished and this was said in a flat tone that did not invite argument.

I hadn't taken into account the suddenness with which her mood could change. I'd been wrong to suppose my task would be simple. Every single sentence addressed to Lucy represented a throw of a dice as far as the speaker was concerned. You might win; you might lose.

With this last reply I suspected she was parroting the opinion voiced by others. We were walking along quite briskly and I must say she looked perfectly fit to me, at least physically. Mentally, of course, I had yet to judge but so far she only appeared to be lonely and unhappy. Any number of people might be so described; and if they were all to be declared insane and locked away the country would be full of asylums. Perhaps it was? At any rate, I wouldn't allow Lucy to be shut away in one, either Dr Lefebre's luxury version for the wealthy or any other. Perhaps my first task would be to persuade Lucy herself that she wasn't ill. But I would wait until I had spent more time in her company.

'I used to like Uncle Charles,' said Lucy suddenly, 'and I thought he liked me, but they have frightened him off me.

Anyway, he was horrible to poor James. I can't forgive him for that.'

This was the first mention by anyone of the absent James Craven. I wanted to ask Lucy how her uncle had been 'horrible'; also where and how she had met her husband and much more besides. But I already knew blunt questions upset her. If I were patient, in time she might speak freely.

As it happened we found ourselves approaching the church. It was a sturdy old building with a stubby tower. Jackdaws wheeled above it uttering their discordant cries. Surrounding it was an untidy burial ground. We stopped at the entry before its ancient lych-gate, roofed with mossy shingles sheltering a pair of wooden benches set either side of the path. Here the funeral procession, mourners and the departed, might take refuge in inclement weather, huddled together one last time to complain about the rain.

'This is our parish church,' Lucy indicated the building, 'it's said to be interesting by people who know about such things. Would you like to see inside it? It may be locked, of course. The village is about half a mile further on, which is inconvenient – for the villagers, I mean.'

I said I would like to see inside the church and we passed under the lych-gate and down the stony path to the porch. But the building was locked.

'We could fetch the key from the sexton,' said Lucy in her careless way, 'but you'll see inside on Sunday, anyway.'

We turned back and instead of walking straight towards the lych-gate and the road beyond, took a little path between headstones. Some leaned at a perilous angle and were very old, the lettering on them almost completely obliterated by lichen and the action of the elements. Insects buzzed around our ears and the quietness of the place and its atmosphere had an almost soporific effect.

I took advantage of the calm to ask, 'Have you recent news of Mr Craven?'

'I shall have a letter soon,' returned Lucy pettishly. 'It takes a very long time for a letter to reach England from China, you know. Anyway, I dare say they keep him so busy he has no time to write.'

Not even a scribbled note to his new young wife? Ben's words rang in my head. 'There is something fishy about this business!' Curious though I was, it didn't seem prudent to pursue the subject now.

Just at that moment I was distracted. A movement caught the corner of my eye. There was a big old yew tree growing some distance away and throwing a wide shade. It seemed to me that, in its dark shadow, something moved. I paused to stare in that direction but at first I could see nothing. Then a separate shadow distinguishable only by movement flitted across the space beneath the branches. It wasn't a bird. Though vague, the shape, if it could even be called that, was too large. There was someone there, watching us.

A churchyard is a public place and someone had come to tend a grave; that was the most likely explanation. The person was perhaps grieving and didn't want company.

Lucy had drawn a little ahead as I loitered so I hastened to join her. She'd stopped and I thought at first she waited for me. But there was another reason, as I soon saw. We stood before a little grave and a tiny headstone surmounted by a carved praying angel.

Louisa, infant daughter of James Craven and Lucy his wife, read the inscription.

I reached out and took Lucy's hand. 'I'm so very sorry, my dear,' I said gently.

She shook my hand away impatiently. '*That's* not my baby. How can you be so silly? *They've* put up that headstone but it's not *my* baby buried there. How can it be when my baby's alive? They've hidden her, you know.'

An audible catch of the breath escaped me. Dr Lefebre had warned me the poor young mother simply didn't accept her loss. But to hear Lucy say the words aloud chilled my blood.

Without warning she darted forward and seized my hand back in a desperate grip. 'Lizzie, you say you want to be my friend. Do you know where they've hidden my baby? I've looked everywhere here. I went to every house in the village and knocked on the doors. I asked if they'd seen my baby but they hadn't. Now the village mothers are afraid of me and won't let me look at their babies for fear I'll bewitch them. They don't understand and I can't make them. They think I'm mad. Sometimes I've got so cross when they wouldn't listen or try and understand what I wanted, I've felt as if my head would burst. Even the village children call me the madwoman and run away if they see me. If you do know where my baby is, please tell me!'

I don't think anything could have been worse than the intensity of her pleading eyes and the awful earnestness of her manner.

'Lucy,' I began tentatively, 'it is very hard for you to bear but—'

I wasn't allowed to finish. She flew into a rage little indicated by her previous way of talking. Her pale face reddened and she stamped her foot with anger on the soft earth. She released my hand, pushing me back with such unexpected force that I staggered.

'Don't begin to tell me more lies! Tell me if you really don't know where my baby is, but don't pretend my baby's buried there in that grave. Oh, it's too much! Isn't it enough that everyone else lies to me but they have to bring you and that doctor to add to them?'

'Why should I lie to you?' I returned calmly. 'Or, indeed, why should anyone lie to you or to me? Who are "they"?'

She blinked and appeared momentarily nonplussed. Her rage evaporated and she said in a sulky tone, 'My aunts, my uncle Roche, all the doctors they bring to see me, that stupid nurse, even the rector of this church here.'

She flung her hand out to indicate the little stone church behind us. 'When the village women complained about me to him, he went to see my aunts. They discussed me. I wasn't there, of course, I never am when they want to talk about me but I'm very good at eavesdropping, you know.' She said this with pride. 'They'd left open the window because the day was so warm, so I leaned out of the window in the room above and they raised their voices after a while, in an argument. The rector kept saying he "couldn't have it", as if my comings and goings had anything to do with him! I must be kept out of the village, he said. They must keep me in the house and grounds. They must face up to their responsibilities regarding me. Aunt Christina got very cross at that and told him a Roche always knew his or her responsibilities. They would make arrangements so that I shouldn't be left to roam. *Roam*, that was the word she used. Am I one of the forest ponies?'

'No, Lucy,' I said, because she paused and glared at me to demand an answer.

It satisfied her. 'Well, then,' she went on. 'I am a married woman and if James were here they would have nothing to say at all. As it was, they called me downstairs when the silly old rector had gone, and told me I must stay in the house and grounds or there would be consequences.'

'What consequences?' I asked.

She scowled. 'They said that, if I wouldn't do as bid, they'd be forced to lock me in my room "for my own good and safety". I demanded to know how this could be for my safety. Aunt Christina said the village women were afraid of me and thought me out of my senses. I might be attacked. Besides I was "sullying the Roche name" with my behaviour. "Outlandish", my aunt called it. Well, it wasn't the first time they'd accused me of that! They said the same when I married James. Aunt Christina and I had a terrible quarrel, but in the end I had to agree. If my Aunt Christina says a thing she means it. If I didn't "act normally", my aunt told me, they would seek specialist help. So I have stayed around the house and garden and that little bit of beach beyond. Yet still they've brought that doctor down from London to peer at me and listen to me . . .'

And they have brought me down to keep an eye on you when you leave the house and grounds I thought grimly. *I am to prevent any more embarrassing scenes with the villagers.*

'It's been hard for you,' I sympathised aloud, 'unable to go out for walks.'

Lucy frowned. 'They don't seem to mind if I walk on the beach – or they didn't until . . .'

Lucy's voice trailed off momentarily and she stubbed her boot against a tussock of coarse thin grass. 'They want me to agree my baby's dead and I won't. That's why Lefebre's here. But how can I say she is when I know she lives? In the end they'll all say I'm out of my wits. But it's a lie. *I'm not!* It isn't only about my baby they spin falsehoods, you know. They'll tell you wicked stories about James, too.'

Her anger was mounting again. Her eyes blazed as they had when she first caught sight of Lefebre. 'They will say James doesn't love me! But he does! He's the only person who ever wanted me.' Tears filled her eyes. 'I was nothing, *nothing* before I met James. He made me someone! He gave me his name so that I wasn't a Roche any more. But they didn't like that, did they? *They* sent him away to China. *He* didn't want to go. He wanted to stay with *me*.'

With that she picked up her skirts and ran off down the path. I hurried after her, calling her name, but she ignored me and carried on until we reached the lych-gate where I eventually caught up with her.

She was panting and looked quite wild, whirling to face me defiantly beneath the shingled roof. Her fair hair had fallen loose and framed her face beneath the hat-brim. Her temples glittered with beads of perspiration but she was dry-eyed now.

I indicated the wooden pews. 'Let's sit down for a little,' I suggested. 'I won't say anything to annoy you, I promise.'

Lucy threw herself down angrily on to one bench and I took the opposite one. She took off her hat and fanned herself for a moment with it before laying it down beside her. So we sat for a minute or two, avoiding one another's gaze.

Eventually Lucy, staring down at her hands, muttered sullenly, 'It's not your fault. You don't know them. But I know James loves me. When he comes home they'll have to admit it! James is very clever. He'll find my baby. We'll be together, all three of us.'

She seemed near to tears again so I said soothingly, 'Yes, yes, of course.'

At this she cheered up as suddenly as she had flown into a passion. It was as if she had forgotten the whole conversation. She even smiled. 'Do you want to go further? The village is very dull, as I told you. If we go back, there's a gate in the hedge in the far right-hand corner of the garden. It opens on to the beach and lets me go that way to walk. We could walk there now.'

That seemed a good idea and I quickly agreed. Lucy picked up her hat and crammed it back on her head with an abandon that made me smile.

'Do I look comical?' she asked anxiously.

'No, no, only let me tie the ribbons for you, there.'

She submitted with good grace and we set off back the way we had come. The road was as lonely as before, except for a solitary gypsy woman carrying a basket. She made as if to approach us, with hand already outstretched to beg. But then she saw Lucy's face. She abandoned her attempt to accost us and hurried on towards the village. As she did, she made a surreptitious gesture, warding away something unseen.

She thinks we're unlucky I mused wryly. But I'd no time to worry about trivial incidents like that. Shore House had come into sight and my precarious truce with Lucy was broken.

Dr Lefebre stood in front of the gate, looking up and down the road. The suspicion entered my mind he was looking for us. I fancy Lucy thought the same.

'Horrid, horrid man!' she shouted at him with every intention he hear her.

'Hush . . .' I gripped her arm in alarm. It wouldn't help her if he were to write in his notes that she'd abused him on the open road with the energy of a London street urchin.

She turned on me in another burst of that sudden passion I'd witnessed in the churchyard. 'Oh, you see, you'll take his part. No one will take mine! Well, *I* won't meet him. *I* won't talk to him. *I* won't see him!'

To my horror she then stooped, scooped up a stone from the

highway and threw it at Lefebre, screaming again, 'Go away, do you hear me?'

Fortunately her aim was poor. The pebble fell well short and bounced along the surface to rest a few feet from him. Lefebre gazed down at it with a detached interest and no show of surprise.

The thought raced through my brain: well, he will write *that* down in his notes.

'Lucy!' I hissed. 'Don't you see what harm you're doing to your own cause?'

She burst into tears. 'Leave me alone, all of you! Don't follow me, Lizzie, do you hear?'

Grasping her skirts, away she ran again, straight past the doctor without looking at him, through the gates and down a path beside the house.

'Dear me,' I heard him murmur as he stared after her. He turned to me as I came up to him and raised his eyebrows.

'We visited the child's grave,' I explained, 'so please excuse her. Why are you standing here? Were you looking for us? Because if you were, I really wish you'd kept out of the way. You can see how the sight of you upsets her. Is it to be wondered at? She believes you've come to take her to your madhouse.'

'Clinic,' he protested mildly. 'No, I wasn't waiting for you and Mrs Craven. As it happens, I'm waiting while Greenaway saddles a horse for me. I intend to ride out over the heath.'

I realised then that he wore riding breeches and top boots, although he still had his neatly buttoned black coat and shiny hat. His gloves had been changed for those of pigskin.

Oh, Lizzie! I thought ruefully. Perhaps I ought to apologise for accusing him but before I could, he spoke again.

'I agree Mrs Craven did seem a little put out. She recognised the grave as her child's?'

But I'd no intention of telling him of Lucy's behaviour and accusations in the churchyard.

'I've told you,' I reminded him, 'I won't be your spy. I won't report to you or anyone else on any conversation I may have with Mrs Craven. She needs to feel she can trust someone, that there is someone she can confide in who won't gossip and won't be prejudiced in any way about her state of mind or anything else.'

'Oh, I respect that,' he replied hastily. 'I agree, she does need a friend whom she can trust.'

There was an awkward moment. 'Dr Lefebre,' I began, highly embarrassed, 'although I can't confide in you, there is one matter I would like to ask you about, if you'll allow me, of course. I do appreciate I propose an unfair trade. I'll quite understand if you tell me to mind my own business.'

He raised his eyebrows but said nothing. I was forced to blunder on.

'It concerns James Craven and his going to China. It seems so odd to have sent the young man away like that. Charles Roche is your friend. Doesn't it seem strange to you?'

Dr Lefebre put his hand to his chin and rubbed his whiskers. 'Mrs Craven's told you, no doubt, that he'll come back to her? No, no, don't answer that. You won't do so, anyway, will you?' He smiled. 'You're right and it is an unfair trade. *I* should supply your curiosity. *You* are quite like a father confessor. You listen to others' sins and troubles but your lips are sealed. Well, a doctor is like that, too.'

I felt myself blush furiously.

He held up his hand and went on, 'However, James Craven isn't my patient so nothing prevents me speaking of him.

'So, let me tell you about Craven, since you ask and since that *is* the beginning of all the trouble. It's right, better, you should know the facts. Craven is one of those good-looking, likeable young men without fortune but with a quick brain, a pleasing manner and no scruples.'

'Have you met him?' I asked. 'Or has someone told you this of him?'

'You and I, dear lady, met only yesterday,' Lefebre said with gentle reproof, 'but I fancy you should already know me better than that. Believe me, Miss Martin; I do not rely on the judgement of others. It is my own opinion based on the opportunity I've had to observe the misery the wretched youth has caused to all and sundry.'

'Yes, of course,' I muttered, both humbled and annoyed to feel so.

He nodded. 'I also met the young fellow on several occasions.' Lefebre's face grew grim. 'He arrived in London just over two years ago rather like Dick Whittington, to seek his fortune. His first step was to approach Charles Roche with whom he claimed some kinship. I think he hoped Roche would take him into the business – in a small way, of course. I dare say at first he had no more than a hope of a clerkship. He was frank that he was without funds but he didn't mention that he was seriously encumbered with debts; some of them run up through gambling. In the course of my professional life, I've had to deal with several cases of people brought low by an addiction to gaming, driven right out of their minds by it. Most of them, at the outset of their careers, displayed the happy, sanguine disposition of young Craven.

'My friend Roche is a kind-hearted and generous man and Craven has the knack of charming the birds out of the trees. Before we all knew it, he was living under my friend's roof in Chelsea – and there he met Lucy Roche, as she then was, barely sixteen and only a few weeks earlier arrived from boarding school.

'Craven saw his opportunity. There, I can say it no other way than bluntly. It would be the biggest gamble of his life so far; but he reckoned the odds to be reasonably stacked in his favour. The girl had no experience of the world. She had probably never met any young men socially or certainly none like Craven. She had no mama or older sisters to look out for her. She was doubtless anxious to escape the chaperonage of her aunts. The ladies regard young persons rather as they would regard those ponies roaming freely on the heath here: unpredictable, only half tame, and liable to be obstinate.

'The young man declared his love for her and she believed him completely. But no family likes a fortune hunter and the Roche family is particularly zealous in defending its interests. So he made sure his offer wouldn't be rejected out of hand, *could* not be rejected, if you follow me?'

He paused and raised his eyebrows.

'I think I do,' I said with sinking heart. Craven had seduced her. Perhaps it hadn't been so very difficult. Lucy's curiosity about sex had already been awakened by her eager study of her uncle's 'collection'.

'Quite so. She was duly found to be with child. Now Craven showed his true colours. He approached Charles Roche with what I might almost call a shopping list of requests. He would marry Lucy but at a price, although he did not express it so baldly. Firstly, all his debts must be settled before any ceremony took place. As to the future, he argued that he and his wife would need a new house in a smart part of London. They would need to live in some style. Roche would be required to allow his niece a generous income and at the same time pay Craven a magnificent salary for some position in the business far above that of a mere clerk. There was no mention, mark you, of Craven earning the salary he felt he could command. He clearly expected the post to be a sinecure.'

'Charles Roche has taken him into the business,' I pointed out. 'Does that mean he agreed to everything?'

'What else could he do? Allow Craven to ruin the girl's reputation and her whole future? To say nothing of breaking her heart? The child believed in the wretch and still does.'

'But Craven's reputation would also be ruined if he abandoned her,' I protested.

Lefebre shook his head. 'My dear Miss Martin, believe me, a rogue like that, whatever his past history, will always find a new victim eager to succumb to his charm and blandishments. Lucy would be tainted as a fallen woman and her child suffer ignominy as a bastard, but the world, my dear Miss Martin, treats a man very differently.'

I knew this to be true and nodded.

'Charles Roche was obliged to save his niece's good name and that of the house of Roche, to say nothing of calming his sisters whose reaction to the unwelcome news you can imagine. But he's not a fool. Craven didn't get all he asked for – or at least not in the way he asked. He was told he would be taken into the business, but not in London. He would be despatched to the company's tea offices and warehouses in Canton. He would indeed receive a fine salary . . . but only for as long as he remained abroad. His wife would be placed in the care of the Roche ladies and all her financial requirements directly taken care of by her uncle, without the intervention of her husband. James Craven is, to put it in a nutshell, a remittance man. He won't be without plenty of similar companionship where he is now. The ports of the Far East have quite a population of European families' black sheep. All are awaiting the regular allowance from home; and all of them well aware they are expected never to return there.'

I took a few moments to digest all this. 'Mr Charles Roche,' I said slowly, 'rather let me understand that Mr Craven would eventually run the tea business.'

'That is the fiction put about for public consumption, Miss Martin. But no, James Craven will never run anything. He will be allowed to dissipate his time in Canton where there's already a competent agent. He will never be allowed to make a decision of any importance and certainly not permitted to get his fingers near the till.'

I must have looked surprised at the crudeness of this last image. Lefebre grimaced. 'I've succeeded in shocking you.'

'No, no,' I said, 'but it's all very distressing. Lucy believes—' I broke off because I had been about to do what I had told him I would not do: reveal some of my conversation with Lucy.

He didn't need me to tell him. He was shaking his head. 'She believes he loves her and will return to England to be with her. But no, he will not. She'll never see him again and I doubt even hear from him. If he cared a jot for her he would never have agreed to be sent away from her, certainly not to such an unhealthy spot for Europeans. The death toll is high. That's why single men are usually sent out there. Craven could have refused on those grounds but then he would have no money to spend as he saw fit. If he remained here with his wife, Roche would require their household bills to be sent directly to him for settlement and that would be it. Every item would need to be accounted for.

'Lucy's own money, you understand, comes from her inherited share in the business and is in trust. As such, all outgoings must have the approval of her Uncle Charles and his fellow-shareholders, chiefly his sisters, who act as trustees. It was arranged like that before her parents left on their unlucky voyage.

They had in mind the risk she might be left an orphan. The arrangement cannot be reviewed until she is twenty-one, whether she is married by then or not. The reasoning behind it was to protect the commercial interests of the house of Roche and, as things turned out, it protected her fortune against Craven's ambitions, at least for the moment. He wasn't best pleased to learn there would be no guineas for him to jingle in his pocket and toss on to the baize of the gaming tables. I fancy he was surprised to find himself outmanoeuvred. But he accepted without too much argument when he saw that was all he was going to get and off he went.'

Lefebre turned and looked again after Lucy. 'It is not unknown, when the truth is unbearable, to take refuge in fantasy. I've seen all too many cases of that.'

Before I could reply to this he added briskly, 'But Greenaway will be wondering where I've got to. I'll see you later, Miss Martin.'

With that he touched the brim of his hat and walked smartly away.

Chapter Seven

Elizabeth Martin

I WASN'T sure what to do next. Lucy might have run into the house. If so, she'd probably locked herself in her room. She wouldn't open the door for me until she'd calmed down.

But she knew the rat-catcher was expected that morning. She wouldn't risk encountering either him or, in her present state, her aunts. Where else then, might she run?

To the beach! I thought. She'd told me of the gate in the laurel hedge at the bottom of the garden. Dr Lefebre had spoken at breakfast of strolling through the garden to the beach the previous evening after dinner. If he'd found the exit, and by moonlight, it couldn't be so hard to discover.

Yet if I hadn't known it was there I might have passed it by. I was surprised the doctor had discovered it at night. It was only a small wooden wicket gate and the large strong leaves of the laurels disguised it. It couldn't be much used, yet some of the laurel twigs had snapped. I paused to examine them. The fresh breaks could have been caused by Lefebre . . . or by the mystery man with the white dog? Had he entered the property this way? The older healed breaks might be Lucy's doing. I pushed at the gate. The encroaching hedge resisted, but the hinges were oiled (another surprise) and a really good shove on my part forced it open. I stepped through on to the shore.

The sun shone brightly in my face. I paused to enjoy its warmth and take in the wonderful sight of the glittering spots of light dancing across the water, some way away because the tide was out again. The coastline of the Isle of Wight with its hills and the buildings appeared to beckon. But the nearness of the island was an illusion.

I'm sorry to confess that for ten minutes or so I quite forgot I was looking for Lucy. Perhaps I wanted to put the whole wretched business out of mind for a while. I liked Lucy and wanted to help her but I didn't know what to believe or whom, here, I could trust to tell me the truth. Lucy was frankly spoken to the point of naivety; but her sudden changes of mood made it difficult if not downright impossible to discuss anything with her. 'I'm good at eavesdropping', she'd announced without any embarrassment. So perhaps subterfuge was not entirely beyond her.

As for Lefebre, he appeared an honourable man but I thought, with a smile, he'd be a good chess player. Perhaps he'd play a match with one of the Roche sisters during his stay. They appeared to like the game.

The wildness of shoreline, its hotch-potch of unfamiliar objects tossed down in abandon, together with the extraordinary clarity of the light, seduced me away from my complicated musings. I began to crunch my way over the pebbles holding my skirts clear, lacking the means to pin them up, and careful not to turn my ankle. The beach was mostly of scoured pale grey or light brown pebbles cast up in drifts by the sea and kept in place at intervals by lines of wooden groynes. They marched stoutly down the shore and out into the water, like rows of blackened rotted teeth. But between the patches of rapidly drying ridged shingle were areas of damp sand so smooth and flat they might have been ironed. The retreating waves had left them speckled with worm casts and scattered with sea shells, both whole and in myriad fragments resembling nothing so much as crushed eggshells. Among them lay strange objects of whiteness so pure it almost seemed luminescent. When I picked them up to examine them, I recognised them as the skeletons of cuttlefish that cage bird owners wedge in the bars for the feathered inmates to peck at.

Equally fascinating were the lengths of seaweed washed up in great tangled clumps or single strands. Some of it was dark brown, some bright green, some shiny and delicate, some coarse and covered with bubbles. I picked up a piece and pressed one between my fingers; the bubble popped in a satisfactory manner oozing some substance giving off a strong ammonia-like smell. I dropped it quickly. There was other debris too, bits of wood and oddments of fish and scraps of fishing net. Among it all searched the gulls, ignoring my presence.

I stooped to pick up another piece of cuttlefish and then gave a cry and stumbled back. My fingers had almost brushed against the bloated body of a dead rat, perhaps washed ashore from a ship's hold. I retreated clear of it.

The encounter made me think of Brennan the rat-catcher and that in turn made me remember, with a start of guilt, that I was here looking for Lucy.

Shielding my eyes against the glare of light from the water, I peered in both directions along the shoreline but could see no sign of her. A few hundred yards away a clump of flat-topped pines clustered in a huddled group edging towards the sea like nervous bathers. At high tide their roots must almost stretch to the water's edge. The exposure to the wind had led to them inclining their trunks shoreward. At their base, brambles straggled untidily. Perhaps she had hidden herself away in that thicket?

I began to make my way towards the spot and as I neared it a small white dog of terrier type ran out from the trees and scampered towards me, barking.

I thought it was one of Brennan's dogs. I stopped, hoping he was nearby to call it off, because they'd struck me as snappy little beasts. Almost at once, to my relief, I heard a man shout and a male figure took shadowy form among the leaning pines and undergrowth.

'Stay, Spot!' he called sharply and the little dog obediently sank to its haunches. I saw it wasn't one of the rat-catcher's dogs, although similar in breed. This one had a coat brushed clean, a neat leather collar and was obviously a pet. It looked up at me with bright inquisitive gaze, tongue lolling.

'Why,' I said to it, bending over it, 'you're a very fine fellow!'

The dog responded by giving me what I can only describe as a silly grin and thumped its stubby tail. The man, swinging his walking stick to either side to clear the path, emerged from the trees. This was not Brennan.

I reached out to pat the little dog and the man began to hurry towards us, his heavy footsteps crunching noisily on the shingle. 'Lucy?' he called eagerly.

I stood up and he saw his mistake. He was only a few feet away now and stopped with such a patent look of disappointment on his face that I had to hide a smile.

'I'm sorry,' I said. 'I'm not Mrs Craven. I'm Elizabeth Martin and I've just arrived at Shore House to be Mrs Craven's companion.'

He rallied and pulled his bowler hat from his curly hair. 'I beg your pardon, Miss Martin. I'm very pleased to make your acquaintance. I'm Andrew Beresford. I own some land hereabouts and live nearby.' He gestured vaguely with his cane. 'I farm,' he added.

It seemed to me that with his well-tailored suit of expensive lightweight woollen material, educated voice and indeed his whole manner, he was what is usually called 'a gentleman farmer', overseeing the efforts of others. Still, his face was sunburned and he looked a solid sort of man used to taking plenty of exercise in the fresh air. I put his age at about thirty-two.

I thought of the oiled hinges of the gate from Shore House to the beach.

'I was walking with Mrs Craven earlier but she's gone indoors,' I said.

His tanned cheeks grew redder. His eyes searched my face. 'Is she well? She hasn't gone into the house because she's been taken unwell?'

There was genuine anxiety in his voice. This is a complication, I thought to myself.

'She's quite well, thank you, Mr Beresford.'

'Please tell her I send my best compliments and . . .'

At this point he stumbled into awkward silence and I rescued him.

'We passed fields yesterday on our way across the health. Is that your estate?'

'Some of it,' he said immediately, glad to seize the escape route. 'But please don't imagine I'm one of the great landowners hereabouts. Beside the farmland itself, there is only the farmhouse where my manager lives; its outbuildings; a row of labourers' cottages; my own house and a paddock or two.'

'Was Shore House ever part of your estate?' I asked on the spur of the moment.

He shook his head. 'That belonged to someone who had inherited it but had no use for it. It stood empty for some years until about five years ago Mr Charles Roche bought it. The villagers were very pleased to think that it would be occupied again. It made a sad sight standing alone and empty and, of course, there would be work to be had in the employ of the new owners.'

Beresford indicated the countryside behind us. 'You can see for yourself there's little work here but on the land. Not so very long ago, less than a hundred years, this was a great coast for smuggling, although the currents are treacherous. A good many people earned a living from it.' He pulled a wry face. 'In fact, whole villages were given over to it to the extent that hardly anyone was to be seen about during the day – they all got up at nightfall and went about their business then. Those days are gone although some old people still remember them. My butler will tell you how, as a child, he was warned never to speak of those midnight comings and goings, and how even the most respectable housewife thought nothing of buying her tea surreptitiously from a contraband cargo. Now there's great poverty here, I'm afraid.

'But folk were disappointed if they had hopes of Shore House. Roche explained to me, when he called on me to introduce himself, that it was not for his own use but to be a home for his sisters. They were of a retiring nature and wanted somewhere quiet. They brought a housekeeper from London together with a cook and their personal maid. From the local population they employ only a couple of housemaids, a groom and a boy . . . and a gardener, of course. Charles Roche's niece, Mrs Craven, joined her aunts about six months ago.'

He threw a wistful look towards the laurel hedge bounding the property. 'I didn't meet her when she first arrived as she was nearing the time of her lying-in. I have met her several times since, here on the beach, by chance, of course,' he added hurriedly.

'I'm glad to hear she meets anyone,' I said. 'This lonely house might suit the older ladies. But I can't think it's the best place for a young woman, especially someone like Lucy, who'd benefit from more lively company.' I hesitated, unsure how to word what I wanted to say. 'You'll be aware she's had troubles,' I said. 'She needs distraction but not more complexities.'

Beresford gave me a long level look. 'I hope you will be able to help Lucy – Mrs Craven. I'm well aware her life of late has not been happy. She's in need of younger female companionship. I'm not criticising the Roche ladies, of course. But shall we say they are somewhat set in their ways?'

'I also hope I'll be able to help Mrs Craven,' I told him. 'That's why I'm here, after all. I'm pleased to have met you, Mr Beresford.'

'Oh, yes, likewise . . .' He replaced his bowler hat. 'I hope we'll meet again, Miss – er – Martin. Come, Spot!'

He whistled to the little dog, which jumped up and trotted off at his heels.

I made my way slowly back to the gate. What was I to make of all this? Lucy liked to walk on the beach and obviously Andrew Beresford liked to hang about there in the hope of encountering her. So who had oiled the hinges of the garden gate? His interest in her was plain. The hope in his voice when he had called out; his familiarity in using her first name; together with the disappointment in his face when he saw someone else: all that made it clear.

It didn't make it better. If anything, it made the situation worse. James Craven might be frittering away his remittance money in Canton's gambling palaces, drinking dens and, for all I knew, opium houses. But he was still Lucy's husband. That was why I'd spoken as I had to Beresford. It was perhaps presumptuous of me to do so and on so slight an acquaintance. He'd have been quite entitled to take offence. But poor Lucy was already confused enough.

'Oh, dear,' I murmured aloud to myself in an unconscious echo of Dr Lefebre.

This was not only a further complication but a puzzle, too. Lucy appeared to be devoted to her absent husband. But someone the previous night had made an assignation in the garden with a person owning a small white terrier dog. Had the beach promenades (and the meetings with Beresford) been reported to Charles Roche? Had that led to his engaging me to be his niece's companion? Two might be tempted to dally: three were a crowd.

I set off back. As I squeezed through the little gate into the property it occurred to me that if Lucy hadn't gone into the house, as I suspected she hadn't, and hadn't gone down to the shore, then the garden was another place she might have taken refuge. I set off towards the far end where a dense shrubbery of rhododendrons might offer concealment.

As I neared the spot I heard a curious sound, high-pitched and desolate to the point of eeriness. It stopped me in my tracks. After a moment I identified it as the whining of a small dog. The distress in that whine sent a shiver up my spine. I hurried forward, calling, 'Lucy! Lucy, are you there? It's Lizzie. Please reply if you hear me, and don't hide!'

There was no human answer, only the increased whining of the dog and then, a second, strange noise was added it, a little like a whine but coming in short, sharp bursts like tiny yelps.

I rounded the biggest of the dark green rhododendrons and stopped in horror.

In a small clear patch among the bushes, a little like a den, Lucy was crouched, pressed into the background of green leaves and dark dusty branches. Her blue skirts were crumpled in disarray. Her broad-brimmed hat lay some distance away and her hair had fallen loose round her face. Her eyes, opened as wide as they could go and turned towards me, were wild and filled with horror. From her open mouth issued the staccato noises I had taken for canine yelps but were in fact the inarticulate gasps of a woman about to break into the screams of hysteria.

One of Brennan's terriers crouched by the sprawled body of its master. The rat-catcher lay on his back. His eyes were as wide open as Lucy's but his expression was one of extreme astonishment. Both arms were bent at the elbow and rested on his chest with the fingers curled claw-like at his garish red neckerchief. It was as if he reached for the object protruding from his neck just above the scarf but panic or something else had prevented his finding it. The thing he had so vainly scrabbled for resembled the hilt of an ornamental dagger. It had been driven in above the collarbone until the blade disappeared completely. Brighter by far than his neckerchief was the glistening scarlet flood that had oozed from the wound.

Blood! Oh dear heaven, it was everywhere on his upper body, drenching shirt and moleskin waistcoat, his jacket and even the surrounding grass. The butcher's shop odour of it crept into my nostrils. The sun sparkled on it. Already curious flies were gathering and the soft persistent buzz of their excitement filled the air.

Shock froze me in a moment of strange detachment. Illustrations from my father's medical textbooks sprang to my mind from far back in the mists of childhood. I thought: *the carotid artery's severed. But the blood's stopped pumping out. The heart's stopped. He's dead.*

Lucy moved and I saw that her sleeves and bodice were smeared with gore. Slowly she stretched out bloodstained hands to me.

'I didn't do it,' she whispered in a tortured hoarse voice, 'please tell them, Lizzie, I didn't do this.'

The little terrier put back its head, raised its pointed muzzle to the sky and let out a long, wailing howl.

Lucy began to shriek.

Chapter Eight

Elizabeth Martin

THE SHRILL sound of Lucy's cries broke my momentary paralysis. I hurried forward and seized her arms, trying to pull her to her feet. My intention was to get her away from the body but she sagged in my embrace and I found myself supporting her.

'Come along, Lucy,' I urged, tugging desperately at the inert form in my arms. 'Let's go indoors and I'll tell them about this. Someone else will deal with it.'

Who'd have thought that slightly built girl could have weighed so much? I'd have had as much chance of moving the dead man. But others had already heard her screams and it wouldn't be necessary for me to haul Lucy indoors or carry the shocking news there. People came running from all directions. From the house came the housekeeper, Mrs Williams, her black skirts flapping. Behind her came the shirt-sleeved figure of a gardener, grasping a spade at the ready should it be needed as a weapon. From the beach came Andrew Beresford running full tilt, his dog scampering behind him.

The arrival of all these people, especially another dog, had an immediate effect on Brennan's ratter. It jumped up and rolled back its upper lip in a snarl revealing its sharp yellow teeth; then took up a protective stance before the body of its fallen master and began to utter hideous growls.

Mrs Williams ran straight to us and wrested Lucy from my arms.

'There, there, my precious,' she crooned, smoothing Lucy's hair, 'Williams will take care of you. Williams will take care of everything. Only come indoors with me and I'll get you to your bed. Come along, Miss Lucy . . .'

Lucy Craven seemed to respond to the familiar voice. She whimpered and made an effort to stand up. Supported by Williams, she allowed herself to be led away towards the house.

'What the devil's happened here?' demanded Beresford of me.

'I know no more than you! Only that Brennan there is dead and I found Lucy by the body.'

'Damn it!' he shouted, advancing on me, his face red with fury. 'You're not suggesting *Lucy* had anything to do with this? That's outrageous!'

My frayed nerves snapped. 'I'm saying nothing of the sort. I'm only telling you what I saw.'

We faced up to one another like a pair of fighting cockerels until the gardener spoke, drawing our attention.

'His little dog will have been digging that out,' he said.

Both Beresford and I turned to look and saw the man standing a little way off pointing downwards to where the roots of the rhododendron bush reached into a bank of soft, sandy soil. Natural erosion had led to the roots being partly exposed, forming a twisting net. Busy paws had further excavated the earth and it was strewn all around. Revealed by the terrier's efforts was a rat's nest, tucked in among the cat's cradle of roots. In it huddled the rat babies, pale white, blind and bloated. They looked disgusting and I turned away, my gorge rising, as the gardener raised his spade. From behind me came a sickening *thump*.

'What are you doing here, sir?'

The new voice cut through the air like the crack of a whip. We all spun round.

Miss Roche had arrived. She was glaring at Beresford in fury. 'Be so good as to leave this property, sir!'

'I came because I heard Mrs Craven cry out . . .' he began.

Miss Roche's face whitened. 'I've forbidden you this house and its grounds, as you very well know. Mrs Craven is my niece and in my care and any matter concerning her will be dealt with by me without your assistance, sir.'

Beresford, I was glad to see, stood his ground. He indicated the body. 'That fellow's dead. With the greatest respect, I suggest this isn't a matter with which you can deal, ma'am. It's one for the competent authorities, that's to say the police. I suggest that I—'

He was not allowed to continue.

'*At once!* Do you hear me? Neither you nor your help is needed here. You shall go at once or Callow there will throw you out!'

It seemed Callow was the gardener and he looked distinctly alarmed at the prospect of wrestling with a healthy muscular fellow like Beresford. Nor, I fancy, did he like the idea of threatening a local landowner with a spade.

This time Beresford accepted his dismissal, albeit reluctantly. 'I'll go at once, Miss Roche, since you ask me to. But I hope you won't hesitate to call on me if you find, after all, there is some way I can help.'

'That is unlikely,' he was informed.

Beresford, hat in hand, bowed politely and strode towards the shore gate with his little dog at his heels. Brennan's dog continued to growl fiercely. The gardener, Callow, had turned his attention to the animal.

He raised his spade again and I cried out, 'No!' so fiercely he stopped with it high in the air and stared at me in surprise.

'No more killing.' My voice shook with emotion but they all knew I meant it.

Callow lowered his spade and for a brief moment even Miss Roche looked at me almost with respect. Then she twitched an eyebrow in the familiar way.

'Take the dog away, Callow,' she ordered.

This order discomfited the gardener almost as much as her previous one. 'We'll have to get a net, ma'am, to throw over him. There will be no getting near him like he is. Nasty savage little beast, that is, at the best of times. I got some netting in my shed, over in the kitchen garden. I'll go and fetch it. But don't either of you ladies try and get near Brennan there or the dog will have you. You had better go in the house, ma'am, and the other lady. This ain't no sight for you.' He hesitated. 'Shall us fetch Constable Gosling? Likely this *is* his business.'

'Whatever for?' asked Miss Roche.

'This is murder, ma'am,' I whispered to her.

'Well, it's nothing to do with us. Someone got into the garden, probably someone with a grudge against Brennan.'

'But the constable must be sent for, Miss Roche,' I insisted. 'Mr Beresford may well inform him himself and if we haven't, it will look odd.' I played my trump card. 'People will talk.'

That threat, as I suspected, weighed with her. Gossip would be furious anyway once the news got out. But she would want to be seen to have done the right thing.

'Oh, very well,' she said crossly. 'If you will have it so. Callow, tell Greenaway to ride for the constable.'

'I fancy Lye Greenaway is out riding with the gentleman,' said Callow.

'Then send him when he gets back. Whatever is the matter with everyone?' Miss Roche whirled round and set off briskly back to the house.

I had no wish to linger here any longer with corpse, snarling dog or rat's nest. I followed her quickly. Besides, there was something I needed to do.

Miss Roche was in the house ahead of me and by the sound of distraught wails coming from the drawing room was telling Miss Phoebe what had happened. I hurried to the hall table and looked among the objects there. Earlier that morning when I had put my letter to Ben in the postbox, the ornamental dagger had still been lying by the silver tray. I would swear to it. But it was not there now.

I turned at the rustle of a woman's skirts. Mrs Williams was coming down the stairs. Bundled in her arms was Lucy's bloodstained dress. She paused in her descent to treat me to an accusing stare.

'I asked you particularly, Miss Martin, not to let Mrs Craven come back while the rat-catcher was here.'

'I couldn't prevent her,' I returned sharply. 'She didn't return to the house where we thought Brennan was at work, anyway, but to the garden. Why was Brennan in the garden? I understood his business was indoors.'

'The dog couldn't pick up any scent of a rat here.' Mrs Williams indicated the hall and general downstairs area with a jerk of her chin. 'Brennan thought one might have come in from the stables. To flush it out he'd need both dogs and would have to return to his camp to fetch the other one. So first he thought he'd look in the garden. His other guess was that a rat had made a nest out there and the parent rat had crept into the house seeking food.'

'There is a rat's nest,' I said. 'It's near the body. Have you put Mrs Craven to bed?'

'I have – and dosed her with a little laudanum I had by. She's fallen asleep. The poor lamb was in a dreadful state.'

That meant that when Constable Gosling arrived he wouldn't be able to question her. I wondered whether in dosing Lucy with the opiate, Mrs Williams had been thinking of that. I indicated the bundled stained gown in her arms.

'It would be better if you didn't order that washed before the constable comes. He'll want to see it.'

Williams darted down the remaining stairs, her face working alarmingly. 'Miss Lucy, poor dear, had nothing to do with this. That's a wicked thing to suggest!'

'I am not suggesting it, Mrs Williams. But the gown is what's called evidence and should be preserved as it is until the representative of the law arrives.' I held out my arms. 'Shall I keep it safe?'

'I shall take my instructions from Miss Roche,' Williams retorted. 'Not from you, miss! You're the companion here and no more or less. As I see it, it's no part of a companion's duties to allow this sort of thing to happen.'

She hurried away with the bloody clothing in her arms and I very much feared that Constable Gosling would never see it.

I realised at this point that my own gown was blood smeared from my attempts to get Lucy to her feet. I hurried upstairs to change it. I'd only just done so, and put the stained patch to soak in some cold water left in the jug on the washstand, when there was a tap at my bedroom door.

I opened it to discover Dr Lefebre, still in riding attire, standing outside. He raised a hand to his lips to enjoin me to silence.

'Miss Martin,' he whispered. 'It's vitally important you tell me privately what happened; before the constable gets here.'

When I hesitated, he took matters into his own hands and stepped briskly into my room, closing the door behind him.

'Dr Lefebre—' I began in protest.

'Don't turn into a simpering miss on me,' he interrupted sharply. 'You're a young woman of sense and believe me, you need to speak up plainly now and tell me every single thing you know about this.'

I'd already decided the doctor was better as a friend than an enemy.

'All right,' I said, 'it's better you hear it from me.'

As far as I knew the sisters were downstairs and he was a shrewd enough man not to have let a servant see him coming into my room. I told him all I felt I could without compromising Lucy any further. So I omitted my meeting and conversation with Andrew Beresford. But I explained I had gone to the shore hoping to find Lucy there and, failing, had begun to seek her in the garden. I had heard strange sounds which led me to the grisly discovery.

'I really don't believe she could have done this,' I added earnestly. 'She is such a little thing and Brennan a strong fellow. Besides, why should she?'

'Where is she now?' Lefebre demanded, ignoring my protests. He'd listened closely to every word I'd said, occasionally muttering into his beard but making no other comment.

I told him she was sleeping, having been given a mix of laudanum and water by the housekeeper on her own initiative.

'Well,' he observed in a sour tone, 'that effectively removes her from examination either by the constable or by me. I would have preferred to have spoken to her before the constable arrived and made some judgement as to her state of mind.'

'State of mind? She was hysterical,' I told him indignantly. 'What can you expect? She gave birth only months ago and is herself nothing but a child.'

He was unsympathetic to this argument. 'She may well have been squawking and wailing; but the condition popularly described as "hysterical" is a complicated matter. The once-held belief that it originates in female disorders, if I may call them so to spare your blushes, is now widely doubted. It can indicate a variety of things to a trained observer.'

'That she is guilty?' I cried angrily.

'Or that she is innocent,' came the cool reply. 'Now I've no way of judging. Williams may have thought she was doing Mrs Craven a favour but take it from me, she's done her a disservice.'

'Williams has also taken Lucy's bloodstained gown,' I admitted. 'I told her it was evidence and shouldn't be washed before the constable arrives, but I'm afraid it's steeping in cold water at this very moment.' I indicated the basin, and the garment draped over it, on my washstand with some embarrassment. 'As is mine. Perhaps I should have left mine, too, as it was. Incidentally, Mrs Williams is laying the blame for all this at my feet. Or, at least, she blames me for Lucy finding the body. Perhaps she's right and I should have kept closer to Lucy, and not stood chatting to you at the front gate.'

'Confound it! That housekeeper is meddling. No doubt in her own mind it's for the best, but it is not. Williams must be made to see that this is a matter for the authorities, however innocently Mrs Craven is involved. As for your actions, there's not the slightest reason for you to shoulder any blame. You're the young woman's companion and not her shadow.'

I was grateful for his support though I still hesitated to tell him the thing that troubled me. But he was right. It was a matter for the authorities and nothing must be hidden. I came to a decision.

'Dr Lefebre, there is one more thing . . .' I told him about the knife missing from the hall table.

'You think it was the same as protruded from Brennan's neck?' His eyes watched mine closely.

'I couldn't swear to it without seeing it again . . . but the hilt was very similar and the knife in the hall isn't there now. It was there on the table by the postbox before breakfast; I could swear to that.'

'Hm,' said Lefebre, smoothing his moustache with thumb and forefinger. 'This is not a matter for a village constable or even for a provincial detective from Southampton. We shall have to send to Scotland Yard.'

'To Scotland Yard!' I gasped.

'Yes, this is not a matter to be dealt with locally, some tavern brawl or armed footpad. If the knife used was taken from the hall here then Brennan was not killed by an intruder in the garden.'

'Someone in this house?' I shook my head. 'Dr Lefebre, Miss Roche will never countenance such an idea.'

'My dear girl, it's not for Miss Roche to say. But I agree she'll refuse to entertain any such a scandalous suggestion. In the circumstances, a local man couldn't hope to deal with her. She won't be without influence hereabouts, may even have the ear of the chief constable, certainly of every local magistrate and circuit judge. A local investigator would be impeded at every turn. Someone must come down from the Yard.'

He paused and then went on, half to himself, 'Besides, Roche must be informed. He must hear it from me. Yes, I'll travel up to London today and tell Charles about it before I do anything else.'

He hissed in exasperation. 'But I'll have to wait until the village constable has been before I leave; and I'll need to go through the formality of persuading Miss Roche to agree. While she can't dictate events, she must still be convinced of the necessity of bringing in someone from outside or she'll be difficult and unhelpful. I doubt I'll get to the Yard today; indeed it must be impossible. I'll leave tomorrow, first thing. Pah!'

With this last impatient outburst he glared at me as if I were the obstacle.

'Dr Lefebre,' I said a little nervously, 'I am acquainted with an inspector, plain clothes division, of Scotland Yard.'

'Are you, by George!' he returned in surprise.

'His name is Inspector Benjamin Ross. He's experienced and will know how to go about his enquiries in the house in a manner that won't upset the Roche ladies.'

'You are full of surprises, Miss Martin.' He smoothed his beard. 'Well, then, let us go down and tell Miss Roche.'

With this he opened the door but I signalled he should wait. I put out my head to check if anyone were about, then stepped into the corridor first, motioning him to follow without delay. I thought that if anyone were watching, we must look a real pair of conspirators and the worst of conclusions would be drawn.

We found Christina and Phoebe Roche in the drawing room, seated side by side. They'd taken the brief interval to change their gowns and were now both dressed in black, looking for all the world like a pair of crows on a fence. I was astonished at this unexpected display of mourning for someone who was, after all, only on the premises by chance and whose shocking death had been dismissed so brusquely by Miss Roche only some half an hour earlier. I realised they were observing form, even in these unusual circumstances. Perhaps my words had had something to do with it. At any rate, a death at Shore House was a death. They, or more probably Christina Roche, had decided it must be marked in a suitable way if only for the time Brennan's corpse remained here. Neither Constable Gosling nor anyone else would be able to say the matter hadn't been treated with due respect. They were listening to Williams who was speaking rapidly and with insistence. The housekeeper broke off as we entered and treated both of us to a hostile glare.

'Later,' said Miss Roche to her.

Williams withdrew.

Dr Lefebre moved faultlessly into action and I had to admire him. He commiserated with the ladies on the misfortune come upon them. They must not become even more distressed by attempting to deal with the law. He would take care of that. It was not a suitable task for ladies. 'Police officers,' said Dr Lefebre with an apologetic glance at me, 'are accustomed to deal with some rough persons in the line of their profession. They have little to do with females of refinement such as you.'

'I want the body off the premises,' snapped Miss Roche. 'I have told Williams to tell Greenaway to remove it and put it somewhere out of the way.'

At this Lefebre looked very alarmed and exclaimed, 'Excuse me!' He dashed out after Mrs Williams.

I knew he had gone to countermand the order to move the corpse before the arrival of the constable, and hoped the housekeeper was more in awe of him than of me.

'It's not a bit of good his insisting,' declared Miss Roche, also guessing his purpose. 'I cannot have the body of a rat-catcher lying about in the garden where anyone may fall over it.'

'I said bringing Brennan here would mean bad luck,' burst out Miss Phoebe. 'Oh, Christina, the whole county will talk of nothing else! The gossip, the scandal! We shan't be able to show our faces, not even in church.'

'Pull yourself together, Phoebe. The county will take its lead from us. We must show dignity and restraint and refuse to let ourselves be forced into any change of ways by this wretched occurrence.'

I decided it was time for me to speak up. 'I beg your pardon, Miss Roche, but I have had the misfortune to be involved in a murder investigation once before.'

Miss Phoebe threw up her hands, squeaked and fell back in her chair.

'Have you, indeed?' said her sister in a way that suggested she wasn't a bit surprised to hear it.

'These things cannot remain a private matter. The police will want to ask questions of everyone here.'

'What can any of us tell them?' wailed Miss Phoebe.

'Quite,' said her sister. 'What, indeed? Should Constable Gosling forget himself to the degree that he tries to badger either my sister or myself, I shall put him in his place. Brennan was a rascally fellow. He roamed round the countryside and probably got himself into all kinds of mischief and mixed with some very unsavoury company. No doubt he quarrelled with someone of similar low character as himself, that person pursued him bent on vengeance and by purest mischance came upon him in our garden. None of that can be laid at our door.'

I thought of the knife but decided this was not the moment to mention it. Fortunately Dr Lefebre returned at that moment, somewhat out of breath but triumphant.

'The body will remain as it is until Gosling gets here. After that it can be removed to the nearest suitable place. Is there an undertaker's establishment nearby?'

'No,' said Miss Roche curtly, as if the idea that anyone in the district might require the services of an undertaker was preposterous.

Miss Phoebe whispered, 'There is a carpenter in the village who makes coffins as required. He made a beautiful one for Lucy's baby. It was taken to the churchyard in our carriage while we walked behind. Everything was done very decently.'

An image of the sad little procession leapt into my mind and I recalled the doctor's jest as he and I 'walked the hill' behind the trap on our journey to Shore House.

'I wasn't thinking of burying Brennan,' said the doctor, 'but of preserving his body for a while – for official purposes. Undertakers' premises usually have mortuaries attached to them. However, Gosling, when he deigns to get here, may have an idea.'

I knew he referred to a post-mortem examination but probably the ladies didn't. They looked vaguely perplexed.

The doctor went on more briskly, 'Now then, ladies, I wish to put it to you that this will require the attention of Scotland Yard.'

They both stared at him in silence. Miss Phoebe's expression suggested she did not know what or where Scotland Yard was. Her sister, Christina, looked at Lefebre as if he had gone as mad as the unfortunates for whom he cared.

'Nonsense,' she said.

'Alas, dear lady, it may prove necessary. Besides, I further put it to you that it would be better to have a total stranger come here and make enquiries than someone who may be known locally, perhaps have acquaintances, and be inclined to gossip?'

It was clear this argument made a powerful impression on both sisters. Phoebe leaned forward and touched her sister's arm imploringly. Christina Roche said nothing but waited for the doctor to support his suggestion.

Dr Lefebre hastened to follow up his advantage. He indicated me. 'We are fortunate in that Miss Martin is acquainted with an inspector of Scotland Yard – plain clothes division.'

'Plain clothes?' asked Miss Roche thoughtfully.

'Just so, ma'am. There would be no uniform about the place to occasion comment. Inspector Ross is, Miss Martin tells me, a very gentlemanly officer.'

I hadn't exactly said that. Ben had no pretensions to be a gentleman and might even have considered the suggestion an insult.

'He is very tactful,' I said, 'and educated.'

'Then why is he a policeman?' returned Miss Roche. 'Never mind, don't tell me. I suppose he has been forced into the profession by some scandal in his past.'

The assumption that Ben was no better than James Craven spending his remittance money in Canton caused me to bridle. I'd opened my mouth to refute it when Dr Lefebre caught my eye and shook his head. I stayed silent but mutinous.

'I should like, with your permission and if it's possible,' Dr Lefebre went on, 'to travel up to London by the late train today. That is, if I can get to the railway station in Southampton in time. If not, and as Gosling is taking his time appearing, it looks increasingly doubtful, I'll go first thing in the morning. I shall of course call on your brother to inform him—'

'Oh, good heavens, Charles!' wailed Miss Phoebe. 'What ever will he say?' She fell back again in her chair.

'Do you require smelling salts, Phoebe?' demanded her sister unsympathetically.

'Oh, no, Christina, I only—'

'Then if you can't be sensible, be quiet. Of course Charles will have to be told. Very well, then.' Christina Roche lifted her hand and gestured in the general direction of London. 'Let the man from Scotland Yard be sent for.'

Part Two

Chapter Nine

Inspecter Benjamin Ross

THEY SAY a police officer develops a nose for trouble. I'm not a great one for relying on unfounded instincts myself, preferring something I can demonstrate to a court. Facts turn into evidence and that's what you can produce to nail your villain: not some vague feeling. Defence counsel would soon have you if you tried that. (Not that the gentlemen of the bar are averse to playing on the instincts of juries, but the judge is there to stop that kind of thing.)

However, experience has taught me to know when a witness isn't being frank . . . and when mischief is afoot. That's not something one can demonstrate to the bewigged assembly of learned friends, but only a fool ignores it.

Since Lizzie left London I'd been prey to imprecise but niggling premonitions of disaster. I told myself sternly this was only because I harboured the feelings for Lizzie that I did. I'd been strongly against her going to Hampshire. I'd mistrusted the tale told her by Mr Charles Roche and I didn't like anything in which Mrs Julia Parry had a hand. Mrs Parry, I knew, cared little for inconvenience or risk to others, provided she wasn't troubled herself. She wanted Lizzie out of the house. I understood that and wanted Lizzie out of the Parry household myself – but for quite other reasons. (I had my own plans for the way in which she should leave.)

Mrs Parry was rewarded in her machinations and I was thwarted: partly because of my own clumsiness and partly because of Lizzie's headstrong nature. Not that I wanted my girl any different to the way she was, of course, but I did wish she would listen to me sometimes.

There, now you have it. That's how I felt on the Wednesday morning when I arrived at Scotland Yard. There is one more thing I ought to mention. I'd received by the early post a letter from Hampshire, written by Lizzie on the night of her arrival. She described her journey in an entertaining way but could tell me little of the members of the household, other than that one of the sisters seemed to be a dragon and the other her paler copy. As for the young wife to whom Lizzie was to be companion, she was little more than a schoolgirl. Only one person appeared in this letter in any detail, a Dr Lefebre, and there was far too much about him for my peace of mind.

For this reason my first action on arrival at my place of work was to seek out a copy of a medical directory and look up the dashing doctor. I rather hoped I wouldn't find him, that I'd be able to prove him an impostor. Then I'd rush to Hampshire and arrest him. Quite on what charge I didn't know, since the law of this country is remarkably generous to impostors. One may declare oneself a duke or a king if one has a fancy (or is lunatic enough), and provided one doesn't seek to gain financial advantage from the fact, the law lets you do it.

But no, there he was in the directory in bold type . . . and he was a mad doctor! He had studied in Vienna and Paris, practised his profession in the asylums of both cities and was established in London as an authority on insanity in all its forms. He even ran a private hospital where, I didn't doubt for a considerable fee, the aristocracy and other influential persons might lock away their more embarrassing relatives.

This entry, sparse enough, nevertheless provided me with a great deal to mull over.

'So that is how the land lies!' I thought grimly. 'Little Mrs Craven is out of her senses and the doctor was sent for to declare her so. In which case, Lizzie is companion to a dangerous lunatic and at the mercy of some unexpected fit of frenzy on the mad woman's part. Neither Mrs Parry nor Mr Roche saw fit to mention that when describing her duties.'

This, in itself, was bad enough. But I also knew well enough that doctors had a way of making an impression on female susceptibilities. Not that I thought Lizzie so easily swayed. But her own father had been a doctor and so the medical profession might appear to her in a very favourable light. I didn't know whether Dr Lefebre was married. I suspected not. Not many women would fancy marrying a madhouse keeper, however distinguished his reputation. (There may be some women in the country who've come to believe they *have* inadvertently married madhouse keepers, but that's another matter.)

Lizzie, however, with her medical parentage, might see it otherwise. Surely the prospect of being the wife of a successful and no doubt wealthy physician, whatever his chosen discipline, compared very favourably with that of being married to an impecunious inspector of the Metropolitan Police who never had any free time.

At this point in my gloomy reflections – a little after midday – a message came that Superintendent Dunn wished to see me at once. I hurried along to his office, walked in and – there my rival was. Dr Lefebre! It could be no other. Lizzie had described him in such detail that I couldn't be mistaken, surely? And what a suave debonair-looking fellow he was. The clothes on his back must have cost a year of my wages. His whiskers were immaculate and the top hat sitting on his knees was of finest quality. The sight of him confirmed all my worst suspicions. But what brought him here to the Yard?

I confess I panicked and burst out, before anything was said by anyone, *'What's happened?'*

Obviously something had occurred serious enough to bring the doctor here and my great fear was that it had happened to Lizzie. I then caught Dunn's eye fixed on me in a way that brought me to my senses. I managed to add in a reasonable tone of voice (I thought), 'You wished to see me, sir?'

'Yes, yes,' said Dunn a little irritably. He was a heavily built man with a shock of unruly hair. It generally began the day brushed into submission but rose in revolt as the day went on until, by the end of it, it bristled like a yard brush. At the moment it was just beginning to break loose. Perhaps he ought to let Lefebre's barber get at it.

Dunn indicated the two gentlemen with him. 'Mr Charles Roche and Dr Marius Lefebre. Perhaps their names are familiar to you, eh?' Dunn's eyebrows met as he scowled at me. 'Or has Miss Martin not yet written to you?'

I'd paid little attention to the other gentleman in Dunn's office and turned to look at him now. I saw a big old fellow with silvery mutton-chop whiskers and an anxious expression. His well-tailored black cutaway coat opened to reveal an ample silk brocade waistcoat bedecked with a heavy gold watch chain. Successful man and pillar of the community was announced in every line of his appearance. I stared very hard at him. So this was the man responsible for sending the lady who held my affections off into the countryside to consort with lunatics.

'I had a letter this morning. I'm familiar with both gentlemen's names,' I said politely. (And what a pair they were, influential men of consequence to their fingertips.) 'Am I to understand that some mishap has occurred in Hampshire?'

I afterwards wondered at the outward calm of my demeanour. Inside my head I wanted to yell out, *For pity's sake, will none of you tell me what has happened!*

'I, too, had a communication this morning,' said Dunn, indicating a square of paper spread flat on his desk. 'It's from Superintendent Howard at Southampton and informs me that an itinerant rat-catcher by the name of Jethro Brennan, otherwise called Jed Brennan, has been found murdered in the grounds of Shore House, the residence of the ladies Christina and Phoebe Roche and their niece, Mrs James Craven. This happened yesterday morning at about eleven thirty. The chief constable thought the matter important enough to send this message by means of the Electric Telegraph Company. I was a little puzzled that the murder of a rat-catcher should occasion such alarm, even in the grounds of a respectable household, to say nothing of the considerable cost of a telegraph message. But Dr Lefebre and Mr Roche have now arrived and I have some more detailed information. Doctor?'

He turned to Lefebre, inviting him to tell me what he had told Dunn.

'Mrs Craven was found near the body, in a state of great distress, by Miss Elizabeth Martin, her companion,' said Lefebre to me. 'You need have no fears, Inspector, Miss Martin is quite safe.'

I was grateful for the reassurance but highly irritated at the kindly manner of his delivering it. I was also unsettled by his knowledge of my friendship with Lizzie, but then I supposed that was the reason I'd been sent for.

'The man, Brennan,' Lefebre went on, 'had been called to the house to seek out a rat seen in the drawing room on a couple of occasions. Failing to find it, he'd gone into the garden with his dog to see if he could find a nest. He was stabbed in the neck, severing the carotid artery, and death must have occurred within moments, hastened no doubt, by panic on the part of the wounded man. The weapon seems to have been an ornamental dagger of oriental design that normally lay on the hall table and was used as a letter opener. Miss Martin noticed it early in the day, before breakfast, when it was in its usual place.'

'There would have been a good deal of blood around,' I observed. 'The assailant must have been spattered.'

'I would think so,' agreed Lefebre. 'Anyone in the vicinity of the body would be. Mrs Craven, who discovered the dead man, and Miss Martin who discovered Mrs Craven by the body and took hold of her to draw her away, were both of them stained with blood. There is no obvious culprit but Mrs Craven's health has been of some concern of late . . . her mental health, that is . . .'

Charles Roche stirred and began, 'I must protest, sir, at any attempt to influence the inquiry. My niece is a slip of a girl. Good Lord, Lefebre! What are you suggesting?'

'My good friend, I suggest nothing at all,' replied Lefebre imperturbably. 'But the police must be informed and it might as well be at once. Otherwise it will give the appearance that we've attempted to conceal something.'

Oho! I thought. A shrewd fellow, our Dr Lefebre.

'We're requested to send a detective to Hampshire,' said Dunn, rumbling comfortably over this exchange and addressing me, 'in order to clear up the matter as quickly as possible. As the doctor indicates, Mrs Craven is a little awkwardly placed. But here at the Yard we're accustomed to take all circumstances into account and don't leap to conclusions for which there is no evidence. Mr Roche's sisters, maiden ladies of delicate sensibilities, are deeply alarmed. The entire neighbourhood has been set by the ears. I have recommended you, Ross.'

'I'll leave at once,' I exclaimed.

'We can travel there together, if you wish,' offered Lefebre. 'I can tell you a little more on the way and you can ask me any questions. Miss Martin may also have her own ideas. It's a strange business.'

'I must remain in London for the next week at least,' said Charles Roche fretfully. 'I receive information daily regarding my business interests and must be here to make decisions. Naturally I'd like to go down to Hampshire with you to support my sisters – and my niece. I shall do so, at the first opportunity.'

He paused, gazing at us earnestly, to make sure we understood that however dreadful the circumstances in Hampshire, business must continue to take priority. I supposed that if one of his sisters or his niece had been found dead in the garden, he would have jumped on a train with us. There was no guarantee. I'd met his sort before. He'd keep an eagle eye on all aspects of his business affairs. Domestic emergencies, however, were another matter. In such cases others were despatched to deal with little awkwardnesses: his friend Lefebre, Lizzie, and now me.

Roche, receiving no comment from us, straightened his back and tapped his cane on the floor. 'I wish to make it quite clear again that there is no possibility whatsoever that my niece can have any responsibility for this dreadful deed. She is very young and frail. She was lately delivered of an infant. Sadly the child didn't survive. She's not been well since then. Allowances must be made for that when speaking to her.'

'I understand, sir,' I said.

'My sisters must also be treated sensitively. They've led sheltered lives and are no longer in the first flush of youth. They'll be greatly distressed.'

'All that will be taken into consideration,' I assured him.

He didn't look satisfied but what did he expect me to say? That I wouldn't question either of his sisters or his niece, who'd found the body? It is always the same when the police have to deal with respectable people of some standing in the community. They are the first ones to write to *The Times* and complain of the rampant lawlessness in our cities and the inability of the police to do anything about it. But when the police want their assistance and dare to set a regulation boot over their pristine thresholds, then it is a different matter.

Fortunately Charles Roche was a realist. He harrumphed a little but knew he had to accept it. He took out his splendid gold watch and consulted it. He was a man of business and time mattered. It matters in an investigation, too. It was imperative I get myself down to Hampshire that very day.

Lefebre who, for all my personal reservations about him, seemed a sensible fellow and aware of the urgency, looked at me.

'If it would suit you, Inspector, I could meet you at Waterloo in time to catch the four o' clock express train to Southampton. I'll await you at the gate on to the platform.'

Both gentlemen stood up and took their leave of Dunn. When they had left, the superintendent turned to me.

'Now then, Ross,', he said bluntly, 'you don't need me to spell out the situation here. If Brennan had been killed in a taproom brawl there would be no problem allocating blame. If there were an obvious candidate for his killer among his ruffian acquaintances there would be none. The local constable would have collared the culprit by now and he'd be awaiting trial in Winchester gaol. But unfortunately for us there isn't handy villain and our rat-catcher was struck down in the grounds of a house belonging to people of some consequence in the community. Sitting by the body in some considerable distress was a young woman of unimpeachable background, but unfortunate medical history, with a wealthy uncle of influence in business circles here in the capital. The said local community is consequently in an uproar, and when the news spreads around London, as it will for it concerns the established firm of Roche, well, all that upsets the powers responsible for the smooth running of all corners of Her Majesty's realm however remote. Oil, Ross, is to be poured on troubled waters.'

'And scandal snuffed out,' I said mildly. 'Charles Roche isn't the only one anxious to absolve his niece of any suspicion, her state of mind being what it apparently is.'

'Oh, as to that,' rumbled Dunn, 'doctor or no doctor, you'll have to make up your own mind. Normally I wouldn't be sending *you* as you are acquainted already with a member of the household and personal relationships could muddy the waters. However, if I keep you here you'll be fretting and worrying and that's no use to me. Besides, I know Miss Martin to be more than usually observant. I'm obliged to admit she's been of help to us before. I *am* sending you and trust you'll keep your mind on your job.'

'Of course!' I replied indignantly. 'I'd like to take Sergeant Morris with me, if that's possible.'

'Oh, take him, by all means,' said Dunn. 'I dare say Mrs Morris won't mind his temporary absence. Have you time to get home and pack a bag? You can take a cab and charge the cost to the Yard,

in the circumstances. Superintendent Howard tells me in this . . .'
Dunn waggled his stumpy fingers at the telegraph form as if it
might jump up and bite them '. . . that a room will have been
reserved for you at an inn near the scene of the crime. It's called
The Acorn. They can probably lodge Morris too. I wish to make
it clear, Ross, that although Howard seems to think expense of no
consequence, I do not expect *you* to communicate with me by
electric telegraph unless it's directly to apprehend a fleeing
murderer! You can write – or put Morris on a train with a report.
While you're gone I'll set some enquiries going here regarding the
dead man, Brennan, as he's believed to have lived in London
when not wandering the countryside exterminating vermin – or
getting himself exterminated. Oh, and Ross.'

I was halfway out of the door and turned back.

'Watch yourself,' advised Dunn. 'They're a funny lot in the
country. Tell your young lady to take care as well. She has a great
curiosity to know what's going on and that can be dangerous.'

'Yes, sir,' I replied with feeling.

'And Ross!'

'Yes, sir?'

'Remember,' warned Dunn with awful emphasis. 'The honour
of Scotland Yard is in your hands. I won't have country constables
sniggering at our failure. Come back with a positive result!'

I managed to find Morris at once, thank goodness, and sent him
scurrying off to fetch an overnight bag while I made a similar dash
to my own lodgings. It was a narrow squeak getting to Waterloo to
catch the train but we made it, having with difficulty found the
right platform. I can't imagine how many letters of complaint the
Railway receives from frustrated travellers.

I saw Dr Lefebre awaiting us, surrounded by smoke and steam, hustle and bustle, but still looking as though he had stepped from the pages of a gentleman's magazine, even with a white silk scarf draped like a bridal veil over his expensive hat.

Morris, who hadn't seen him at the Yard, murmured, 'Bless me, is that the cove, sir? Regular fancy man, isn't he?'

I had no time to reply (though I agreed heartily). I advanced on Lefebre looking, as I well knew, red faced and dishevelled, and apologised for cutting it so fine.

'No matter,' said he, 'have you your tickets?'

Then came a moment of embarrassment. We were indeed provided with travel warrants but Scotland Yard being thrifty in the matter of expenses, they were third class. Dr Lefebre, naturally, held a first-class ticket.

'Never mind,' he said. 'Join me in the first-class compartment and I'll pay the difference when the guard comes round.'

I didn't want to lose the opportunity of a long conversation with a material witness about the events at Shore House, but acceptance of his proposal would put me under an obligation to him. That was not only awkward from a personal point of view, but also from a professional one.

I cut the Gordian knot with: 'Sergeant Morris can travel third class. I'll join you, Doctor, in the first-class compartment. I'll pay the difference myself and trust that I'll be recompensed by Scotland Yard.'

There was no guarantee of this; the Yard being in thrall to the taxpayer – who is of the opinion officers can undertake almost any investigation at no cost whatsoever to the citizen. But in the circumstances I trusted Dunn to argue my case.

So Morris, looking somewhat disappointed, went off to find himself a seat in third class and spend the journey fending off smoke and occasional glowing cinders flying through the unglazed windows. I joined Lefebre in the unaccustomed luxury of first.

We were in luck. Only one other person shared the compartment with us, an elderly female entirely swathed in black. She had with her a wicker basket containing a large cat, apparently of the Persian variety. It glared at us through a small barred aperture remarkably like the peephole in a cell door, as if of the opinion we alone were responsible for its incarceration. I fancied it bore a strong resemblance to a house-breaker I'd charged only the previous week.

'Now, Percy, you must be good!' its owner coaxed it. 'You shall have a piece of chicken for your dinner when we arrive. You like chicken, don't you, Percy?'

I wondered if the whole journey would be punctuated with one-sided conversations with Percy but no, the old lady promptly fell asleep as soon as we began to move. Percy settled down in his portable prison and dozed off too.

Dr Lefebre and I began our conversation in subdued tones to a background duet of small snores from the wicker basket and slightly louder ones from the old lady.

The doctor had taken off the silk scarf and put it tidily away in a pocket. He now produced, from another pocket, a small, rather crumpled, folded sheet of paper, which he handed to me. I unfolded it with care and puzzlement and saw it appeared to be a rendering of account from his bootmaker.

'It was all I had to hand,' he explained apologetically. 'It was in my pocket by a piece of luck or they would have moved the body before I could fetch a better sheet.'

I turned the bill over and saw that a rough sketch had been made on the reverse. It showed the outline of a human form, some circles marked as rhododendron bushes and some arrows indicating the direction of the house, the sea shore and the path which Lefebre believed Mrs Craven to have taken round the side of the house into the garden.

'You're a detective, sir,' I said to him. I wasn't being sarcastic; I was impressed.

'No,' he replied, shaking his head. 'I'm a professional man accustomed to make careful observation and take notes as I go along in order to make an accurate diagnosis.'

He then explained how he had been waiting by the front gate while the groom saddled a horse for him, when Mrs Craven and Lizzie had come along the road, returning from their walk. Mrs Craven had taken fright at the sight of him and run away in the direction indicated by the arrows.

'Taken fright?' I asked.

'She believes I'm at Shore House with the purpose of declaring her not of sane mind.'

'And are you there for that purpose?'

'No,' said Lefebre coolly, 'only as an observer on behalf of my old friend, Charles Roche. He isn't able to travel there himself on account of his business commitments. Miss Martin has written to you of Mrs Craven's circumstances?'

'A little,' I said. 'She wrote on the evening of the day of your arrival and had had little time to talk to Mrs Craven.'

'So she won't have told you about James Craven? Ah, I thought not.' Lefebre recounted the history of James Craven, which I was later to learn he had told Lizzie.

'Has anyone heard from young Craven since he left for the Far East?' I asked.

'His wife hasn't, neither has Charles Roche. But he did arrive safely in Canton and presented himself at the Roche *hong* (as they call a warehouse in the East). Roche received a letter from his agent there apprising him of the fact. James Craven is accommodated, free of any cost to himself, in a bungalow with a Chinese manservant to take care of him. The agent has already paid the first instalments of remittance money. For a fellow who had nothing but undeclared debts and not a penny to bless himself with when he first turned up in London, he hasn't done badly, in my view!' concluded Lefebre crisply.

'He'll be lonely, however, so far from home.'

'There will be others of his kind to keep him company and help him gamble away his remittance. Also . . .' Lefebre put a hand to his mouth, coughed gently and glanced at the sleeping old lady. 'Europeans in his situation generally take a concubine and I dare say Craven will do the same, in due course.'

It all sounded highly irregular to me, but I was concerned with those at Shore House not with someone oceans away, relaxing amid tasselled lanterns, opium fumes and silk-clad females.

I looked again at the piece of paper in my hand. 'Where is the body now, do you know?'

'It's been taken to the new military hospital at Netley, just outside Southampton, for post-mortem examination. I took the liberty of sending a letter with it asking that the examination be carried out as a matter of urgency, although I don't anticipate my original diagnosis will be challenged. It should have been done this morning. The hospital, as you probably know, was opened to receive its first patients only last year, '63, and its mortuary is the most modern available. It seemed the best place to keep our corpse until you could arrive. The military authorities have been remarkably cooperative.' For the first time Lefebre looked slightly awkward. 'You may not approve, however.'

'It sounds excellent to me,' I said, albeit a little grudgingly. Why couldn't a police surgeon have carried out the examination? I was well aware that I was coming to this case late, even though the murder had only taken place the previous morning. Events had already started to slip from my control and I must watch out or they'd run away completely. I said briskly, 'I should like to stop in Southampton long enough to visit the hospital before travelling on to Shore House.'

'They will be expecting you.'

'You won't mind, Doctor,' I began next, 'if I take this opportunity of asking you for an account of your activities yesterday morning. You saw Brennan at the house?'

'I saw him arrive a little before ten. He set to work in the downstairs rooms with his dog, seeking out the rat. I'd arranged with Greenaway, who is both head groom and coachman, to ride out with me across the heath. I sent word to the stables I should be ready shortly and he could saddle up as soon as was convenient. I went upstairs and got ready. I was told Greenaway would be another fifteen minutes, so I went downstairs—'

'You saw Brennan again there?'

Lefebre shook his head. 'No, but I heard him talking to the dog, urging it on. I could hear the animal snuffling along the skirting boards. Brennan had a theory the rat had a nest and if it was indoors, it was likely to be behind the skirting.

'I can tell you frankly I didn't care for what I'd seen of Brennan. Miss Martin may have written in her letter to you that we met Brennan with his wife on the heath on our way to Shore House. Greenaway told us that the man was considered honest in his way and not given to pilfering. However, there was a distinct slyness in his manner. In my judgement he wasn't a fellow one could trust. There's more than one way of being dishonest, as you'll know, Inspector. Now, as I was saying, I decided to go outside and smoke a cigarette. I walked down to the front gate.'

'Forgive me interrupting again,' I broke in, 'but you didn't take a turn in the garden?'

'No. I stood at the gate for a while. No traffic passed me except a gypsy woman with a basket of pegs. She asked me if she might offer them for sale at the kitchen door. I told her that she certainly might do so as far as I was concerned.'

'And she entered the property?' I asked sharply.

'She did. She went round to the back of the house where the kitchen would be. But she was not gone long, eight minutes at the most. Then she came back. I gathered she'd made no sale. She offered to read my palm. I told her I had no wish to know my future but I gave her a sixpenny piece and she blessed me.' Lefebre grimaced.

'Where did she go then?'

'She set off in the direction of the village. The village is about three quarters of a mile from Shore House. The church lies between, no more than a quarter of a mile from the house. The church is ancient and I'd guess it predates the houses in the village. That is why it isn't central to the place but lies outside. There must have been an earlier village, around the church, possibly abandoned at the time of the Black Death. The site of the later present-day settlement may owe something to an unwillingness to rebuild on the site of the legendary plague. Country folk are superstitious. There's a bend in the road, so I soon lost sight of the gypsy. I smoked a second cigarette. Then Mrs Craven and Miss Martin came into sight. I understand they'd visited the church but found it shut up. Mrs Craven, as I've already explained, ran away at the sight of me. Miss Martin and I exchanged a few words and she then went in search of Mrs Craven.

'The stable boy arrived at that point and told me Greenaway was saddled up and ready to leave. So I went to the stables and we rode over the heath for about an hour or a few minutes less. When we returned the stable boy told us what had happened. That is to say,' Lefebre corrected himself pedantically, 'he told us the rat-catcher was dead in the garden and everyone in a great to-do. They'd got the rat-catcher's dog there at the stables, caught up in some netting. It was the only way, the lad said, they could get it away from the body. The beast was still snarling and trying to disentangle itself. I told the boy he should stay away from it. Greenaway's opinion was that they should throw a bucket of water over it to calm it down and shut it in one of the empty loose boxes. I left them to it. I went into the house, sought out Miss Martin and asked her what had happened. I wanted a clear account before I saw the Roche ladies and I knew Miss Martin would give that.'

I wasn't surprised he already appreciated Lizzie's clarity of recollection but I hoped his admiration for her went no further.

Morris would be able to verify most of the doctor's story with Greenaway and the stable boy, and ask in the kitchen about the visit of the gypsy. I was curious about the gypsy woman. If she'd walked on towards the village, Lizzie and Lucy, returning from the church, might have seen her.

There was a silence while I mulled over what he had told me and also began to consider the matter of the knife. If the murder weapon came from the hall table, as Lizzie had suggested to Lefebre, it did indicate a member of the household. But possibly Brennan himself could have removed it and taken it into the garden with him for some purpose – or even because he thought it of value, the sort of knick-knack which could be profitably sold on. He might even have wanted to keep it. Greenaway may have told Lizzie and Lefebre that the rat-catcher was no pilferer. Certainly if it was thought Brennan was light fingered, he wouldn't get work in well-to-do residences. But a fancy knife might have appealed to him.

'Had Brennan caught rats in or around the house before?' I asked.

'It was the impression I received. The Roche ladies certainly knew who he was. Brennan himself, during our meeting on the heath, asked Greenaway to tell his employers he was in the neighbourhood.'

'Well, even the rich have rats,' I said drily.

'Quite so,' returned Lefebre in his smooth way.

Perhaps this talk of rats had seeped through to Percy in his slumbers, for at this point he awoke, let out a tremendous yowl of frustration and began scratching at his basket walls. The old lady awoke too and began to soothe him with more promises of chicken. Our conversation ceased.

Chapter Ten

Inspector Benjamin Ross

OUR FIRST sight of the spanking new military hospital at Netley was certainly impressive. The huge main red-brick block ran almost out of sight for a quarter of a mile at least, and stood in a fine park of many acres running down to the waterside. We descended before its magnificent entrance and stood in awe.

'Regular palace,' observed Sergeant Morris, clearly impressed. 'And stuck out here in quite a gentleman's estate. Not much like a hospital as we know 'em in London, sir, is it? Army done itself all right, if you ask me.'

Lefebre smiled at him. 'Believe me, Sergeant Morris, the need for such a place as this was sorely lacking when we went to war in the Crimea. It was because there was nowhere to bring the many casualties of that sad affair that the government caused this to be built for future conflicts.'

'The assumption being that there would be some – and with a similar high casualty rate,' I remarked.

'You and I,' Lefebre said to me, 'are men of caution. But there are always men in power who see waving a flag, and sending others to be shot or sabred, as a matter of sound policy and honour as well. As a police officer you must have seen a pair of bullies square up to one another inside or outside a public house and beat each other to a pulp in the name of "settling the thing". But violence seldom does "settle the thing".'

'You are a man of peace, Dr Lefebre,' I exclaimed, much surprised by the warmth with which he spoke.

He raised his shoulders in an eloquent shrug. 'I know what I believe isn't fashionable. I confess I'd hesitate to air my views here. In most quarters it would be considered unpatriotic. I am a patriot but I am also a medical man. I seek to preserve life, not blast it into oblivion.'

'But you treat the mind,' I said curiously. 'You do not repair bodies.'

Lefebre turned his head and gave me a curious look. 'And do you think,' he asked, 'that mind and body are separable entities? That one may be whole if the other is not?'

I was spared answering this by the arrival of a tall man with fair hair clipped very short but sporting a splendid moustache.

'Ah, Inspector! We're very pleased to welcome you to Netley. I'm Dr Frazer and I carried out the post-mortem examination of your man.' He shook my hand heartily. 'Brought your sergeant along, I see. Splendid, splendid. Good to see you again, too, Doctor. Come along then. You'll be anxious to view our handiwork. Still, no hurry! Chap won't run away, eh?'

He wheeled and made off at a fast pace while we scrambled behind him in some disorder. We progressed briskly down long spotless corridors past men on crutches, men with bandages, but also men with no sign of outward injury who must be here for some good reason. We encountered white-coated male orderlies, whom I would have expected, and lady nurses I'd not expected. These maidens had a gaze in their eyes that cut like a lancet and so much starch in their aprons they crackled as they passed by us. There was medical paraphernalia of every kind and everything brand new. It was quite unlike the chaos of the hospital wards I'd had occasion to view before, every surface battered and scraped and all enveloped in an air of despair.

Morris had respect and admiration written deep on his features. I suspected that when we got back to London, Mrs Morris would hear of nothing but this visit for days, if not years, to come. He was, however, unlucky enough to bump into a trolley, fortunately untenanted, and send it careering off to crash into a wall. Scarlet with embarrassment he scuttled after it to retrieve it, apologising profusely. One of the viragos in a starched apron descended on him and snapped, 'The wheels have just been oiled!'

'Don't worry, Sergeant.' Frazer looked over his shoulder at the mortified Morris and grinned. 'This is the army. If it doesn't move, paint it. If it does move, oil it!'

'I'm surprised to see ladies working as nurses here,' I remarked.

I'd nearly said 'respectable women' and had substituted 'ladies' in the nick of time. I knew, of course, that 'trained nurses' were appearing in London hospitals. So different from the illiterate slatterns and drunken crones who had formed the majority of the nursing sorority during most of my life. This brand-new breed originated with those brave women who followed Florence Nightingale to the Crimea. Decent young women were now learning their profession in the school she'd set up.

'We were lucky in persuading a few to join us from St Thomas's hospital in London. But we are setting up our own training programme,' confided Frazer without slackening his pace. 'We are modelling it on the system introduced at St Thomas's by Miss Nightingale in '60. She's given us much valuable advice.'

I felt I had to ask some intelligent question. He was so obviously and rightly proud of the hospital. 'How many patients could you treat here at any one time?'

'Up to a thousand, at least. Could squeeze in a few more if we had to, I dare say, but Miss Nightingale's very keen on not overcrowding. We have one hundred and thirty-eight wards. The Queen, God bless her, laid the foundation stone back in '56. Ah, here we are.'

'Some of the patients show no sign of injury,' I remarked.

Frazer looked back and exchanged a glance with Dr Lefebre. 'Not all injuries are physical, Inspector. Some are of the mind.'

So I was put in my place for a second time.

I fancied, however, it explained how Brennan came to be lodged here. Lefebre, a specialist in mental disorders, was known to the hospital and had been able to request a favour. I wasn't altogether sure I liked this but the local Hampshire constabulary had presumably approved it. Once again I was made aware that I was a stranger here in more ways than one. I was far from my home 'patch' with its familiar ways and familiar villains. The professional and respectable classes of this place were connected by threads spun over many years. Their first loyalty would not necessarily be to the truth, but rather to maintaining the status quo. Certainly, the death of an itinerant rat-catcher wouldn't be allowed to shake it. This was why I, an outsider, had been sent here. On the one hand, I'd be free from influence brought to bear by anyone local. On the other hand, I'd be excluded from their club. Not since I'd arrived in London from Derbyshire at the age of eighteen had I felt myself in such an alien world. Perhaps in this new place I'd be able to trust only Lizzie.

We had arrived.

I have been in a few morgues and dissecting rooms in my time but nothing like this one. Some of the places where I've viewed a corpse have been little better than sheds, dirty and stinking of blood and decomposing flesh. Here the late Jed Brennan lay on a table, covered by a white sheet, in finer surroundings than he had ever tenanted in life. All blood and other signs of the mutilation of the body had been washed away. The surfaces here were as polished as any others in the hospital. The army required both the living and the dead to keep things neat. There was not even the usual miasma in the air. However there was a smell, and I sniffed.

'Carbolic!' I said.

'They believe here,' Lefebre murmured to me, 'that, as Dr Lister has found in Glasgow, a carbolic spray does much to reduce infections.'

'Orderly!' called Frazer.

The sheet was whipped from the corpse and it lay before us.

I've seen a few dead bodies, too. They never fail to move me to pity, even when the deceased is a rogue or murderer. No doubt Brennan had been a fine strong fellow but here he lay, as naked as the day he was born and, like all dead things, pitiful. The thing that struck me first was that he had corns on his toes. Tramping miles around the south of the country, it wasn't surprising but I found myself thinking: *Poor fellow, every step must have hurt.*

'We had a good look,' said Frazer happily. 'Tidied him up for you, as you see.' He indicated with some pride a line of stitches down the centre of the torso that would have done credit to a seamstress. 'We do a good job of suturing here. No cobbling together. Death was due to severing of the carotid artery. The stomach contained elements of his last meal, which I suggest was rabbit. Otherwise the internal organs were in poor condition, almost certainly due to imbibing rotgut liquor. Men of his sort are invariably heavy drinkers. If he hadn't died violently, organ failure would have killed him in the end.'

'He bought cheap from backstreet distilleries, I expect,' said Morris unexpectedly in a lugubrious voice.

'Quite so,' agreed the surgeon. 'The army warns the troops against that sort of thing.'

The orderly had temporarily vanished but now returned holding two large brown paper envelopes.

'Here we are!' declared the ever-cheerful Frazer. 'This 'un is my report, all the details there. This one . . .' He shook it and it rattled. 'Murder weapon.'

'The knife!' I exclaimed.

'Malay workmanship,' said Frazer growing, if possible, even more enthusiastic, 'what they call a *kris*. Got a similar couple of 'em myself. Good quality. You find them all over the Straits Settlements, Dutch East Indies, other places in the Far East.'

He opened the packet and shook it. The knife fell out and by chance landed by Brennan's ear, pretty much by the wound. It was an extraordinary-looking thing with a very elaborate enamelled handle and a blade unlike any I'd seen before, not straight on either side but wavy.

I picked it up. 'You own two of these, do you, Dr Frazer? Does that mean they come in pairs?'

He shook his head. 'No two *kris* are the same. Each is special to the man for whom it was originally made: fashioned according to his height and build, his social standing. As a result they vary considerably in length of blade and the value of the materials in the handle. But all have the wavy blade and intricate workmanship. Beautiful, ain't it?' He sounded unexpectedly wistful. 'I have a collection of oriental swords and daggers. Wouldn't mind adding that one to it.'

'It's certainly got a sharp enough point.' I touched it gingerly.

'I've seen before what a *kris* can do,' said our buoyant host. 'First-class killing weapon. Slip in like a knife in butter.'

I suppose if you're accustomed to carve up dead human bodies you acquire a certain detachment; but I still disliked his cavalier tone and returned the knife to the bag.

'We're obliged to you,' I told Frazer.

'My dear fellow,' he replied warmly, shaking me by the hand, 'it's been most interesting. No trouble at all. By the way, when this is all over and you have your murderer . . .' He cleared his throat and for the first time showed some embarrassment. 'Thing is, I don't know what you do with evidence like that knife. If it's returned to its original owner, and they don't require it, or if the police don't require it, well, I wouldn't mind having it in my collection.'

'Alistair Frazer is a very fine pathologist,' said Lefebre to me as we left, sounding a little apologetic.

So he might be but I thought him something of a ghoul. Still, it takes all sorts.

'I thought the knife was Indian,' added Lefebre as we drove away. 'But I'm no authority, obviously.'

'Is there much oriental knick-knackery about the house?' I asked him.

'Not a great deal, for a family with such strong trade links with that part of the world.'

I thought this over. Lizzie had apparently identified the knife as the one previously on the hall table, now missing. But she had only seen the handle protruding from Brennan's neck. I'd have to show her the thing again, not a pleasant task. It would also have to be shown to the Roche ladies who, according to Lefebre, were as yet unaware of the missing knife. At least I now knew there would not be another identical *kris* anywhere. Yet the knowledge was of limited value since to a layman one *kris* would look much like another without Dr Frazer's collector's eye. Lizzie might declare it the same one and still be wrong. The same thing went for the Roche sisters even though they owned the weapon. The housekeeper and the maids must also be shown the *kris*. The person who dusts an object regularly knows it better than anyone.

But could there be such knives in other houses in the neighbourhood? It was not impossible. Oriental artefacts flooded into the country by one route or another, often brought in by returning soldiers or sailors. Frazer had a whole collection of them. While unusual, they were not exactly rare. It seemed very likely this was the missing hall-table knife, but I shouldn't assume anything.

It was vital to settle the identification. It could point to the murderer having been in the house that morning. If the knife had come from elsewhere, so might the murderer.

'The dead man's wife,' I said, 'Mrs Brennan. Where is she? What did she have to say?'

'I have no idea,' Lefebre said. 'You'll have to speak to Constable Gosling about that. He took the bad news to her, I understand.'

Constable Gosling. A lot might be learned from the local man. I looked forward to meeting him.

Chapter Eleven

Inspector Benjamin Ross

WE SET down Dr Lefebre at Shore House. It was now getting late; daylight was fading, and in the dusk the house appeared a gloomy building. On the ground floor the curtains weren't yet drawn but there was lighting in the rooms. Not bright enough for gas, however. This was a more muted glow; I guessed at oil lamps. They wouldn't have gas out here. I hoped that perhaps Lizzie might have heard the rumble of wheels and would show herself at one of the windows, but nobody had the curiosity to look out, or possibly our arrival hadn't been heard within. Perhaps, in the morning, the setting – no doubt beautiful but at the moment hardly discernible – would improve its general appearance. And I'd see Lizzie.

We were all of us tired. Even Dr Lefebre looked a little weary. But he'd travelled up to London from Southampton by the earliest train, and to catch that he must have risen soon after dawn. It wasn't surprising that he was showing some sign of strain. We arranged that Morris and I should call the following day at eleven. I would be presented to the Misses Roche and interview them. Morris would interview the servants. We'd also be able to observe the scene of the crime in good light.

The fly then carried us on to The Acorn where we were to be lodged. It set us down with our bags at the door where a reception committee awaited us; brought outside in some haste, it seemed, by the rumble of the wheels. Lined up before us were a stalwart member of the Hampshire constabulary with well-polished boots who was almost bursting his buttons with anticipation; a plump female in a blue and yellow print gown hastily tying the strings of a clean apron behind her back; and a potboy with red face, spiky hair and a grin from ear to ear.

As the fly rattled away the constable saluted, the female in the print gown dropped a curtsy and the potboy, probably feeling he ought to do something but not sure what, put two fingers to his mouth and let out a piercing whistle. It was as if we were being piped aboard one of Her Majesty's ships of the line.

'Lord love us!' murmured Morris behind me, 'do they think we're royalty?'

'Constable Gosling, sir!' declared that worthy, stepping forward. 'Welcome to the New Forest, Inspector Ross. This is Mrs Garvey, the landlady.' He indicated the female in the print gown.

'Honoured to have you under my roof,' said Mrs Garvey. 'Here, you, William! Take the gentlemen's bags up to their room.'

Room? Only one? I hoped at least that I was not expected to share a bed with Morris, who was of substantial build.

The potboy darted forward, grabbed our bags and disappeared inside with them. Mrs Garvey, with smiles and gestures, urged us after him.

The inn was a very old building with low ceilings and walls bulging out of true. We were in the main taproom where there was as yet no company but two old men ensconced on settles against the far wall and smoking clay pipes. They stared at us solemnly. I nodded to them in greeting. One of them took out his pipe and waved the stem at me in return salutation. The other just continued smoking. Gosling took off his helmet, placed it under his arm, and stood to attention by the door.

'You'll take some refreshment, sirs, after your journey?' urged Mrs Garvey.

I looked round. I needed to hear Gosling's report. That could not wait until morning. But I didn't need an audience.

'Is there somewhere private?' I asked.

'Bless you, sir, of course. You can have the snug.' Mrs Garvey flung open the door to a room about the size of a generous broom cupboard. 'Make yourselves at home and I'll bring something directly. What will you take?'

'Tea,' I said firmly. 'If you would be so kind.' In truth I could have done with something stronger and I dare say so could Morris, but we needed clear heads.

In due course the tea arrived together with an oil lamp threatening us with its blue smoke and smell. When the door had closed behind our hostess and we were seated cosily (there was no other way) round the table in the snug, I began. 'Well, Constable, let's hear what you have to tell us.'

'It's a bad business,' said Gosling lugubriously. He'd set his helmet on the floor by his feet and his head was revealed to be perfectly round. 'We don't have murder in these parts, not in the normal way of things. Brennan, of course, wasn't from these parts. He came down from London.'

It occurred to the constable that we too had come down from London. He turned scarlet with embarrassment and his head glowed like a Christmas lantern. The reflection from the flame of the oil lamp encouraged the fancy. I asked him to tell us everything he had observed from the moment he was called to the house.

Gosling delivered his report capably enough but there wasn't much to it. The groom, Greenaway, had fetched him. He told him that Brennan was lying dead in the garden. There had followed a small delay because Gosling didn't live in this village but in the next one. It had been a quiet day and the constable had employed it digging over his garden. Thus when the groom arrived, he'd been obliged to go into his house, wash the dirt from his hands and change into his uniform. On arrival at Shore House he'd gone straight to the garden. The body lay by some rhododendron bushes and he could show us the spot. The gardener and the stable lad had removed Brennan's dog and Gosling, kneeling by the body, observed that the handle of a knife protruded from the dead man's neck. He had returned to the house and spoken with the housekeeper who explained that Brennan had been in the house earlier, but then gone into the garden. She had not seen any strangers about that morning other than a gypsy woman who had come selling pegs. But they hadn't needed any pegs and the woman was sent on her way.

'Mrs Williams is a very straight-spoken woman,' said Gosling. 'She was very upset about it being young Mrs Craven who had found the body. She told me I couldn't speak to the lady because she was sleeping, dosed with laudanum. She, I mean Mrs Williams, kept on about it not having anything to do with Mrs Craven and I was not to badger her. Well, I couldn't speak to her anyway, her being dead to the world on account of the laudanum, but I did say you would wish to see the lady, sir, when you got here.'

'How did Mrs Williams take that?'

'Not very well,' admitted Gosling.

'It wasn't Brennan's first visit to this village,' I observed next.

'No, sir. He came regular and pitched his little tent up on the heath. Village people deal with their own rats, mostly, but we do have a few big houses in the neighbourhood. Shore House, for one, and Oakwood House for another. That belongs to Mr Beresford. Then there's old Sir Henry Meacham about three mile off and a couple of others.'

'Was Brennan liked?'

Gosling considered this question at some length. 'I wouldn't say he was, but there again, I couldn't say anyone had anything particular thing against him. People were used to him. He was a good customer in here.'

'A drunkard?' I remembered Frazer's remark about the state of the dead man's liver.

'Not the sort that causes trouble. He seemed able to hold it. He was a bit unsteady on his feet when he left but no one ever found him lying in the road.'

That seemed a fair enough judgement. Gosling, however, looked a little uneasy. 'Thing is, sir,' he blurted, 'when I said he wasn't disliked, well, that was true. But people were wary of him and generally left him alone. For a start his two dogs are snappy little beasts so you didn't approach too near when he had them with him, which he generally did. People are a little suspicious of any stranger in a small place like this and some of 'em thought him a bird of ill omen. Then he didn't talk much. But he had a way of sitting by the fire and smiling at you, not saying anything, just smiling. After a while, it made folk a bit twitchy, if you know what I mean. It was as if he had some private joke or other that kept him amused.'

'No one ever asked him what it was?'

'Shouldn't think so,' said Gosling frankly, 'he wasn't the sort you would mess with. Big fellow and I dare say quick with his fists if he had to be.'

'Yet,' I said, 'someone was able to come up to him in the garden and drive a knife into his throat.'

Gosling nodded his head slowly. 'That's been worrying me too, sir. It was as if—'

'Yes?' I urged. 'You're a local man, Gosling. You know the way of things here. I value your opinion.'

The constable's head was so red by now it seemed there was a real danger it would combust. 'Fact is,' he burst out, 'I reckon it was someone he knew and didn't have reason to fear.'

I nodded. 'Did he ever quarrel with anyone, either here in The Acorn or in the village, even in what might seem a minor sort of way?'

'They wouldn't quarrel with him, sir. They would just keep clear.'

'Tell me about the ladies at Shore House!' I ordered abruptly.

Gosling blinked. 'Very quiet pair of ladies. They've been living here about five or six years. The house was empty before that. You don't see them about much. Their brother, Mr Charles Roche, comes down from London from time to time to visit. A few months ago, Mrs Craven, their niece as we understand it, came to Shore House for her lying-in. Baby died, sir, very sad.'

'I believe the infant was not stillborn but died some twenty-four hours later?'

'Don't ask me,' said Gosling. 'You want Mrs Garvey. She'll know all about it. That sort of thing is women's business, isn't it? I did hear tell the poor little soul was found dead in its cradle. Natural causes was what Dr Barton wrote on the certificate and the coroner was happy to accept that.'

'Talking of women, what of Mrs Brennan? How did she take the news of her husband's violent death?'

'Very quiet,' said Gosling after a moment's thought. 'Lye

Greenaway took me up on to the heath to the place where they were camped. He'd been there earlier to fetch Brennan to the house. The woman wasn't there when we arrived. We waited for a while and she came back with an armful of firewood, just bits of fallen branches and so on. It's not lawful to cut wood in the Forest but picking up odd scraps just lying around is allowed.

'When she saw me she did take fright a little. The uniform, you see. She thought her man had got himself into some trouble and might have been taken off to gaol. Funnily enough, it seemed to worry her less that he was dead. She only nodded and sighed.'

'She didn't ask how he had died?'

'Well, no, she didn't. That was strange, if you ask me. I had to tell her it all again, how he'd been attacked but we didn't know by whom. She took that fairly quiet too, until I told her it had been in the grounds of Shore House. That did scare her. I could see it in her eyes. But she clammed up and said nothing. I told her she must stay in the locality and not go away where we couldn't find her. There would be an inquest, I told her, and she must appear. It was delayed because police officers were coming from London. She seemed bewildered. I felt sorry for the poor soul. It's my opinion, sirs . . .' Gosling leaned forward confidentially and tapped his scarlet brow solemnly. 'She's not quite all right up here, if you follow me. On the simple side.'

Unlikely to impress a jury, then, I thought, or Superintendent Dunn, come to that. 'I must speak to her, all the same,' I said. 'Perhaps you could bring her here?'

'Do my best, sir,' said Gosling gloomily. 'If she hasn't run off halfway across the county by now.'

We let Gosling go home after that. Mrs Garvey came to ask what we would like to eat. She had a freshly baked steak pie. I realised I was ravenous and told her that would do very well. So in the privacy of the snug Morris and I dined on the pie with boiled potatoes and carrots, followed by a blackberry and apple tart accompanied by a large jug of cream, and all washed down with porter.

'Mrs Morris will be missing you, Sergeant,' I said as we tucked in. 'I am sorry to have brought you away from home.'

'Mrs Morris's sister is visiting,' returned Morris. 'I shan't be missed. This is a very good fruit tart, this.'

Mrs Garvey reappeared and asked if all was well. We assured her it was. She then asked if we would like coffee and perhaps a little gin and hot water?

'There is nothing for settling the stomach and sending you off to sleep like gin and hot water,' she opined.

Regretfully we declined and at last rose from the snug table and made our way back out into the taproom.

In our absence it had filled up to such a point I don't think they could have squeezed anyone else in. Tobacco smoke filled the air and also a degree of what I might call country odours such as sour milk. There had been a buzz of conversation but as soon as Morris and I appeared, a dead silence fell and every pair of eyes there turned to us. Word of our arrival had spread and they'd come from near and far to see these exotic persons from the nation's capital. We were studied from head to toe and our progress across the room to the staircase minutely noted. Still closely observed, we climbed the lower staircase and when we turned a bend in it and were lost to view to those below, we heard an excited gabble of voices immediately break out again.

'I don't know about you, Mr Ross, but I feel like a travelling freak show,' grumbled Morris.

Our room was small but I was relieved to see there were two beds. One was a four-poster and the other a much smaller single bed pushed against the wall. Morris, observing the dictates of rank if not of physical build, made for the single bed. I took possession of the four-poster feeling quite lordly. That didn't last long. The mattress was both lumpy and damp. I regretted having turned down the offer of gin and hot water.

Morris, after one murmured remark made to the ceiling, 'Decent young women like that, nursing soldiers, it don't seem right to me!' fell asleep at once with his mouth open, breathing noisily.

I made myself as comfortable as possible and hoped I would not wake up in the morning to find myself incapacitated by rheumatism.

Despite everything I slept very well. Perhaps it was the sea air from the Solent not half a mile away. We ate a hearty breakfast downstairs in the snug, which had been set aside solely for our use at any time of the day. I was feeling cheerful and optimistic because I'd be seeing Lizzie again. Also, I have to admit, because the case intrigued me. I wanted to get to grips with it. I knew, too, that a lot rested on my shoulders: the reputation of Scotland Yard, for a start. If I came down here from London and made a complete mess of things, my reception on my return didn't bear imagining.

We set out for Shore House on foot, giving ourselves good time to observe the countryside and the general topography. We came upon the church after some half a mile.

'Pretty,' observed Morris. He glanced round him uneasily. 'It's mortal quiet, sir.'

'It's a churchyard,' I pointed out.

'I mean everywhere. Where are all the people? Not just the dead ones like that lot there.' He indicated the jumble of burials. 'I mean the living.'

'They are at work, I dare say. You're in the country, Sergeant. They begin the day early. Cows to be milked and so forth.'

'It don't seem natural,' objected Morris. 'I'd rather be in Limehouse with villains, drunken sailors and riff-raff all around me. At least I'd hear a human voice and have a fair idea what might happen next. Here there's no way of knowing.'

Like me, Morris felt displaced. We'd both lost our familiar points of reference and had quickly to develop new ones. It wouldn't be easy.

We reached the house soon enough and it did nothing to improve Sergeant Morris's poor opinion of country life.

'It's a nice enough house, I grant you, pretty big and fit for nobs. But it seems a funny sort of choice for a pair of maiden ladies. What do they do all day?'

'Unlike you and me, Morris, they like a quiet life.'

'It's not natural,' said Morris firmly. 'Women like visiting their friends and taking tea and such, gossiping. Why, these ladies can't see a new face from one month's end to another!'

We were admitted by the housekeeper, a formidable woman in black whose eyes glittered at us with hostility.

'You are expected, gentlemen,' she said, and started towards the door at the end of the hall.

I prevented her with, 'One moment if you please, Mrs Williams. It *is* Mrs Williams, is it not?'

She nodded silently, her eyes watchful.

'This is the hall table where normally a Malay knife, called a *kris*, is kept?' I pointed to the spot.

'It is, though I didn't know the proper name for it. *Kris*, you say? It's used as a letter knife. I don't know who told you of it.' Her mouth twitched in suppressed anger. 'Unless it was Miss Martin.'

'It does not matter who told me. The knife is missing. Is that correct? At any rate, I don't see it.'

'It's been mislaid,' said Williams firmly. 'Now, will you come this way? And if you'll wait a moment, Sergeant, I'll take you to meet the staff.'

Morris waited to be led to the kitchen quarters and I was conducted into the presence of the Roche sisters.

I had hoped to find Lizzie with them but she was not in the room and I was disappointed again. I told myself to attend to business and concentrated on the sisters. Lizzie's description of them in her letter had been remarkably accurate. There they sat gowned alike in violet silk with crocheted collars at their necks. The elder sister's hair was drawn back severely beneath a lace cap. The younger, Miss Phoebe, wore false ringlets. Either she had dressed her hair in haste that morning, or her mind had been occupied with other matters, because the ringlets had been attached at different levels so that one dangled lower than the other. It gave her a distracted look.

I introduced myself and Williams glided away. I was not invited to sit down and so remained standing before the two ladies like a schoolboy in disgrace. I made some suitable remarks of sympathy with their unfortunate situation and expressed the wish I would be able to get to the bottom of matters soon.

'I should hope so,' said Miss Roche icily. 'It is not our custom, Inspector Ross, to receive police officers in our drawing room.' She hesitated and then, reluctantly, gestured towards a chair. 'Sit down. You might as well.'

I accepted the seat so grudgingly offered. 'If I might ask you,' I said, 'to give me your account of what happened that morning? Start, if you would, with the arrival of Brennan at the house. Who sent for him?'

'Haven't you spoken to Gosling?' asked Miss Roche. 'Hasn't he told you what happened? Why must we repeat it?'

'Because, ma'am, I fancy you may be more observant than Constable Gosling,' I said artfully.

I did Gosling a disservice. He'd struck me as being a competent fellow rather wasted in a backwater. But flattery might get me somewhat further than mere insistence.

'Oh, very well,' said Miss Roche sourly. 'I sent for Brennan because I'd seen a rat up here in the drawing room, in broad daylight, twice.'

I glanced at Miss Phoebe, hoping to draw her into the conversation.

'I didn't see it,' she said. 'But then, I expect I was reading.'

'What does it matter whether my sister saw it or not?' demanded Miss Christina. 'I saw it. Isn't that enough? Now then, I sent for the rat-catcher and he came. I didn't want to watch him at work and went upstairs to my room where I occupied myself with reading my daily chapter of Scripture.'

'And you, ma'am?' I asked Miss Phoebe.

'Oh, I breakfast in my room,' she assured me breathlessly. 'I never come down before eleven. I knew Brennan was here. I don't like him – didn't like him.' She faltered. 'He was such a rough fellow and on his last visit one of his dogs killed the kitchen cat.' She swallowed nervously. 'So I stayed in my room.'

I juggled the positions of all these people in my head. The Roche ladies each in their rooms upstairs. Lizzie and Mrs Craven walking to or coming from the church. Dr Lefebre out by the entrance on the road, smoking his cigarette and waiting for a message from the stables.

'But Brennan then went out into the garden,' I remarked.

'You will have to ask Williams about that,' returned Miss

Roche. 'I have no idea what he did. I was brought downstairs by the sounds of a commotion in the garden below. I went out and found quite a crowd of people clustered about Brennan, who lay on the ground.' There was an almost imperceptible pause before she went on, 'One of them was Mr Andrew Beresford, a neighbour, and I ordered him from the property.'

'Why?' I asked.

'He's been told before his presence here is not welcome. There is no cause for you to know the reason.' She drew a deep breath. 'My niece, Mrs Craven, was there, understandably much distressed. Williams took her indoors. Miss Martin, the companion, followed them. I went inside to tell my sister what had happened. Callow – the gardener – dealt with the dog, Brennan's terrier. It was a danger to anyone approaching the body. He had then to await Greenaway's return to order him to harness up the trap and fetch Gosling. Dr Lefebre returned with Greenaway – they had been riding over the heath. He, the doctor, took a look at the body, I understand, and confirmed the man was dead. That's all I can tell you.'

'And the body of the rat-catcher?' I asked.

Miss Roche raised her eyebrows. 'Dr Lefebre ordered it should not be moved before Gosling saw it. Later it was moved to a mortuary somewhere. My only concern was that it left the premises. I had no interest in where it was taken.'

'I meant, ma'am, that before the return of Greenaway with Gosling, the body seems to have been left unattended for some time,' I suggested.

'Should it not have been? Anyway, Callow came back with a net to snare the dog, so he was there for some minutes.'

The trickiest moment had come. 'I must ask you to look at this, ladies. I'm sorry but it is necessary.' I took the envelope containing the *kris* from my pocket and slid the knife out on to the palm of my hand.

Miss Roche eyed it with distaste. 'That is the weapon?'

Miss Phoebe gave a little moan and turned her head aside.

'I must ask you whether you recognise it, ma'am.'

'I recognise the style of it.'

'Miss Phoebe?' I prompted gently.

She took her hand from her eyes, leaned forward and exclaimed, 'Why, Christina, it's our letter opener!'

'It *looks* like our letter opener,' corrected her sister.

'I understand the letter opener is missing from the hall table,' I said to Miss Roche.

'So Williams has told me. However, that does not mean the one you have there is ours. Ours will be about the place somewhere.'

So much for my hope of surprising the ladies with the knife. Williams had been there before me to inform them of its loss and allow them time to prepare their response to my question. Whatever her motives, Williams appeared intent on frustrating us. Upper servants, in my experience, often present more of a problem than their employers. No one is more zealous in preserving the good name of a household than its butler – or housekeeper.

At that moment the door opened. 'Ah,' said Miss Roche, 'here is Miss Martin, who has been engaged to be companion to my niece and with whom I believe you already have some acquaintance. If you have further questions perhaps you would direct them to her.'

Something in my face must have told her she'd taken a step too far in her arrogance. More graciously, she went on, 'We wish to be of any help we can, naturally. I shall tell Lycurgus Greenaway that the stables are at your disposal. If you need a horse, just order one saddled for you. Or, if you prefer, Greenaway can drive you in the pony and trap anywhere you need to go.'

I stood up and thanked her. Now I could turn and there was Lizzie in the doorway. I had regained one of my points of reference, my most important.

Anxiously I scanned her features and saw that she was pale but composed.

'Good morning, Inspector Ross,' she said politely. 'I hope you had a trouble-free journey?'

I had expected no less than to find her steadfast under fire; but I had hoped she might show some delight at the sight of me and so my own pleasure was spoiled by a twinge of disappointment.

'Thank you, Miss Martin, yes,' I returned with equal formality. 'I wonder if I could ask you to show me in the garden exactly where you found—'

Miss Phoebe squeaked.

'Yes, of course,' Lizzie said quickly. 'Please, Inspector Ross, follow me.'

I bowed to the Roche sisters, thanked them for their cooperation, and followed Lizzie out into the garden with what I hoped was a measured step.

Chapter Twelve

Elizabeth Martin

I HAVEN'T the words to describe to you the relief I felt when I saw Ben Ross with the Roche sisters; and the difficulty I had at concealing it before the two women. Any expression of joy would have been badly viewed by Miss Roche and prejudiced her against both Ben and me even more than was already the case. But now at last someone had come who would make sense of this horrible business, if any sense could be made of murder.

Conscious of Miss Roche's eyes on me, I managed to greet Ben with suitable restraint. But as soon as we'd made our way into the garden and were out of sight of the drawing-room windows, I burst out,

'Oh, Ben! I'm *so* glad you're here. I was afraid they'd send someone else.'

He seized both my hands. 'And I can't tell you how glad I am to see you unharmed, Lizzie.'

If he'd only left it there, our reunion would have been perfect. But no, he had to go on, 'I had a bad feeling about this whole business. I did tell you so, didn't I, Lizzie? You will admit I was right?'

Now, no one likes to hear 'I told you so' from anyone. But particularly no lady likes to hear it from the gentleman with whom she is supposed to be walking out. Not that we were likely to be doing any walking out here, but I dare say you know what I mean.

'I don't believe you expected murder,' I said, pulling my hands from his.

He reddened. 'Now, Lizzie, don't take offence. I'm sorry if I was – tactless. Please, I've not come all this way just for us to quarrel.'

'Of course not!' I said quickly. 'I admit I did fancy there were some things I wasn't being told, but I certainly didn't expect anything as dreadful as murder, either.' I cleared my throat and wondered how to go on, as he seemed to be waiting. 'Are you and Sergeant Morris quite comfortable at The Acorn?'

'Quite comfortable, thank you, although we are something of a circus show as far as the locals are concerned.'

An awkward silence followed. In it we eyed one another, both fearful of saying the wrong thing, so that we were unable to chat as easily as we'd have liked. I realised how much I'd missed Ben. But, of course, it had to be police work that had brought about our reunion. On the other hand, without Brennan's death, Ben wouldn't be here. It was as though we were always fated to meet over a corpse.

At last Ben said, 'Well, perhaps you'd show me where you came upon Mrs Craven and the body? Tell me everything from that moment on, if you would.'

I almost replied, 'Yes, officer!' Instead I drew a deep breath and said, 'All right. Let's see.'

So what *had* happened? Some of it he would already have heard from Lefebre. How Lucy had been taken up to her room by

Williams and hidden away from all of us. How Lefebre and I had a brief discussion (I didn't mention this had taken place in my room and was pretty sure Lefebre wouldn't have mentioned this detail either). We'd decided to advise the Roche women that Scotland Yard should be called in. I'd suggested the name of Ben himself.

'Thank you,' said Ben on hearing this.

'Oh, but I wanted to make sure they didn't send someone else,' I explained.

His face lit up and he even smiled. 'Really, Lizzie?'

'Yes, of course. You're the very best detective they have at Scotland Yard.'

His face fell. 'Oh, is that the only reason? I was hoping . . . Well, I'm grateful for your vote of confidence. But Dunn may not agree with it if I go home having failed to solve this particular crime.'

'You'll solve it!' I declared stoutly, 'and if I can help, I will. And, and I am so very happy to see you here, Ben, in any case. You know that.'

This time Ben didn't answer, only looked at me, so I took breath and continued with my account.

Constable Gosling had arrived. I'd taken him, as I was now leading Ben, to the place in the garden where I'd come upon Lucy and the dead man. Lefebre had been successful in preventing the body's removal. The wretched Brennan lay where he'd been abandoned in grotesque fashion among the rhododendrons. At least someone had had the decency to cover him with a horse blanket. Personally, like Miss Roche, I'd have preferred the corpse to be taken away somewhere. Unlike her, I understood why it had to be left. I'd tried in vain not to look, indicating it to Gosling with my head averted, but it was no good. It drew my gaze with horrid fascination. The sight was pitiful as well as shocking. I told myself that what lay beneath the blanket was not a dead man but only some garden rubbish. But Brennan's boots protruded, toes pointing skywards, so I couldn't ease my mind with this hopeless pretence. The dog had been taken away.

I'd explained briefly to the constable how Lucy had run away from me. To be honest, I told Gosling, as I told Ben now, that Lucy and I had 'parted company'. (I couldn't control what Lefebre, who'd witnessed Lucy's flight, might have told Gosling or, indeed, Ben, but he'd get only the bare facts from me.) Seeking her, I'd first searched on the shore and then in the garden where I'd come upon the scene. I'd pointed out to Gosling the direction of my footsteps.

'Thank you, miss,' Gosling had replied. 'You can go back to the house now. I won't need to talk to you again. Not a nice business this for you, you being a delicate female.'

Usually I'd have retorted I was perfectly robust in mind and body. But I had to admit to myself I was feeling somewhat queasy. 'Thank you, Constable,' I'd said.

Gosling's somewhat pop-eyed gaze contemplated the blanketed heap on the grass and then turned to the rat's nest containing the now motionless rat babies.

'Very nasty,' he observed.

Dr Lefebre reappeared at that moment and fell into conversation with the constable. That released me and I quit the scene as fast as my legs would carry me. I'd felt duty bound to stop by the drawing room and ask if I could do anything for the sisters.

My solicitude had been brushed aside.

The following details of the conversion with the sisters I omitted to recount to Ben.

Miss Roche had fixed me with a cold eye. 'How well are you acquainted with this police inspector at Scotland Yard?'

'Quite well, ma'am, Inspector Ross is—'

I wasn't allowed to finish.

'It sounds to me,' said Miss Roche, 'a very unsuitable acquaintance for a young woman of respectable background. You and Dr Lefebre between you have persuaded me to allow this Inspector Ross to be sent for. But it is largely on your recommendation, Miss Martin, and I trust you've not misled us as to his abilities.'

I'd nearly burst out, 'Thank God Ben is coming!' but managed to stop myself just in time and substituted, 'I do assure you, Miss Roche, you can have every confidence in the inspector's talent and dedication.'

Her eyebrow twitched. 'Really?' she said. 'We shall see.'

With that and a nod I'd been dismissed. I wasn't sorry to leave them to whatever discussion they wanted to have together. I'd not come to Shore House to minister to them. They had not engaged my services, their brother had, and I realised very well they resented my presence. But a huge weight had been lifted from my mind by the news that Lefebre would ask for Ben to be sent down here.

Not all concern, however. My chief worry was Lucy, whose companion I was meant to be. The laudanum given her by Williams meant that I didn't see her for all the rest of that day. I kept away from the sisters except at lunch, a dismal affair of cold mutton pie and boiled potatoes. The kitchen must be in some disarray. Gosling had probably been there quizzing the cook and maids. Dinner had been little better, with a pudding of lumpy semolina and stewed prunes. I was glad to retire early.

I took up my narrative to Ben again at this point. I hadn't been able to sleep. I'd tossed restlessly for some time, the vision of what I'd seen in the garden dancing before my eyes. At last I got up, threw a shawl round my shoulders and went to sit by the open window hoping the night breeze and soothing lapping of the water would help.

The garden had been in darkness. I couldn't help but recall seeing two mysterious forms out there the night of my arrival, and hearing their whispered conversation.

'You didn't write to me about this,' Ben interrupted at this point.

'I'd already finished my letter and sealed it up. Anyway, I didn't then know it was important. Perhaps it wasn't – isn't,' I defended myself.

Ben heaved a sigh. 'Go on.'

A little tetchily I continued, describing how I'd pushed the casement open wider and leaned out. The distinct odour of the sea filled my nostrils. The tide was coming in again and very fast. The moon glittered on the rolling waves. An owl swooped by, on his way to hunt, quite making me jump.

(Ben started to look a little restless at this point and I realised this counted as description of the scenery.)

I'd been about to pull in my head when I glimpsed, far away to my left on the shore, a flickering light. It wasn't a lantern; that would have been a steady pinpoint. It was an erratic, dancing glow that waxed and waned, rose up into the air and then fell back again. Above the smell of the incoming sea, I identified something else. Smoke. There was a fire down there on the beach. My sight of it was briefly cut off as something dark passed before it. Then it returned, passing between the fire and me again. Someone was down there and moved round the blaze. If it was a vagrant who'd pitched his camp, he'd find it and his fire washed away by the incoming tide. Perhaps he was a stranger to this shoreline.

I went back to my bed with new thoughts running round my brain. The open heath and adjoining countryside, which had appeared so empty when we travelled across it in the trap, was in reality sprinkled with an unseen nomadic population, day and night. There were those too poor to afford any transport or the price of a bed at an inn, and forced to walk to their destinations, taking days over the journey and sleeping beneath the stars. Others, like Brennan, made their way from spot to spot offering their own peculiar skills. There were labourers without employment seeking a new place or at least a day's work, wandering musicians, pedlars, tramps and gypsies. Brennan and his wife had made camp on the heath. Another traveller had made his camp on the shore. Could Miss Roche be right? Had one of these made his way into the garden perhaps intending to beg at the kitchen door, and encountered Brennan? Had there been a dispute and . . .

But the knife, I thought. Such an intruder would not be armed with the knife from the hall table.

Perhaps the knife was not the hall one? Or possibly Brennan had slipped it into his pocket earlier in a petty theft and, arguing with a trespasser in the garden, had pulled it out and threatened the unknown man with it. There had been a struggle, the trespasser had wrested the knife from Brennan and plunged it into his neck . . .

'Stop, stop, Lizzie!' I'd muttered aloud.

I could have conjectured like this endlessly. I'd made an effort to clear my mind, settled on the pillows and eventually fallen into uneasy slumber.

★   ★   ★

171

On Wednesday, when Dr Lefebre had gone up to London to inform Charles Roche what had happened and visit Scotland Yard, Lucy had still not appeared at breakfast. The laudanum must have worn off by now. I went up and knocked at her door and enquired through the panels how she was.

'Go away! I won't open the door and I won't come out!' had been the fierce reply.

Two can play at that game. I tapped at the door again more sharply and in a raised voice called, 'I shan't go away. I shall sit here until you open the door and you'll know I'm here. This is nonsense, Lucy, and a waste of your time and mine.'

There was a pause, a scuffle and rustle of skirts, and the key clicked as it was turned. It was left to me to push open the door and by the time I had entered the room, Lucy had scurried away to the far side to a window seat. She sat huddled on it with her arms wrapped round her body.

I'd been relieved to see she was fully dressed and her hair was brushed. It curled loosely on her shoulders, making her look even younger, and as if she really did belong in the schoolroom. There was a tea tray nearby brought, I suspected, by Williams earlier. She looked very pale and although her attitude was almost as if she had been frozen yet her eyes still held that wild look. It worried me.

She'd greeted me with, 'I know they are bringing policemen from Scotland Yard to arrest me! I won't let them in.'

'They're not coming to arrest you, Lucy. What nonsense. You . . .' Here I paused to pick my words carefully. On the one hand Lucy appeared to believe any stranger arriving at Shore House had come to take her away, whether it be Lefebre or Ben Ross. On the other hand, she was sensitive about being disbelieved. This made it difficult to refute her charge.

'I have previous acquaintance with Inspector Ross. I've seen him at work. He's careful, very methodical, not given in any way to impulse. Also he's intelligent. He won't bully you. You'll find him courteous and understanding.'

(I swear Ben blushed at this point of my narrative although he put up his hand as if to stifle a cough, in order to hide it.)

'He may be all the things you say,' returned Lucy vehemently, 'but I still won't see him. I won't come downstairs and they shan't come in here. I shall lock the door and if they try to break it down, I shall – I shall push the chest of drawers in front of it, there!'

'Let's not talk of it any more now,' I soothed her. 'They don't arrive until tomorrow. Let us go out for a little walk. The fresh air—'

But I got no further. Lucy interrupted me with a repeat of her intention to stay in her room and that was that. An offer to sit with her, perhaps read to her, was equally rebuffed.

'I don't want to be watched!' she shouted at me.

This was a sulky child and best left to work out her bad mood. I, at least, could go for a walk and breathe fresh air so I'd left her and gone to my room to collect a hat. When I stepped out again and turned towards the head of the stairs I received quite a shock.

The corridor in which my room was located, to the right at the top of the stairs, was always dark because there was no window. But the corridor to the left was lighter, due to a window at the far end. Both corridors had been empty when I went into my room, of that I was certain. I had only been moments picking up my hat. But I was no longer alone.

A female figure in a dark dress stood motionless at the head of the staircase, facing towards me. Because I was in gloom, and the waiting figure lit from behind by the window at that end of the house, I couldn't make out anything at all, not one feature. It was a form as mysterious as that figure I had seen slip into the house from the garden on my first night here. The waiting woman had been so still and silent, I confess I felt a moment of panic and even had a foolish impulse to turn and run back into my room. But I told myself sternly it was only a trick of the lighting that gave the figure such a sinister aspect. I forced myself to walk briskly towards her (although I did half wonder if she would disappear before I reached her).

When I was closer I'd been able to see (with some relief) that it was Phoebe Roche. I had wondered if it would turn out to be the dowdy self-effacing woman who acted as lady's maid to both sisters, although she would have no reason to wait for me as the figure clearly had been doing. I remembered that Miss Phoebe breakfasted in her room and didn't come downstairs until mid-morning. She must just have emerged from her early seclusion. With the departure of the corpse from the premises, the sisters had promptly laid aside their mourning black. Today's gown, as I could now see, was magenta in colour. I fully expected that when I saw Christina Roche, her dress would be the same. Did they agree this the night before, I wondered? 'Good morning, Miss Phoebe,' I said, my voice seeming to echo along the upper landing and reverberate away down the corridor behind her.

'Good morning, Miss Martin.' Phoebe peered up at me in a way that might have to do with the poor light or, it struck me, meant she was very short sighted. I hadn't so far seen her wearing spectacles. But neither had I seen her reading despite her sister Christina's claim that Phoebe 'always had her nose in a book'. Perhaps she read in the privacy of her bedroom and that was why she came downstairs so late each morning. 'I was about to knock at my niece's door. Do you know, by any chance, if she's in her room?' she asked.

'She is and I've spoken to her, but she's still very upset. I wanted her to come out with me for a walk but she refuses. Perhaps you can persuade her?'

I waited to see if she'd take up the suggestion, but after only the very shortest of hesitations, Phoebe Roche shook her head. 'My niece is obstinate. I do believe it's her only failing. Even as a small child there was no moving her once her mind was made up. Add to that a natural youthful impetuosity . . .' She sighed and shook her head resignedly. 'My sister and I have done our very best for dear Lucy,' she went on abruptly. 'I know Charles, my brother, sent you because he felt Lucy might benefit from younger, more lively, company in whom she might confide. We all worry about her. I think Charles believes, that is, he feels we did not prevent—'

She broke off in some confusion. I guessed she had been about to refer to the hasty marriage between Lucy and James Craven.

'I'm sure you have always done all you can, ma'am.'

It was not their fault they were completely unsuited to deal with Lucy's troubles. As to whether they could have prevented the love affair, that was another matter. Young lovers sometimes seem to thrive on opposition and are ingenious in finding ways to meet. From what I had been told by Lefebre regarding James Craven, the sisters would have been hard put to it to prevent him outmanoeuvring them. An elopement might have been the result.

Again, I pruned the conversation of the following exchange that I saw no reason to repeat to Ben.

Miss Phoebe had now eyed me slowly up and down in a way not offensive but certainly disconcerting. 'You carry yourself very well, Miss Martin, and although you are not a beauty, you are handsome. You have a certain presence; I think it would be called that.'

All this had been so innocently uttered I decided the speech was intended to be complimentary and took it as such. But I'd no idea what could have inspired it.

Miss Phoebe's next words were, 'My niece is very pretty, don't you think?'

'Indeed she is,' I agreed.

'When she's quite well she's beautiful, I've always thought. She's not well now. She hasn't been well since the baby died. Even before that, from the moment Mr Craven left for China, she fell into a decline. My sister upbraided her for moping. She told her a Roche should show more strength of character. I was very sorry about the baby.' She sighed. 'I, of course, was never a beauty, always a plain child and a plain young woman. Now I'm a plain old one.'

I thought Miss Phoebe no more than fifty or so. As a woman fast approaching thirty myself I didn't view that as very old. I reflected with some annoyance that society considered a single gentleman of fifty still perfectly eligible. One of thirty was still a sprig of a lad! Why should women be so cruelly placed 'on the shelf'? I waited in silence because I guessed there was something she wanted to say to me.

She leaned forward and lowered her voice as one about to impart a confidence. 'I've often thought myself fortunate to be so plain. Not when I was younger, of course. Then I wanted to be pretty, as Lucy is. But now, when I consider my niece's sad situation, I do believe it's a blessing for a woman to be born without good looks. One is spared so much distress and sorrow.'

With that, Miss Phoebe smiled sweetly at me, and began to walk downstairs, apparently abandoning her plan to knock at Lucy's door.

I was left perplexed and wondering if she had been trying to indicate something rather more than her words had expressed. Perhaps it was Phoebe who needed someone to confide in? In the end, I put the whole thing out of my mind, following her downstairs.

Ben was scowling down at the ground and appeared to be mulling over what I'd recounted so I broke off my tale for a while.

Chapter Thirteen

Elizabeth Martin

THERE WERE things I hadn't yet told Ben, partly because a natural break in our conversation had arrived and partly because I was uneasily aware my loyalties were divided. Of course, Ben would say that in such a serious inquiry there was nothing that should be kept from the police. But I was well aware of Lucy's fragile state of mind. She needed a friend and I'd promised her I'd be that friend.

I thought back to that curious meeting with Phoebe Roche. But was it so odd? She'd come to ask after her niece. Nothing could be more natural.

'Will you go on?' prompted Ben gently.

'What? Oh, yes, of course. Where was I?'

'Outside Mrs Craven's door, talking to her Aunt Phoebe.'

I picked up my story. I'd followed Phoebe downstairs. By the time I'd reached the hall below, the drawing-room door was closing on her. I'd tied on my hat before the mirror to make sure it wasn't crooked and set out.

My footsteps had turned automatically towards the church and I'd wondered whether today I might find it open. It had been a fine morning and I'd felt very sorry I hadn't been able to persuade Lucy to come with me. It could hardly be good for her to be shut away in her room in the state she was in.

The church slumbered in the sunshine like a recumbent elderly giant. I tugged at the great metal ring in the oak door in vain and decided the sexton must be too lazy to come and open up when there was no service to be held. I began to stroll along the narrow paths between the plots in the churchyard, stopping from time to time to read an inscription. As is usual in country burial places, the same few names reappeared over and over again. Most tombstones were modest in nature but there were a few more ornate ones. One quite grand vault surrounded by wrought-iron railings belonged to the Beresford family. I saw they'd been at least a hundred years in the district. Another, curiously built in the shape of a pyramid, was a memorial to a Captain Meager R N who had taken part in the Battle of the Nile and survived that engagement to perish of the fever in the West Indies. These were the local families, the gentry and the farm labourers and servants who had worked for them. Here lay the squire, village blacksmith, grocer, baker, cobbler and midwife, all linked by kinship and old acquaintance or by employment. 'A place for everything and everything in its place.' Lucy had told me that was Miss Roche's favourite saying. For 'everything' one might substitute 'everyone'. Yet, in this little community, the Roche sisters had arrived as strangers and remained as such. I wondered again at their self-imposed isolation.

I'd turned aside and made my way back to simpler resting places until I again found myself standing before the little stone commemorating Lucy and James Craven's infant child. I'd been prepared for it to inspire me with sadness but not to surprise me; yet it did. For the second time that morning something startled me.

Placed carefully upon the tiny mound was a small tribute of hedgerow grasses and flowers. I couldn't imagine who might have done such a thing. Not Lucy, who denied her baby rested here. A village child, perhaps? There was something childishly naive about the simplicity of the tiny bouquet. It was tied together with a scrap of grubby red ribbon. Someone had taken great trouble; someone who had no access to garden flowers or a greenhouse.

A sudden idea had occurred to me and I'd whirled round, looking towards the spreading yew tree. But today nothing had moved in its dark shadows. I'd turned back and wondered what I should do about the offering. Should I remove it? If Lucy came here and saw it, it might distress her. But who was I to remove a gift surely made in respect and in love? I'd left it there and walked slowly back to Shore House deep in thought.

Ben had fallen silent and thoughtful again. He emerged from his reverie, gave his head a shake as if to clear it and asked, 'Anything more?'

'Very little,' I told him. 'But the spot where I found Lucy and – and the dead man is just over here.'

Despite my offer to help, I could show Ben where Brennan's body had sprawled more easily than I could supply him with much new information likely to be of use. I could tell him how I'd heard people talking in the garden that first night. But I couldn't guess who it might have been. I hadn't mentioned seeing a white dog; in truth I didn't know whether it had been Brennan's terrier or Beresford's and if the latter, anything I said might require an embarrassing explanation from Lucy. I decided that if it became necessary I'd tell Ben about the dog later.

'This is the place,' I said now to Ben. We had reached the rhododendrons where I had come upon Lucy and Brennan.

Ross took a scrap of paper from his pocket and studied it, looking up from time to time, as if to check something.

'What's that?' I asked curiously. One is not meant to quiz officers about their duty, but I wanted to know.

'Dr Lefebre drew me a map, a diagram, showing where the body lay, Mrs Craven sat and the relationship of it all to the house. I'm obliged to him and to you because you've confirmed it. Not to have seen the body *in situ* myself is a nuisance. But I'm fortunate that I have such excellent witnesses in you and the doctor.' He tucked the paper away in his pocket. 'Miss Roche told me that someone called Beresford was at the scene when she arrived and she sent him packing. What do you know of that?'

'He's a local landowner. He was walking on the beach shortly before all this. I saw him there and spoke to him. He must have heard Lucy screaming and he came running, as the others did. I fancy—' I hesitated. 'I fancy there's some difference of opinion between him and the Roche women. Well, between him and Miss Christina, at least, and her word is law at Shore House. She ordered him off the premises.'

'Mm. Well, I'm afraid I must interview Mrs Craven.'

'Must it be today?' I begged. 'She really is so frightened. She'll become hysterical and make no sense.'

'So, what do you suggest?'

I thought quickly. 'Perhaps I could persuade her out for a little walk tomorrow morning? I can't guarantee it, but she must be thoroughly tired of being cooped up in her room most of the time. If we walked to the churchyard, you could be there, just by chance, and meet us.'

We settled that was how we should do it. Then Ben asked, 'When you and Mrs Craven walked to the church on the morning of the murder, or were coming back from there, did you chance to see a gypsy woman? She would have had a basket on her arm. She was selling pegs. Lefebre saw her. She called at the kitchen here.'

'There was one,' I remembered. 'She passed us going in the direction of the village. I think she meant to offer to read our fortunes or some such, but she seemed to take fright at the sight of Lucy and scurried away.'

I seized the nettle. He would be told the gossip soon enough. 'People around here are – are quite wrongly wary of Lucy. She's a harmless child, Ben. Why can't they see it's only pining for her husband and her grief over her baby that make her act oddly from time to time? Who would not?'

'No one else, then?' asked Ben, without comment on my defence of Lucy.

'No, but wait! That morning, before the discovery of Brennan's body, someone was in the churchyard when Lucy and I were there by the grave. There's a big yew tree nearby and someone was hiding in its shadow watching us. That's why, when I found the posy on the grave, I looked that way again. Only that second time there was no one there.'

'Hiding? Was it a man or a woman?' His dark eyes lit with enthusiasm. This wasn't description of the scenery: this was a fact. Ben Ross! I thought crossly. You do so like *facts*!

'I can't tell you. I only noticed a dark shape. There was almost no light beneath the tree. It's a vast thing, hundreds of years old, I don't doubt. But someone was there,' I insisted. 'I saw a movement. it may mean nothing. It was probably only a villager nervous of interrupting us.'

'But,' Ben said, 'the second time you visited the churchyard, after your meeting with Phoebe Roche outside Mrs Craven's room, you found that someone had left a little bouquet of wild flowers on the baby's grave. Who could that be, do you think? According to your account, Mrs Craven had no opportunity to pay another visit to the grave without you.'

'No, she didn't. But in any case, Lucy denies it's her baby lying there so why should she place flowers? I don't see either of the Roche sisters placing such a poor little bunch, or indeed any kind of tribute. There seems to be an agreement that Lucy's child isn't spoken of under the roof of Shore House.'

To myself I thought, it's as if the poor little soul has just been not so much forgotten as erased like a mistake in a drawing. Phoebe only dared to whisper her regret in that dark corridor where no one could see or overhear. Even Lucy waited until we were out of the house, in the churchyard where she could show me the grave, before she could talk of her loss. It was her way of introducing the subject, as if she couldn't refer to her baby without some excuse.

Aloud I said, 'Please try not to use the word "loss" when you speak to her, Ben. She won't accept the baby's dead and if you talk as if it is, she gets very agitated. But with the Roche sisters behaving as if the child never existed and offering her no sympathy or support in her bereavement at all, is it surprising? Lucy's dealing with the appalling situation by just denying it's happened. This is a very – very unhealthy house, Ben. That's my feeling about it all.'

'Mrs Craven's state of mind . . .' Ben began. But he got no further. He suddenly flung up his arm into the air and pointed into the distance towards the heath.

'What's that? Is it a fire?'

I had my back towards the heath and had to turn to look in that direction. A plume of dark smoke spiralled up some way off and was slowly spreading like a dark stain into the blue sky. It could only come from the expanse of bone-dry heather and gorse.

At that moment we heard the rumble of cartwheels approaching at a great pace. We hurried up the side of the house and round to the gate just in time to see a farm wagon rattle and sway past, the horses at a canter. The wagon was gaily painted and carried a group of rustics all armed with birch brooms. The sight was extraordinary. They looked like a coven of male witches setting out for some unearthly ride.

Greenaway came puffing towards us at that moment. 'Fire up on the hearth, sir – and Miss Martin. Those chaps have gone off to beat it out. Mr Beresford, he has it all organised and ready that if anyone sees smoke, he gets together his farm workers and off they go straight away. Better than any fire service, they are. Not that we have a fire engine here. The nearest is at Hythe.'

He squinted into the distance and turned to Ben, looking worried. 'Fact is, sir, where you see that smoke, that's about the spot where Brennan and his wife had their tent set up. The poor woman is still camped there. Gosling told her she wasn't to leave. I can't say I like it, sir.'

'What?' cried Ben. 'I must get up there immediately! Can you guide me?'

'Ah, I'll saddle up, then,' offered Greenaway. 'We'll have to ride up there, sir. It's off the road and I can't take the trap. We could walk but it would take us a while.'

I saw an almost comical dismay enter Ben's face. 'I am no horseman, Greenaway.'

Greenaway peered into his face. 'Well, tell you what, I'll saddle the pony for you, if you don't mind. Thing is, she's quieter than the horses and there's the advantage that if you do come off, there isn't so far to fall.'

Ben looked far from encouraged. He bid me a hasty goodbye

and followed Greenaway in the direction of the stables. The lawn by the gate was dry, so I sat down with my skirts about me, and watched the spreading haze of the smoke as I waited for Ben and Greenaway to return mounted. I prayed the blaze didn't mean some harm had befallen Mrs Brennan. I couldn't forget that poor defeated-looking woman. I fancied now I could smell the burning gorse and heather as the wind veered round and sent the sinister mass billowing in my direction. My eyes stung with small particles borne on the breeze from the fire. I rubbed them and wondered if I ought to go indoors. I also wondered how far and how fast the blaze could spread. Were we safe here?

Soon I heard the clatter of hoofs and the two men reappeared. Greenaway rode what I suspected was one of the carriage horses, currently without work in view of the cracked axle. Ben, looking ill at ease, trotted along beside him on the ewe-necked mare that had pulled the trap.

'I would take off my hat and wave it to you, Miss Martin,' he called as they passed by me. 'But I need both hands to hold on to the mane!'

I smiled and waved at them, though in truth the occasion was no matter for amusement. They had gone. I scrambled to my feet, dusted my skirts down and made hurriedly for the house, glad to be out of the smoke-tinged air. I did hope Ben would be all right. Horses feared fire. Perhaps his pony would bolt. My mind occupied with all these thoughts, I entered the house through the main door.

As I came into the hall I heard voices through the panels of the closed door to my right. It led, I knew, into the small parlour where Lucy had hidden from the breakfasting Lefebre. I'd peeped into the room earlier and seen it was gloomy and cluttered. It didn't surprise me it wasn't much used. Yet a man and a woman were talking in there now. All at once my senses were alive with expectation. I'd heard a man and a woman in the garden, the night I had arrived. Could this be the same pair? There was only one way to find out. Discretion and good manners meant I shouldn't interrupt. My curiosity would not be satisfied unless I did. I threw open the door.

The speakers stood close together and appeared to have been in some very earnest discussion. They broke off their conversation at once and turned towards me: Dr Lefebre and Mrs Williams.

My arrival had clearly disconcerted them. They moved sharply apart. Lefebre recovered first.

'Miss Martin! Mrs Williams and I were looking at the smoke from the window here. Mrs Williams is of the opinion it's a gorse fire.'

'Andrew Beresford's sent his farm workers to beat it out,' I told him. 'And Inspector Ross has gone up there, too, with Greenaway.'

They could have seen as much from the window. I told them nothing new. Williams murmured an excuse and hurried from the room, her gaze averted.

'Is the inspector interested in fires?' asked Lefebre, raising his eyebrows and watching me closely.

'No, only in this one. Greenaway thinks it must be at about the spot where the Brennans made their camp. Mrs Brennan should still be there. I think Greenaway is afraid she could be in some danger.'

'Indeed? Perhaps I should inform Miss Roche. Will you excuse me?'

I watched him go and went to the window. From here one could see the smoke spiralling into the sky but little else. The laurel hedges surrounding the property were in the way. If they had gone upstairs they would have had a far better view from an upper window. That mattered little, however, as whatever they'd been discussing, I didn't think it was the fire.

And what was it about their attitudes, standing so close and talking almost as equals, which made me fancy their acquaintance was older than they might wish me to believe?

Chapter Fourteen

Inspector Benjamin Ross

I LIKE horses but that's not to say I like being aboard one. I watched with envy Greenaway atop the larger horse, trotting ahead of me. His sturdy form appeared to be at one with the movement of the beast beneath him. As for me, it seemed as though when the saddle went down, I went up, and vice versa, so that at every other moment the saddle and I made painful collision. I fancy the pony could feel it too because she shook her head, throwing it up, ears laid back, and turning it so that one large white eye fixed me with a reproachful stare. After a while, however, I realised the mare was docile enough and wouldn't try to set me on the ground out of sheer mischief or spite. If I had come off, more out of my own incompetence than any fault on the part of my steed, the landing would have been soft enough on the peaty soil. I felt myself relax, got more the hang of the thing, finding I could, if I didn't try so hard, move in unison with the animal. If our errand hadn't been so serious, I would quite have enjoyed the experience.

We covered the ground fairly quickly. As we neared the seat of the fire the pungent smell of the burning gorse and heather filled my nostrils. Particles of blackened vegetation swirled in the air and stung my eyes.

Greenaway turned and shouted out, 'Tie your handkerchief over your mouth and nose, sir!'

He took his own advice and I hastened to follow suit. Masked like a pair of Sardinian bandits, we approached the very edge of the area where we saw the farm cart.

Now we could hear the fire as well as see it. It roared and crackled. The horse and my pony grew nervous and tossed their heads.

'Hold fast!' called Greenaway. He jumped down from the saddle and fastened the reins of his mount to the tail of the cart. Coughing as smoke found its way into his mouth, the groom came over to me and aided me to dismount by hauling me from the saddle like a sack of potatoes.

'Thank you, Greenaway,' I said with as much dignity as I could muster. I staggered slightly, finding it odd for a few seconds to be on my own feet.

Greenaway tied my pony alongside the horse and I saw that a man was approaching us. Like us, he wore a handkerchief tied over his face. When he reached us, he pulled it down and his face was comically divided into halves, the top quite blackened with smoke and the lower half pale.

'How goes it, Mr Beresford?' shouted Greenaway.

So this was Beresford, the neighbour so unwelcome on the property of Shore House.

'We'll manage it but we could do with some more help,' was his reply to Greenaway's question. He glanced at me and asked, 'Are you the inspector from London? I can't shake your hand, mine is too dirty.'

Both the groom and I hastened to offer our services.

'Good, good!' exclaimed Beresford. 'You'll find a couple of brooms in there.'

We stripped off our jackets and threw them with our hats into the cart, then armed ourselves with a birch broom each and followed Beresford. He shouted hoarse explanations and instructions as we went, waving his arms to indicate direction.

'We're in luck. The wind is driving the fire towards boggy ground and when it reaches there, it will dampen down and fizzle out of its own accord. But we must prevent it spreading to either side. My men are positioned in a semicircle round it and beating the ground ahead of them as they move inwards. Find a place in the circle!'

'Have you seen anything of the Brennan woman?' I cried out as he ran off.

'No one!' came the shout back to us, barely audible against the cracking of wood and the growl of the flames as the fire took hold of each new patch of heather and gorse.

After that it was all hands, I can't say 'to the pump' because sadly a pump was what we didn't have. But it was everyone to the task. We worked steadily. The sweat rolled off me. My boots grew hotter and hotter from contact with the smouldering ground and the pain in my feet would have been torturing if I'd had time to concentrate on it. I knew my face and clothes were getting as filthy as those of the men to either side of me. My arms ached with swinging the birch broom. From time to time my weapon itself would catch fire and I'd have to beat that out. But gradually as time wore on we drove the conflagration back and eventually it began to splutter and die down, as Beresford had predicted. The ground was soft beneath my feet and rank brown liquid oozed up through the mud. We had reached the boggy area.

At long last, late in the afternoon, we rested our brooms, or what remained of them, on the ground and drew deep ragged breaths. Our throats were sore. We could barely speak and croaked at one another. We were a band of identical brothers in blackened clothing and smeared faces. To me, who had begun life as a pit boy in my native Derbyshire, the experience was extraordinary. I was transported back to the scenes of my youth, when the shifts ended and the colliers emerged, black from head to toe with coal dust, from the belly of the mine.

'I'm grateful to you!' said Beresford hoarsely, coming up to me. He held out a blackened hand and briefly grasped mine. 'I'm afraid I didn't greet you very civilly back there.'

'You had more important things on your mind,' I gasped back. 'I was intending to call on you but now I've met you here. This isn't the time to talk, however.'

'Come to dinner tonight,' he invited me. 'Come about eight, or whenever you're ready. You'd better get yourself off back to The Acorn and have them heat you a bath.'

'I can't leave yet,' I told him. 'Greenaway says the widow of the murdered man was at their camp, just about here. I must find out what happened to her.'

'We'll search the area!' said Beresford promptly.

He rallied his weary troops and they set off again, slowly and methodically covering the area of the fire. After a while Greenaway and I, standing at the edge of the fire where the ground was soggy with underlying water, saw a man approaching us, carrying something wrapped in a piece of clothing.

He held it out as he reached us. 'Looks like a saucepan, sir. Mind now! 'Tis mortal hot.'

The article was gingerly passed to Greenaway who immediately took it a little way off and dropped it into what looked like a puddle of water. To my surprise, with a loud sizzle, the pot disappeared completely beneath the surface. Greenaway reached in and pulled it, now cooled, out. He handed the waistcoat, as the piece of clothing proved to be, back to its owner, and the pot to me.

It was still very warm, despite its bath.

'That's a very deep hole,' I remarked, indicating it.

'Ah, that's not natural,' returned Greenaway. 'That's what we call a gypsy well.'

I must have looked puzzled because he explained. 'Say you're camped near here where there isn't any running water. What do you do? There's water under the surface, so you dig a deep hole. You go away for a while and when you come back, the water will have filled your little pit. But mind! That water is no good, it's foul. So you ladle it out until the hole is empty again and go away and wait again. The second time you come back, the water will have filled the hole like before, but this time it's fit for use, to drink or cook with. The first water seeped through the soil and took out all the badness, filtered it. See . . .' He scooped up some water from the hole and sipped it, before rubbing it over his grimy face.

Rather uncertainly I followed his example. The water had a brackish taste but wasn't undrinkable.

Greenaway nodded. 'That's what we call a gypsy well. That's what the travelling people do if they haven't any other water source.'

'So gypsies dug this?'

'Very likely,' said Greenaway.

'Might Brennan have dug it? He was camped near here?'

'He might.' Then, looking down mournfully at the excavation, Greenaway went on, 'Ah, that's a danger to a horse, though. If a horse puts a foot in that down he goes and can break a leg. If it's a ridden horse, then off comes the rider and will be lucky not to break his collarbone or neck.'

Beresford joined us. 'There is no sign of the woman,' he said, 'only that pot and a couple of tin plates, warped by the heat.' He stared directly at me. 'We found a charred body but it was that of a pony. It must have been dead before the fire caught it, I fancy. The ponies can generally outrun a heath fire and only rarely get trapped. No human remains, at any rate.'

'I suppose that's good news,' I said. 'Thank you for organising the search. But I'd dearly like to know where she is.'

'I must get back and my fellows too,' said Beresford. 'I'll see you later, at eight.'

Greenaway and I rode slowly homeward. Previously I'd felt somewhat at a disadvantage looking up from my pony to the groom looming over me on the bigger horse. But now there was a relaxed atmosphere as between those who have shared an arduous task. I wouldn't get a better opportunity to talk to him than this.

I began, 'Tell me about Brennan. I understand he wasn't much liked, although there was no real reason for it.'

'That's true, sir. Some people round here, especially the older ones, are inclined to be a bit superstitious.' Greenaway threw me an apologetic glance. 'They thought he brought bad luck. It was because he made his livelihood out of rats, most likely, that and his being an outsider. Some of the mothers, the more foolish of them, would even threaten their naughty children with "Jed Brennan will take you away!" Even the most difficult child was as meek as a lamb afterwards.'

'What sort of bad luck?' I persisted.

Now Greenaway was obviously embarrassed and mumbled 'Ah . . .' two or three times before declaring, 'Most of it was nonsense like I said. If a maid broke a jug while he was in the neighbourhood, she'd blame it on the rat-catcher. Any little thing like that, if he was nearby or not! Of course if anything did happen and he *was* there . . .'

The groom's voice trailed away and he leaned forward to pat his horse's neck.

'Such as?' I asked as casually as I was able.

'Nothing of any interest, sir.'

'But?' I persisted gently.

Greenaway shifted his seat in the saddle. 'One of his terriers killed the kitchen cat at Shore House.'

'How did that happen?'

'Blessed if I know, sir. Cook swore she had shut the cat in. We'd had a couple of rats about the stables and the 'catcher came with his two little dogs to flush them out. They were very neat and quick about their business, those dogs. Fair marvel to watch them at work and the speed of them you wouldn't believe. One of 'em would jump in and grab a rat, give it a quick shake or two to snap its neck and the vermin was dead. Then the dog would drop it and dash off after another. They cleared the stables in no time.'

Greenaway broke off his narrative and didn't appear disposed to add to it.

On the face of it there ought to have been little to add, except for the cat, which had yet to figure in the story. I urged him to go on.

Greenaway stroked the horse's neck again. 'Ah . . .'

Nervousness on the part of a witness, in my experience, means you are getting to the nub of the matter. I waited.

Greenaway burst out, 'Suddenly young Joe – that's the stable lad – shouts out "That's not a rat!" Brennan and I ran to see what was amiss and there were the two dogs, tugging at something between them. Brennan roared at them to drop it and when they didn't he fetched them a kick or two. They let it go then and I saw it was a dead cat, our cat. I knew it because it was black with white paws and a white bib in front, neat as you please. Only it wasn't so trim now, a real mess it was, all bloodied and torn about.

'Brennan started to swear in a way no Christian man ought to know how. Of course, he was afraid he'd blamed. He reckoned the cat was dead when the dogs found it. The cat scent had got them excited and that was why they'd been tossing it about and worrying it. He pointed out they hadn't worried any rat's body like it. Well, whatever had happened, it was dead. Sam Callow, the gardener, buried it somewhere. He told me the skull was all smashed in. Those dogs have strong jaws.'

'But Cook insisted she'd shut the animal in the kitchen?'

'She didn't want to be blamed either, I reckon,' observed Greenaway. 'Likely she did shut the creature in, but cats being cats, if they want to get out and they see half a chance, they're gone.'

'Quite,' I agreed. I hadn't expected more on the subject from Greenaway as it seemed it was one he was anxious to drop. But to my surprise he spoke again.

'Thing is, sir, we called it the kitchen cat, but really it was Miss Lucy's – I should say Mrs Craven's – pet. When she first got it she made a real fuss of it and was very attached to it. Only Miss Roche—'

'Go on,' I encouraged.

'I'll be speaking out of turn, sir.' His voice was obstinate.

I wondered whether insisting I was a police officer would impress him. I fancied not. But he did have something more to tell. It might turn out to be trivial, but I wanted to hear it all the same.

'Lye,' I began, 'you and I have spent the last few hours working together as part of a team to beat out a gorse fire. Murder is like a fire. It springs up anywhere at any time, generally without warning. Sometimes people declare they can think of no cause. It's a mystery. But there's always a cause. In the fire we've just dealt with it was clear enough: dry gorse and a hot sun. As yet I can't see a cause for Brennan's death but there is one, be sure of that. I have to find it. That's my job. It's urgent that I'm as quick about it as I can be because murder, like any flame, has a way of spreading. I can't manage it alone. It's only by all working together we can put it out.'

'You've got a way with words!' said Greenaway with admiration. 'I'll say that for you. It'll be coming from London that does it, I dare say. You wouldn't catch Nat Gosling putting it that way. But I doubt the parson could've made a better speech than that.'

I burst out laughing, though it hurt my smoke-sore throat. 'All right, Lye, don't overdo it. Just tell me about Miss Roche and the cat. I'm a police officer and I know how to keep information to myself if need be.'

'Ah, 'tisn't anything much,' returned Greenaway, sounding sheepish now. 'Miss Roche didn't like having the cat in the drawing room or anywhere above stairs. It climbed on the furniture and up the curtains. She reckoned its claws did a good deal of damage. Cats will scratch at a thing, sometimes, you know, and although their claws are tiny they're powerful sharp. Also, it wasn't quite what you'd call house trained. One day it made its mess right in the middle of a Persian rug. "That's it!" says Miss Roche. "The cat goes." I can't say as I blame her.

'But Miss Lucy, sorry, Mrs Craven didn't like to think of anyone drowning her pet or any harm coming to it. So in the end, the cat was banished to the kitchen where Cook was pleased to have it, because it proved a fine mouser.' Greenaway added, 'I'm all for animals earning their keep, myself. But then, I'm a countryman.

'At first Mrs Craven was always coming to the kitchen to visit it, playing with it and feeding it titbits. But after a little while, so Cook told me, she seemed to lose interest in it and didn't come any more. Well, she was getting near her time—'

Greenaway put his fist to his mouth and coughed discreetly behind it. 'You'll know what I mean, sir. The young lady would have had other things on her mind. Still, I believe she was sorry when Mrs Williams told her the cat was dead.'

'That's it?' I asked.

'Yes, sir, that's it.'

I've talked to too many witnesses. I know when there is some little thing still unsaid.

'Team work, Lye,' I chided him.

Greenaway fell to fiddling with his horse's mane. 'It was just my fancy, nothing more.'

I waited. Greenaway glanced slyly down at me to judge whether I'd given up quizzing him or not. Seeing I hadn't, he sighed.

'It was only I wondered if the real reason Miss Roche took against the cat was because Mr Beresford had given it to Mrs Craven.'

'He had?' I exclaimed. This was startling news.

'Yes, sir. It seems not long after Mrs Craven came down here from London for her lying-in, and before her time was due, she was walking on the shore and met Mr Beresford. They passed the time of day and she mentioned being lonely. The next time she went walking there, up pops Mr Beresford, by chance like, you know . . .' Greenaway forgot himself so far as to chuckle. '"I've got something for you," he says. "To keep you company." He puts his hand in the pocket of his greatcoat and takes out this biggish kitten. Mrs Craven was delighted. Why, the young lady is nothing but a child. She took it home as pleased as punch. But Miss Roche wasn't near so happy about it. I'll always think the reason she wanted rid of the cat was because of where it had come from, if you take my meaning.'

'I do,' I said thoughtfully.

'Ah, now you've heard all I've got to say,' declared the groom. 'There's no more so don't waste any of your fine speeches on me.'

Nor did I. I was lost in conjectures. I'd come here to investigate one death. But there had been three at Shore House recently, if only one was murder.

First, Mrs Craven's cat had died. Then Mrs Craven's child. Lastly the rat-catcher.

A fire, I thought, had been smouldering here for a good time before Brennan died . . . and someone had fanned it into life.

'Lye,' I said, 'I have no more questions but I do have a favour to ask. If you would be so good, ask Callow to dig up the cat for me.'

'Dig it up?' cried Greenaway, twisting round in the saddle to stare down at me, his eyes popping.

'Yes, he must remember where he buried it. Tell no one I asked you or him to do this, if you would. It's a private matter. Tell him too not to speak of it or let anyone see him do it.'

'It'll be nothing but a few bones by now,' protested Greenaway.

'Yes, and ask Callow to be very careful not to damage them further in disinterring them. I don't want him chopping bits off with his spade or breaking any. Tell him to take it to his shed and send word to me or to Sergeant Morris and one of us will come and have a look at it.'

'It's a funny old business is police work, if you ask me,' replied Greenaway. 'Or the way you do it in London must be. I don't see Nat Gosling wanting dead cats dug up. Still, I'll tell Callow.'

My return to The Acorn caused a bigger sensation than my original arrival.

'Lord bless us!' cried Mrs Garvey. 'Jenny! Jenny! Run and put every kettle and pot you can find on to boil. Inspector Ross needs a bath!'

I couldn't wait for the hot water to begin my ablutions so I went round to the stable yard, stripped off my coat and shirt and, while Morris worked the pump handle, washed my hair and head beneath it.

Meantime, my bath had been set up in a corner of the yard: a large tin tub decorously surrounded by a hedge made of wooden clothes horses draped with blankets so that I'd be shielded from the vulgar gaze.

I climbed into it, and very pleasant it was to sink into the warm water. 'Morris!' I called.

His head and shoulders appeared on the other side of the blanket fence.

'Mrs Brennan has gone missing,' I said as I applied liberally the large bar of soap provided by Mrs Garvey. 'But I have learned something of interest.' I told him about the dead cat.

'Now consider this, if you will, Morris. Some time ago Brennan arrives on his regular visit. While he's here the cat is killed, possibly by his terriers. A little later and he's here again. This time it coincides with Mrs Craven's lying-in. The baby dies in its cradle. We must seek out the doctor and hear what he has to say about the infant's death. Brennan leaves and there are no more tragic incidents at the house until he returns yet again. This time,

Brennan himself dies, and all these deaths occur at Shore House. The events may be completely unrelated. But I dislike too many coincidences.'

Morris too, as it turned out, had been doing some judicious gossiping. He confirmed that Brennan was held to be a harbinger of ill fortune. 'Mrs Garvey has been telling me tales of two-headed calves, and sows overlying their litters, not long after he's arrived on one of his visits. They're almighty credulous around here, sir. She reckons that last year a potman she used to employ fell off the roof and broke his leg just as Brennan entered the taproom.'

'What was the potman doing on the roof? Do they keep the ale up there with the chimneys?'

'No, sir, he was replacing tiles brought down in a storm.'

'Then he slipped and fell. The pigman wasn't paying attention to a sow that had just farrowed. The two-headed calf . . . I don't know about that. Sounds like the sort of curiosity displayed for a penny at fairgrounds. See here, it seems to me this place brought Brennan bad luck rather than the other way around.'

'I had a chat with the maid responsible for dusting the hall table, too, sir, and showed her the murder weapon. She identifies the knife as definitely the one that used to be kept there. It was used for opening letters and cutting parcel string. She reckons she knows it by a chip in the enamel. She seemed sensible enough, a woman of a certain age and not a silly girl. All the same, you never can tell. She might have been anxious to look as if she had something important to say. I've come across that before,' finished Morris grimly. 'Life's generally pretty quiet around here, I reckon, apart from the occasional accident like a fellow falling off a roof.'

We'd all suffered from a witness's desire to be in the limelight, if only for a few hours. Yet mistakes could be made in all sincerity. How many times had I heard a witness swear to something that later turned out to be wrong? How often had a fleeing suspect been described by those around as being tall, short, stocky, very thin, wearing top boots and breeches, pantaloons, a frockcoat and shirtless?

'Well, perhaps we are a step forward,' I said to encourage Morris.

I recollected time was getting on. 'Pass me the towel if you would be so good, Sergeant. I am to dine with gentry this evening.'

'Rather you than me,' returned Morris, handing over the towel. 'Mrs Garvey has a boiled ham *and* a currant pudding – and there won't be any footman standing over me watching to see if I use the wrong knife! Not that I'm suggesting, Inspector Ross, that you'd do anything like that.'

'Thank you for your confidence, Sergeant.'

Chapter Fifteen

Inspector Benjamin Ross

FOR ALL I was sure Beresford would keep a good table, I couldn't help envying Morris the boiled ham and the currant pudding in the privacy of the snug. He could eat it at his ease. Although Beresford appeared a decent sort of fellow I was, after all, about to dine with the local squire.

But Beresford greeted me heartily at his door and led me inside down a hallway lined with a motley collection of trophies from sporting expeditions. Glass eyes observed our progress: stuffed birds, a snarling fox and a huge fish. ('Only plaster, that, the original one rotted,' Beresford told me.) Assorted paintings and prints covered the walls: hunting scenes, shooting ones, a couple of seascapes and a Royal Navy ship of the line or two. All the accumulated junk, in fact, you'd expect to find in the family home of a country gentleman and landowner.

The dining room, however, when we entered that, held something rather different.

'Good heavens!' I couldn't help but exclaim. 'That's a fine collection.'

Above the fireplace at the far end of the room the entire wall was festooned with daggers, swords, dirks and small arms, some, to my eye, looking quite ancient.

'Oh that,' said Beresford carelessly, 'my housekeeper tells me the maid grumbles about having to climb up and dust those. But I can hardly take them down. They represent the family history in their own strange way. My uncle, Sir Henry Meager, has a similar array but more extensive. Beresfords and Meagers have been linked by marriage for centuries. Meagers always send their younger sons to sea. We Beresfords are landlubbers to a man! So a lot of the stuff you'll see round the place is a testament to that family link.'

'I wonder . . .' I began rather hesitantly.

But he was ahead of me. 'You are wondering if, by chance, one piece might be missing? I can assure you they're all present and correct. Believe me, I ran home after – after I saw that fellow Brennan lying dead with a knife in his throat – and searched the whole lot. I quite . . . you will think this strange . . .' Here he faltered to a halt.

It was my turn to read his mind. 'You quite hoped some pilferer might have taken an ornamental dagger from your collection and the one in Brennan's neck couldn't have come from Shore House.'

'Of course I hoped it, prayed it,' he returned quietly but with emotion quivering in his voice. 'Not that it came from here particularly but that it came from anywhere other than there.'

He recovered his sang-froid, met my expression with a quizzical look of his own and added wryly, 'You see, I place my cards upon the table, Inspector Ross.'

He did and I appreciated his frankness. But I wondered how well Beresford knew each individual piece and its exact position in the warlike display on the wall. Would he realise, for example, if a few had been moved around to disguise a gap?

Speaking of tables, the dining table wasn't a large one. That was fortunate as my host and I faced one another from either end of it. It seemed a silly arrangement to me since what kind of conversation can be had calling down a length of polished rosewood like that? Perhaps it served a purpose. It put a distance between us and any such gap discourages intimacy. Had Beresford calculated I couldn't very easily interrogate him (however politely) from this seat? At any rate he had effectively robbed me of my best chance to play policeman. But not all chance. A policeman is always a policeman, even when he isn't about his duty, as Lizzie would be the first to agree. Sooner or later I had to talk to Beresford about what had happened on his neighbour's property and tonight remained my best opportunity to do so.

Our relative positions also gave me a chance to study him unobtrusively. He was in his thirties, with short-trimmed light brown hair and square jaw. His nose was short and his complexion ruddy. Later in life when he might have put on weight and become less athletic he would probably turn into a real John Bull. In figure he was well built and clearly used to an outdoor life. He probably spent little time in his own house and the state of it reflected that. I don't mean it wasn't clean and tidy but it was full of the inherited knick-knacks of other people. It lacked his own personal imprint. Some people, mostly women, would have said he needed a wife.

The lack of a wife to run his house was underlined by the reappearance of the elderly butler, now attended by a clumsy girl, all elbows and crooked mobcap. She looked as though she might have been directed into table attendance from her normal duties for the purpose of this evening. They removed our soup dishes, the girl rattling the china alarmingly.

When we were alone again, Beresford spoke. 'I want you to

know, Ross, that there is not the slightest possibility that Mrs Craven could have done this awful thing.'

He paused and looked at me expectantly, waiting for my answer.

When I remained silent, he went on, 'She couldn't! She's too weak, too small. She wouldn't have the strength or resolve either physically or mentally. Why should she do something so – violent? Motive, you fellows call it, don't you? Well, what motive could Mrs Craven have to attack a labourer, *a rat-catcher*, for pity's sake!'

'I'm not accusing Mrs Craven,' I said. 'For the simple reason I'm not accusing anyone as yet. But since you ask me to suggest a motive, might I point out that the last time Brennan was in the district, his visit coincided with the birth and soon thereafter the death of Mrs Craven's child. Perhaps in some way she connects him with that sad loss. In local circles I understand he was believed to bring ill fortune.'

'Pah!' exploded Beresford, his face reddening. 'Farm labourers and their womenfolk might believe that. Lucy Craven wouldn't. Are you seriously suggesting she might think Brennan bewitched her child? She would have to be crazy to believe it and *she is not that*!'

His voice had been rising. He placed both hands palms flat on the table and leaned towards me aggressively.

We were interrupted at that point by the re-entry of the two servants, bearing between them a joint of roast pork and a pair of steaming vegetable tureens balanced uneasily on a tray carried by the awkward girl. The butler set the pork on a sideboard. Beresford sank back in his chair and waved a hand. It wasn't clear whether he meant to brush away his tone or indicate to the butler he should proceed. The girl deposited the tureens with a clatter.

'I eat plainly,' Beresford in a voice of stiff apology. 'I hope you don't mind?'

'I'm glad of it!' I told him. 'After today's labours I admit I'm quite famished.'

He relaxed and spoke more warmly. 'Thank you for your help today. We get these fires from time to time in this weather. We haven't seen much rain for a good while. That helps the farmer get the harvest in but the heath dries out and is like tinder. That's why I keep my little fire-fighting force at the ready.'

'Apple sauce, sir? enquired the girl of me and proceeded to daub it liberally over my helping of pork.

'On the side of the plate, Susan!' hissed the old man.

The girl was immediately all confusion, just missing my ear with one of her elbows, and dithered as if contemplating somehow removing the sauce.

'It's quite all right,' I soothed her.

When they had left the room, Beresford managed another wry smile. 'You see I only keep a small staff. I'm a bachelor and don't need more. I employ a couple; the husband you have just seen. He acts as a butler and general factotum; his wife is cook-housekeeper. The maid is a niece of theirs. She isn't particularly bright and I employ her for their sakes.'

Beresford was indeed a decent fellow. It was a great pity Lucy Roche had not chosen him instead of the absent James Craven. But perhaps she hadn't met him early enough. I would consult Lizzie about this. Women know more about that sort of thing.

Beresford was about to reintroduce the subject of Mrs Craven but was clearly anxious not to antagonise me. 'You must excuse me if I sounded somewhat heated just now. It is a matter very close to me and you'll have seen I make no pretence about that. You suggested that perhaps Lucy – Mrs Craven – might associate Brennan with the loss of her infant. It's true she's taken that loss very hard. They couldn't persuade her to attend the burial. For a while . . .' He hesitated and then set his jaw determinedly and went on. 'I'm not telling you anything that others won't tell you. For a while Lucy wandered about the village and the lanes in a distraught state. Everyone pitied her. She would run up to any woman with a baby bundled in a shawl and demand to be shown the child. It upset the local mothers, understandably enough. I believe some of them, or their menfolk, complained to the rector. He took himself off to Shore House to make a fuss. After that Lucy stopped accosting people or, at least, she stopped coming into the village. Her aunts had a hand in that, I fancy, egged on by the rector, who's more of an old woman than any of them.'

Beresford appeared to think he had perhaps been critical of his neighbours because he added hastily, 'Good women, the aunts, I don't doubt, but sticklers for respectability and by nature as dry as dust. Dr Barton, our local sawbones, said it was the shock of losing her child and the aftermath of puerperal fever that made Lucy act so wildly. But she's all right now. Believe me, I've talked to her . . .'

He looked a little embarrassed. 'I've continued to meet her from time to time on the beach. Quite by chance, of course! I walk my dog there. She likes to walk there too. I don't think she is very happy with her aunts. Not their fault, of course, but well, they're a real pair of old spinsters, as I said, who have no idea how to amuse her or comfort her or – or anything.'

Whereas you, I thought to myself, fancy you could do a lot better in that department.

'I'm quite sure,' Beresford said firmly, 'Lucy Craven is as sane as you or I. Rather given to melancholy perhaps, but what young woman in her situation wouldn't be? I don't know why her family had to fetch that doctor down here from London.'

His tone grew fierce again. I thought with a little amusement that both he and I disliked Lefebre being in the company of ladies we admired.

'You've met Dr Lefebre?' I asked.

'Not yet. But I intend to make his acquaintance before he returns to London and tell him that his advice and interference aren't needed!' was the brisk reply.

Perhaps I ought to change the subject. 'You've never employed Brennan as a rat-catcher yourself?'

'What?' Beresford appeared to have gone off into some private dream in which he despatched Dr Lefebre back to London never to return. 'Brennan? Oh, never. I have a terrier of my own.'

He indicated the dog in question, which sprawled a little way off head on paws, and watched us intently with its boot-button eyes.

'I don't remember when we last had a rat in the house. They scent the dog and keep away. Get 'em in the stable yard, of course . . . and out at the farm. But the farm dogs usually do a good job of catching them.'

'So Brennan never called here?'

'No, though I'll ask Gregson if either he or his wife saw anything of him this visit.'

At that point the elderly butler returned.

'Gregson!' his employer asked him. 'Did you see Brennan or his wife anywhere about the village before he died?'

'No, sir,' was the prompt reply. 'I never encouraged the fellow. I believed him a rogue and sorry though I am to speak ill of the dead, to my mind he was a rogue to the last. He knew I was of that opinion and he never showed his face here.'

'Why did you believe him a rogue?' I asked.

'You only had to look at him! A nasty shifty sort of face, he had. No one liked him, that's a fact. He came from London, too, and everyone knows that's a place full of knaves and tricksters.'

Beresford gave me an apologetic look but I didn't disagree with Gregson. London was indeed full of crooks, large and small, and it had been my misfortune to encounter a fair number of the fraternity. But Gregson's dislike of Brennan seemed more to be rooted in the general mistrust the rat-catcher had inspired round here than in any single hard fact.

'How about a gypsy woman, selling pegs?' I asked the old man. 'Did you or your wife see her recently? She might have come to the kitchen door on Tuesday last.'

Gregson contemplated me. 'The day of the murder, that would be? Well now, I didn't see her. But I'll ask my wife.'

A little later the information arrived with the port that a gypsy woman had indeed called on Tuesday, late in the morning. Mrs Gregson had bought a few pegs.

'But my wife saw nothing of Brennan nor of that woman he liked to call his wife.' Gregson gave us a knowing look.

'I have to find Brennan's wife,' I said to Beresford, when the butler had shuffled out again. 'It's a matter of urgency. She can't have vanished. I'd like to find that mysterious gypsy woman, too.'

Beresford promised he would do his best to organise help.

'I'm glad we found no sign Mrs Brennan perished in the fire today. But I'm as anxious as you to know she's not come to harm,' he remarked. 'Her man's death will have left her quite destitute, I dare say, and she may need some money.'

My reasons for finding her were less altruistic, but I agreed.

Later I walked back to the inn through the night with only the stars and a lantern lent me by my host to guide me. It was so quiet that I shared the instinctive unease earlier expressed by Morris at the churchyard. The loneliness oppressed me. In the Derbyshire mining village of my childhood it had never been like this, even at night. Men leaving one shift passed others setting out for the pit. A flickering lantern or the crunch of heavy workboots marked the approach of those coal-blackened figures, otherwise invisible in the darkness. Yet one always knew they were there, trudging wearily homeward, exchanging brief words with their replacements as they appeared out of the gloom.

Here? Here I felt I had been marooned like a shipwrecked mariner on a foreign shore. (Lizzie later told me she had felt the same way when she arrived. She had now learned, as I might have warned her, that the natives were not necessarily friendly.)

Where were they all, as Morris had demanded? London was always busy. At that very moment, I knew, the streets gleamed in the gaslight and the population of day had been replaced by the myriad inhabitants of the night. The air was hardly ever silent from the rumble of wheels and clatter of footsteps, the sudden shout, the whispered discussion, the whistling, tuneful or otherwise, of those who walked home unaccompanied and kept up their spirits as best they could.

Some of these night birds were abroad for innocent reasons, going and returning from places of entertainment or toil. Others, as I well knew, were on more sinister or disreputable errands. Painted women, many as young as Lucy Craven or even younger, beckoned invitations from doorways. Gaslight shone from taverns, eating houses and brothels. Ne'er-do-wells and wastrels reeled homeward with empty pockets and aching heads, relieved of their money in the aforementioned places. Even if no one passed by you in the street, in every alley some homeless wretch was huddled or a drunk sprawled unable to take himself any further. They might stir as the constable walked by with his measured tread, turning the beam of his bull's-eye lantern into nooks and crannies. A thief rifling the pockets of the insensible might slip away before the hand of the Law fell on him. But you were never truly alone. The city never slept.

Here in contrast activity was marked by the rise and setting of the sun. Men and women struggled from their beds with its rays and crawled back into them with its last red glow. It was as if they feared the darkness. Even the wanderers and homeless, one of whose campfires Lizzie might have seen from her window, had found some shelter and wouldn't venture out of it until dawn. The countryside had barred its doors and slept; no one accompanied the odd straggler like me on the road. Only a poacher might lurk out there in the darkness. But fearful of discovery and the gamekeeper, he'd keep well clear of me.

I passed horses in a field to my right and was grateful for the sound of their snorts and the nearness of other living creatures. They followed me on their side of the hedge until I was beyond their patch of ground. I could hear them moving and smell them; even the heat from their bodies struck my face. They were curious about me and perhaps also desirous of my company. I stumbled along, partly because I couldn't see where to put my feet, and partly because of the port, which I was unaccustomed to drink; it had muddled my senses.

I must have seemed an oddity to all creatures of the countryside, human and animal. They were in their place; I wasn't in mine. They were equally strange to me. It made me wonder again quite why I had been requested from London. Was it because those who mattered hereabouts feared a local scandal and, to prevent it, wanted the matter cleared up quickly? Or was it because they feared scandal if the facts *were* discovered by me – and I had been sent here not to succeed but to fail?

If so, they had mistaken their man.

Chapter Sixteen

Inspector Benjamin Ross

THE FOLLOWING morning saw the strategy devised by Lizzie and myself put into action. I went early to the churchyard to await the arrival of the ladies and also because I wanted to look at the grave of Mrs Craven's child. A wilting bunch of wild flowers and foliage lay atop it; otherwise nothing remarkable. I turned back towards the church and heard myself hailed.

'Good morning, sir!'

An elderly man was hobbling rapidly towards me with a gleeful expression on his face. My heart sank. Was this the oldest inhabitant about to relate his life story to me?

'Jarvis!' gasped the old fellow as he reached me. 'I'm the sexton of this fine building.'

'Good morning, Mr Jarvis,' I returned, 'I was just—'

'You're a visitor!' he crowed, rubbing his hands. 'You want to see the church. You'd like me to open it up for you.'

I began to tell him not to bother but changed my mind. I had to give him some explanation for my loitering here and besides, when Lizzie arrived with Mrs Craven, I would need somewhere private to talk to the lady.

'If you would be so kind,' I said.

'Come along, come along, sir!' cried Jarvis, hobbling back the way he'd come and gesturing at me to follow him with wild circular movements of his right arm.

By the time we reached the church porch he was fumbling with a ring of keys similar to a gaoler's and after clanking them impressively and quite unnecessarily, finally opened the old oak door and pushed it creaking inward.

A smell of dusty hassocks, candle wax and stale flower water wafted out. I followed the old man down two worn stone steps and we stood at the foot of the nave.

'This church,' gasped my guide, 'was built by William the Conqueror.'

It was Norman, certainly, as its round arches and massive pillars bore witness. I murmured some expression of interest.

'You'll observe we have no stained glass, sir. It was Cromwell who knocked it out. But there are some fragments in that window there, do you see it? The old rector found them and had them put in the present window. He was a great man for antiquities, was the old rector.'

I wondered when the 'old' rector had held the living. Probably when Jarvis was a stripling and the whole of this coast waited for the Napoleonic fleet to sail up the Solent.

'Down here,' cried Jarvis, waving me onward again, 'there's a very interesting tomb.'

He might as well have been a gaoler and I his prisoner. I followed him meekly and found myself staring down at a plain coffin-shaped stone monument without inscription of any kind.

'It's a crusader tomb!' declared Jarvis, pointing at it triumphantly.

I couldn't argue but I did think the tomb might have been

anyone's. It was very old, however. I expressed proper admiration.

'And on the wall there,' Jarvis's gnarled forefinger directed my gaze upward, 'is a handsome memorial, very fine bit of work that. That's one of the Meager family, sir. They are gentry hereabouts.'

I had at least heard of the Meagers, thanks to Beresford. It prompted me to ask if the Beresford family had any similar memorials. Yes, they did, a whole row of brass tablets.

'They were all very distinguished gentlemen, sir, this one . . .'

I realised I was about to be given the entire Beresford family history followed, no doubt, by the biography of each and every Meager. Jarvis would still be droning on when Lizzie arrived with Mrs Craven.

'Thank you for your trouble,' I broke in, hastily pressing half-a-crown into his hand. 'Perhaps you could leave the church open for a little so that I can study everything in detail?'

'Oh, I won't be back to lock it up again until noon,' he assured me, pocketing his half-a-crown. 'You take all the time you like, sir. I do know who you are, sir. You're the gentleman from London. You're an officer of the law, you are, and I can leave the church safe in your keeping. You won't go scratching your name on the pillars or stealing the prayer books. I dare say that in London you don't have churches half as interesting as this one, eh?' He peered up at me.

'Not quite like this one,' I told him and he seemed happy with that.

I wasn't surprised he had recognised me. I thought now that I identified him as one of the two old men who had been in the taproom of the Acorn when I'd arrived with Morris. He hobbled away and I breathed a sigh of relief.

I hadn't got rid of Jarvis a moment too soon. When I went outside again into the mild sunshine I saw Lizzie and Lucy

Craven approaching the church. I took off my hat and walked to meet them, doing my best to look inoffensive.

'Oh, Lucy,' said Lizzie as I came up, 'this is Inspector Ross, the man I was telling you of. He would like to talk to you.' She took Lucy's hand. 'There's nothing to worry about.'

I'd been curious to see the lady. My first impression was that she was very young, as I'd been forewarned. My second impression was that she was very frightened.

'Don't be alarmed, ma'am,' I urged her. 'I realise all this has been very difficult for you but I should be very grateful for ten minutes of your time.'

She stared at me with remarkable blue eyes. 'Lizzie says you are a nice man,' she said simply.

'I'm grateful for Miss Martin's recommendation. But I'm also a police officer, you know that.'

'Yes, of course I do. You want to talk about that man, Brennan.'

Lizzie had prepared the ground well. Mrs Craven sounded weary but resigned.

'If you'd just give me your account of your discovery,' I encouraged her. 'I'm sorry if it distresses you but I need to hear it from your own lips. Perhaps we could go into the church and sit down? The sexton, Jarvis, was here and opened it for me.'

Lizzie murmured that she would just take a turn round the churchyard and rejoin us in a few minutes. She walked away and Lucy watched her go with dismay.

'Please, ma'am,' I said, indicating the church with my hat. 'Just a few words and it'll all be done and over with.'

She nodded and we began to walk towards the porch but when we reached it she stopped suddenly and asked anxiously, 'Do you think Jarvis will come back?'

'Not until noon, he assured me.'

'I shouldn't like to be locked in. He might think you gone and lock the door with us both inside.'

'Believe me, ma'am, he knows I'm in the church and if he should come back early, he'd hear us talking, anyway. But it will be perfectly all right. I gave him half-a-crown.'

I smiled at her and after a moment's hesitation she returned the smile uncertainly.

'Then it will be a little while before he returns,' she said. 'He will have gone directly to The Acorn.'

I followed her into the dim cool interior and she sat down on a pew at the back within sight of the door, no doubt as a precaution should the sexton after all reappear early.

I took a seat beside her.

'I couldn't bear to be locked in,' she said softly.

'There's really nothing to be frightened of, Mrs Craven,' I said soothingly. But I knew she wasn't talking only of the church.

Fear can both be seen and sensed. Her breathing was shallow and rapid. She'd clasped her hands tightly in her lap. But I felt her terror rather than saw it. She didn't turn her head to look at me.

'Mrs Craven?' I repeated gently.

She turned towards me at last. Pearls of moisture glistened on her upper lip and her eyes stared wildly at me.

When I was a young boy and working in that coalmine, many incidents imprinted themselves on my memory and remain there as fresh as though I witnessed them yesterday, not years ago. I remember the first pony that was brought to work underground. It would have been in 1837 or '38 when I was working as a trapper, though hardly big or strong enough to manoeuvre the heavy wooden doors which controlled the airflow within the mine. Lowering the beast into the shaft presented quite a problem and a large crowd gathered to watch. Even the men going off shift, tired and hungry (and I among them), tarried to see how it would be done.

Two men had come with the pony. They had done the job at other pits and knew how to go about it. The animal was forced to the ground and its legs pushed up under its belly and secured there. Unable now to stand, it lay panting and drenched with sweat. It was then, with some extra help, rolled over on to a padded mat which was wrapped completely around it and tied in position so that only its head stuck out at one end, and its tail at the other. In this parcel-like form, a hook was attached to the bindings and it was winched up so that now it hung straight down, head uppermost, tail dangling. It whinnied shrilly in its fear and distress and threshed its head, its eyes rolling whitely, nostrils flaring. Slowly it was lowered into the shaft and bit by bit sank from our sight, tail first, padded body and finally its head. The stark terror in its eyes as it descended into the dank darkness below where it would spend the rest of its life has haunted me ever since. They took two other ponies down later but I didn't watch.

I thought of it now, sitting here with this young woman who was so obviously in dread of being incarcerated, either in a prison or in a madhouse, to spend the rest of her life unable to breathe free air.

'I haven't come to accuse you,' I said. 'Only to hear your evidence.'

'I didn't like Brennan,' she said frankly. 'I didn't like the way he looked at me. Always laughing, not with his mouth, I mean, but with his eyes. He beat his wife, I know it.'

'How do you know it, ma'am?'

'I saw him strike her.' Lucy raised her arm suddenly and mimicked the blow she had witnessed. 'Like this, and then again.

Mrs Brennan just stood there. She didn't cry out or weep. She stood like a statue, waiting for the blows.'

'When was this?'

Lucy's arm dropped back. She looked vague. 'Some time ago. He came regularly to the district.'

She tilted her chin and went on in a firmer voice, 'But I didn't kill him.'

'No one has suggested you did, ma'am.'

She shook her head angrily. 'No one has suggested it *in words*. But they let it be known in every other way. They think I'm mad. They think the loss of my child has turned my brain. But I'm not mad and when I find my baby they'll have to admit it.'

She turned to me. 'Besides, he was killed with our letter knife, wasn't he? So someone in the house took it and used it. Why shouldn't it be me, the madwoman?'

I thought that young Mrs Craven might be frightened and immature, and deluded with regard to her child's death, but she was far from stupid.

'Just tell me what happened that morning, when Brennan came to the house and you and Miss Martin went out for a walk.'

'Well, we did that, just as you say. We walked to the church and were returning to the house. Then I saw that man, that doctor.' She shivered. 'I ran away from Lizzie and from him.'

'You're speaking of Dr Lefebre?'

'Yes. I don't like his being here. They say it's not on account of me that he's here, but of course it is. It's like everything else; they show it in every other way but words!'

She paused and I waited. Quietly she went on, 'I ran into the garden. I meant to go down to the beach. I did open the gate and step through it, but then I saw Andrew Beresford in the distance with his dog. Do you know him?'

'Yes, Mrs Craven, I've met Mr Beresford.'

'Then you'll know what a good man he is. I didn't want him to
see me in the state I was in. Mr Beresford has been kind to me.
He encourages me to believe I will be well one day. So you see
why I didn't want to meet him just then when I was so panicked
and wild. I turned back into the garden and sat for a minute or
two on a seat to get my breath and settle my mind. Then I thought
Lizzie might come and find me and I didn't want to see her,
either. I couldn't go into the house where I was sure to meet
someone. You would think, wouldn't you, that in such a quiet
place as this it would be easy to be alone? But I find it very
difficult because they follow me about wherever I go. Lizzie has
been sent to watch me. She says she hasn't and I do think she
believes it. But it's the true reason why my Uncle Charles engaged
her.'

She sounded bitter. I thought she was probably right. Whatever
Lizzie thought the reason for her being given this post, in reality
it was to prevent Lucy Craven being alone. But why did they fear
so much to leave Lucy unattended? Did they think she might
harm herself? Or harm others?

'So,' I drew the conversation back to where it had been heading
before this distraction, 'you left the seat in the garden.'

'Yes, and I began to walk about aimlessly. I was still upset. Then
I thought, if I went to the very end of the garden to the shrubbery,
I shouldn't be seen. So I began to go that way. I had almost . . .'

She faltered and fell silent, looking down at her hands. I saw
they were trembling.

'Shall I call Miss Martin?' I asked. 'Would you prefer it if she
were here?'

'No, no, it's all right. I was just remembering . . . I was nearly
there when I heard a noise.'

A tingle ran up my spine. 'What kind of noise?'

'Like – like leaves rustling, I suppose, and a cracking of branches. As if someone was forcing a way through the shrubbery. It's mostly rhododendrons. They've grown tall, taller than I am, and thick but I suppose one could get through. I called out to ask if anyone was there. Then I heard another sound, different, a sort of croak. I saw there was someone; a figure was just visible, coming towards me. I wanted to turn and run but my knees had turned to jelly and I just stood, waiting.

'It was Brennan . . . he came out of the bushes towards me, walking in a funny way, stumbling as if he couldn't drag his feet. His eyes were open wide and staring. He held his hands at this throat. There was red – red blood, spurting between his fingers and running down the backs of his hands. Then he took one hand away and I could see the blood pumping out of a wound in his throat. It was so horrible and I still couldn't move, my brain wouldn't tell my legs to work. He reached out and grasped at my sleeve. I pulled myself away and I – I put out my hands and thrust him back. I should have helped him. But I didn't want to touch him. I just wanted him to keep away from me so I put my fingers against his waistcoat, gave him a good shove, and snatched my hands back again.

'He uttered that croak again and lost his footing. He pitched backwards and lay there. His dog came running out of the bushes and began to sniff at Brennan and paw at him. I sank down on the ground . . . I couldn't run away. I hadn't the strength. I think I started to make some kind of noise myself, a sort of wail, or so Lizzie says. She heard me. She came upon us just then.'

'Thank you,' I said when she fell silent. 'That was well and clearly told. I know it was painful for you. One more thing, if you can help me just a little further. The rustling you heard before

Brennan appeared. You say it sounded like someone pushing through the bushes. Would that be Brennan coming towards you? Or someone hastening away?'

She hesitated. 'I don't know.'

'Very well, we'll leave it at that.'

Relief flooded her face. I hated to wipe it away. But I had a few more questions.

'You'll forgive me, Mrs Craven, if I ask how old you are? I'm afraid a police officer is required by his calling to be impertinent.'

'I shall be eighteen at Christmas,' she returned promptly without appearing to take offence. But at seventeen a birthday is still something to look forward to with optimism.

'And you're an orphan, ma'am, or so I understand?'

'Yes, since I was a baby. My uncle Charles is – was – my guardian, until I married.' This time she spoke the phrase proudly.

Not only almost eighteen but a married woman. I began to understand quite why she had been so determined to marry James Craven. She had acquired a status and a confidence probably lacking before. But she hadn't gained control of her own fortune and I had now to broach the delicate matter of money.

'I have also been given to understand that the inheritance left to you by your parents is held in trust. That your income is controlled by your uncle until you're twenty-one.'

Now a frown crossed her face. 'Yes, it's very vexing, you know, when poor James is in such need. I went to see the lawyer. He's another trustee. He's absolutely Uncle Charles's man. He talked to me as if I were a child. I *am* married. They won't let James have any money.'

But *you would*! I thought with compassion. You'd happily let him spend the lot.

'Your husband's employed by the firm of Roche, is he not? He has his salary.'

She dismissed this quibble. 'Oh yes, but he's obliged to be in China. Uncle Charles has been very mean and unkind.'

It was difficult to know quite what Charles Roche's motives were. On the one hand, he desired to protect his niece. On the other hand, he controlled her money (and her interest in the family firm) for another three years. In that time anything might happen to James Craven in China. The climate, disease, bandits, opium addiction, drinking himself to death . . . Or simply a dangerous sea voyage such as had claimed the lives of Lucy's parents; he might perish in all these ways. Were Lucy a widow by the time she reached twenty-one, she would continue to rely heavily on her Uncle Charles for financial advice and he would be able to look forward to controlling her money, and her share of the firm, for a few years more.

'Thank you, Mrs Craven; you've been very helpful,' I assured her. 'I may need to speak to you again.'

'As you wish,' she said with a sigh.

'And if you think of anything at all, any little thing you may have overlooked . . . tell me or send a message to me at once. Now then, perhaps we can find Miss Martin.'

'Yes, please,' she replied, sounding more like a child looking forward to her eighth birthday than a young matron anticipating her eighteenth.

Chapter Seventeen

Elizabeth Martin

I WATCHED Lucy disappear into the little church with Ben. I knew he would be kind and tactful, but also persist until she had told him all she knew. I hoped Lucy didn't fly into one of those childish fits of anger. I realised they sprang from fear, but others might not.

I couldn't linger by the porch and appear to be eavesdropping but I couldn't leave entirely, either. So I returned to the lychgate and sat down on one of the benches. After a few minutes someone came along the road from the direction of Shore House. The footsteps stopped by me and I heard myself hailed.

'Good morning, Miss Martin.'

It was a woman's voice and I was at first unable to place it. I stood up and walked out into the road and the sunshine and saw the nondescript female who acted as lady's maid to both sisters. She'd hardly addressed a word to me directly before.

Viewed closer to hand, she was a sour-faced woman who looked as if life had treated her far from generously, although to be a lady's maid, even to a pair of spinster sisters, was a good position in a domestic sense. It amazed me that she had been considered suitable to deal with feminine requirements. She was of heavy mannish build and reminded me of those women in men's apparel I'd seen shovelling coal and labouring on the roads. The idea of those square strong hands manipulating a needle to do some delicate mending was incongruous. But perhaps a lady's maid of greater refinement wouldn't have agreed to come to the country.

I knew she'd come from London with the sisters when they first arrived and appeared not to have formed any friendships among the staff. I'd observed already that they were inclined to be unkind about her behind her back. She, in turn, spoke only as necessary and with a Londoner's scorn for the provinces. She let the housemaids see she thought them bumpkins. Little wonder they revenged themselves with inventing preposterous tales about her until they fell into helpless giggles. I recollected her name was Higgins, and returned her greeting.

I expected she would walk on but she stood there, staring at me speculatively. I thought with some alarm that perhaps she meant to go into the church and I'd have to warn her away. If so, I hoped she'd oblige me, as such was the solid mass of her I couldn't have stopped her physically.

I asked, 'Are you out for a walk, Higgins?'

Her mouth twisted into a sneer. 'I get no time for walks, miss! I'm off into the village, as they like to call it, though it's a poor place in my opinion. There's a woman who knits gloves, as I've been told, very well, too. I mentioned it to Miss Christina because she was saying that before the winter came, she and Miss Phoebe and Mrs Craven must be provided with woollen gloves. So I'm sent to enquire if the woman will take the commission. I dare say she will, and charge double for it.'

'As a villager she's fortunate to have some occupation that can bring in a little money,' I said.

Higgins dismissed this with a shrug. A gleam of curiosity entered her mud-coloured eyes. 'Is Mrs Craven not with you, then, miss?'

So that was why she loitered to talk to me. She'd seen Lucy leave with me but then come upon me sitting here alone.

'Yes,' I said. 'She's just looking round the church.'

Higgins's expression clearly showed what a poor reply that was. Why should Lucy, who lived here and probably saw the church interior every Sunday, suddenly take it into her head to visit the church? Then it occurred to me that Higgins was asking from more than idle curiosity. No doubt she was her employer's spy in the household. The story about woollen gloves was an excuse to follow and observe us.

If so, I wasn't about to supply any information for her to take to the sisters. I nodded to her politely and hoped she would walk on. But still she stood there. Her eyes, when I looked up and met their gaze again, held a nuance of mockery.

'So how do you like it here, then, Miss Martin? You've come down from London.'

'I have, but I'm not a Londoner. I grew up in a small town. I think the countryside here very pretty.'

I knew that wasn't what her question was designed to find out. She knew I knew it. Now we fenced openly.

'Quiet as the grave!' she returned brusquely. 'I only stay because of my ladies. I've worked for Miss Christina and Miss Phoebe for twenty years.'

'I'm sure they appreciate your loyalty,' I replied.

'They deserve my loyalty!' she said fiercely. 'They're a fine pair of ladies. It's not right that all this trouble should be visited on them.'

'The police will solve the mystery of Brennan's murder quickly,' I snapped.

'Oh, that fellow's no loss. A rogue, I reckoned him. I wasn't speaking of that, or not of that alone. The trouble they've had with Mrs Craven, Miss Lucy as she was, it's been a real burden on them.'

Now, I meant to show Higgins I was as loyal to Lucy as she claimed to be to her 'ladies'.

'Mrs Craven has suffered a great misfortune,' I said firmly. 'In any case, we ought not—'

The look in Higgins's eyes turned to open mockery. 'Oh, Miss Companion! Been here less than a week and know all about it, do you? You've been taken in, I dare say, by the young lady's pretty face and blue eyes. Let me tell you, I've known her since she was a baby. An awkward, spoiled, contrary child, she was, and nothing has changed in her. You'll see. Such tantrums when she couldn't have her own way and such obstinacy!'

Really angry, I cried out, 'I won't allow you to speak of Mrs Craven like this! Nor is it your place to do so. I won't hear another word. Is this what you call loyalty?'

'As you please. My loyalty is to the ladies; I owe nothing to Mrs Craven.'

'You'd better go on to the village and seek out the knitting woman,' I told her coldly. 'Since you say you were sent out to do that.'

Higgins said nothing for a moment, only gave me a frosty look. She walked on a few steps, then paused and turned. 'You don't know, Miss Companion. You don't know anything. The trouble didn't start with that cobbled-together business of the marriage to save her reputation – and her family's. Did you know they had to take Miss Lucy out of her boarding school, when she was only eleven years old, and find another? The school wrote to Mr Roche and asked him to remove his niece. Her violent tempers were more than they could deal with. Why, she even attacked another pupil during some childish squabble.'

I wanted to order her to be quiet but despite myself I heard myself asking, 'Attacked?'

Triumph flickered in the mud-coloured eyes. She knew she had won our little battle. I had asked for information.

'That's right, miss. She seized a sewing needle and jabbed it into the other girl's arm. Terrible scandal it was, the other girl's parents being set to make real trouble. So Miss Lucy was taken away in disgrace and another school bribed to admit her.'

I opened my mouth but nothing came out.

Higgins nodded at me as amiably as if we'd been having some friendly conversation. 'Well, then, I must be about my business, or there will no woollen gloves this winter!'

She walked off down the road leaving me seething with rage. I glanced towards the church. I had been afraid Lucy would come out with Ben while Higgins had been there to see. At least that hadn't happened.

I couldn't sit still beneath the lych-gate. I wanted to stride up and down and drive out my pent-up anger. I walked down the narrow paths between the graves and gradually found myself calmer. That is to say, I was in control of myself but I can hardly say I felt at ease. Could it be true? Had Lucy attacked another girl at her school? I'd wanted to cry out that I didn't believe it; but I'd seen from the satisfied gleam in Higgins's eyes that she knew her account would be verified if I enquired further.

Such behaviour couldn't be excused. An unhappy orphan child, packed off to be brought up by strangers, might be excused the occasional tantrum. But to take up a sewing needle and drive it into a fellow-pupil's arm? I remembered how she'd picked up stones to throw at Dr Lefebre. A shiver of doubt ran up my spine. Had I indeed been 'taken in'?

My feet had brought me to the grave of the Craven baby. I stopped and looked down at it. The sight of it sobered me and made me more rational. Lucy was suffering from melancholia; even Dr Lefebre had said so. It had been brought on first by the birth and then by the sad loss of her child, to say nothing of the absence of a husband to whom she was devoted despite, or even because of, the poor opinion others had of him. If she behaved strangely it wasn't to be wondered at. She needed time and care and support.

Someone else was coming. I looked up, hoping it wouldn't be Higgins. I didn't trust myself to keep my temper with the woman. But it was a quite different figure.

Although I'm not superstitious, I have to admit I let out a shriek of alarm. With the upsetting conversation with Higgins only just behind me, and standing in this quiet spot surrounded by the dead, the last sight I needed or expected to see was that of an aged man with a scythe over his shoulder approaching me purposefully across the graves. There was eagerness in every line and determination that I shouldn't escape him.

The old man stopped when a few feet away and set his scythe on the ground. He touched the battered brim of his hat. I found the gesture reassuring. However the Grim Reaper greeted his victims, it wasn't, I was sure, in such a servile manner.

'Good day to you, ma'am,' said the old man. 'Jarvis, the sexton, at your service.'

'Oh, Mr Jarvis,' I said, relief flooding through me, 'I've heard of you.'

'Is that so?' he asked, pleased and surprised.

'Well, Inspector Ross, the police officer who has come down

from London, told us – me – that you had opened the church for him.'

'That I did, ma'am. Are you wanting to visit the church yourself?'

'Oh, I'll see it on Sunday, I don't doubt,' I said hastily. 'I'm Miss Martin and I've come to be companion to Mrs Craven at Shore House.'

'There now,' said Jarvis happily. 'I heard someone had come down here for that purpose. What a thing it is to have so many folk from London visiting us all at once!'

He looked past me, down at the earth. 'I dug that one,' he said conversationally.

'Dug . . .?' Oh, goodness, he meant the child's grave.

'I used to dig most of them,' Jarvis went on, with a proprietorial gesture at the graves around us, 'as it was my business to do until my rheumatics got bad. Now I mostly get Walter Wilkes to dig for me. Not that his corners are ever square, but he's not fit for much else but digging holes, Walter, so I give him the job.' He eyed the grave in front of us with undeniable satisfaction. 'That baby's coffin only needed a little hole so I managed that myself. People of quality like those at Shore House are entitled to have square corners.'

Jarvis turned in stately fashion and stared at the church porch. 'Is that Londoner still in there, then?'

'Yes, Mr Jarvis, he is.'

'He must be powerful interested in monuments,' observed the sexton. 'But I dare say they don't have many churches like this one in London. Well, I'll not lock up yet, then. I'll go on back and finish clearing that long grass where the old burials are. That grass grows like nobody's business. Good day to you, ma'am.' He touched his hat-brim again, shouldered his scythe and trudged away.

I heaved a sigh of relief and hoped I didn't have any more unpleasant encounters before Ben had finished talking to Lucy. But here they were at last, emerging from the porch. Lucy looked calm and as if some burden had been lifted from her.

'Thank goodness for that!' I said aloud.

Chapter Eighteen

Inspector Benjamin Ross

I ESCORTED the ladies back to the gates of Shore House and returned to The Acorn. I had only just reached the inn when a clip-clop of hooves caught my ear and turning my head I saw, to my great astonishment, Morris entering the yard astride the scruffy pony belonging to the inn. I'd seen this animal grazing in its small paddock. I'd never imagined Morris tackling the business of riding it, even though I knew we had agreed that he should take on the task of interviewing Dr Barton that morning.

It was not that Barton had been directly involved in events at the time of Brennan's death; but the conviction hadn't left me that the matters leading up to the rat-catcher's violent demise had been set in train some time ago. Everything that had happened during the best part of a year Lucy Craven had spent living with her aunts at Shore House was of interest to me. The murderer was familiar with the house, its contents (including the murderous letter knife), and the grounds. The death of the child suggested another mystery. There Barton could help.

Of course, the person I most wanted to find was Mrs Brennan; not only to know that she was safe but because I suspected she knew why her husband had been killed . . . and when we knew why, we would know who. But her whereabouts remained a mystery even though Gosling had been put in charge of a thorough search. His laboriously written notes on his progress, delivered to me at the inn by a succession of rustic messengers, had not been encouraging. The rat-catcher's wife appeared to have vanished. I was beginning to fear she'd made her way back to London despite being told to stay in the district. So, in the meantime, we scratched around for clues and it was possible the local doctor might shed some light. It was clutching at straws; but time was passing and with every day gone by the murderer gained in confidence and we became more frustrated.

Morris drew his Rosinante to a halt beside me and slipped easily from the saddle in a manner that quite put my poor equestrian skills to shame.

'Well, Sergeant,' I said, 'you are a man of surprises. I wonder you chose the police and didn't enlist in the cavalry.'

Morris patted the pony's neck. 'Well, sir, you see, my old father kept a donkey and cart. Now, a donkey's not a pony, to be sure. But we children were forever scrambling on the poor animal's back and making it canter round with us clinging on. I sort of took to it, if you like. Later on, when I got bigger, I'd beg the coalman or the brewer's dray driver to let me ride their horses in the shafts or I'd go down to the mews and help the grooms out. I like horses. A horse is a good-natured beast unless he's been badly treated. As for enlisting in the cavalry . . .' Morris shook his grizzled head, 'I couldn't do it, not caring for the animals as I do. Horses get shot to pieces and maddened by the cannon fire, just the same as men, only it's worse for them, to my mind. A man knows, when he takes the Queen's shilling, what he's doing, or if he doesn't, he should. A horse doesn't get the choice.

'If you don't mind, sir,' went on Morris, after delivering this oration, 'I'll just return this one to its field and I'll join you directly, if you'd like my report.'

'Join me in the snug,' I suggested. 'I'll ask Mrs Garvey to bring us some fresh coffee.'

In due course, Morris arrived in the snug and we settled down to exchange reports. I told him of my conversation with Mrs Craven. He told me of his visit to Dr Barton, and I'll let him tell it to you, in his own words, as dictated to me. If I'd left him to write it down himself, I'd have got only the barest outline. Morris, although meticulous in reporting anything a witness might say, has a habit of omitting anything he doesn't consider 'proper' in an official report.

Sergeant Frederick Morris

I asked Mrs Garvey where Dr Barton lived and she told me it was about four miles away. I was preparing to walk there when she suggested I take the pony belonging to the inn. Apparently it's hired out to anyone in need of an animal, four shillings for the day and two shillings for the half-day. That seemed a lot to me and I fancy she'd added a little to the normal rate because we aren't locals. But the day is warm. I thought it might look better if I arrived at the doctor's house properly representative of the police force, by which I mean not dusty and sweating. I know you told me, sir, that Miss Roche had offered us a mount from her stable, should we need one. But then everyone at Shore House would know what I was about, so I agreed to hire Mrs Garvey's pony. I trust it is an allowable expense.

The potboy caught the pony. I saddled it up and it struck me, as I did, that the beast showed very little life. To tell the truth it seemed half-asleep. I set out and soon began to think I might have got where I was going just as quickly on my own two feet. The pony's name is Comet and if ever a quadruped had the wrong name, that pony is one. It ambled along and nothing I could do seemed able to make it go faster. There were a lot of flies about and buzzing round the beast's head and mine. So eventually I pulled a spray of leaves off a hedge, as we were creeping past, with the intention of brushing away the flies. But as soon as Comet caught sight of the branch in my hand, he broke into quite a fast trot. So we got to Dr Barton's in good time after all.

I found the house easily enough, as it's on the main road, just set back a little. There was a boy of about twelve years of age, wearing a blue jacket with brass buttons, loitering about outside the door; I enquired of him if the doctor was at home.

'Is it a birth?' asks the cheeky young monkey.

I told him it wasn't his business to know; and repeated my question as to whether Dr Barton was at home.

'Is it a broken leg?' was all the reply I got.

I was beginning to think the lad must be simple. I yelled, 'Dr Barton!' at him and would you believe it, all he replied was, 'A tooth to be pulled?'

It seemed to me the doctor undertook just about any task in the medical line. But if I wasn't to be all day trying to find out if the physician was at home, I had to take some action. I dismounted, handed the reins to the boy, and told him that he should have sixpence for looking after the animal, if I spent any time with the doctor.

'This one?' says the boy as if I'd arrived with half a dozen ponies all tied together, 'that's Ma Garvey's pony.'

'It is,' I said, 'and you will catch it from her if you let the animal wander off.'

It was in my mind that if the pony got free, it would take itself off back home without me. Luckily just then a female looking like a housemaid appeared at the door. I asked her to tell her master Sergeant Morris was here, and would be glad if he could oblige me with a few minutes of his time.

To my relief she did admit he was at home. I was shown into his consulting room. It seemed partly that and partly a private study. It was very cluttered, and if that housemaid has the job of dusting it, well, all I can say is, she is a slapdash worker. The place was full of medical books, all appearing very old to my eye, and a number of indecent-looking things in jars. I chose to avert my gaze from them, sir. But from the look of them they'd been there a few years.

As for Dr Barton himself, he turned out to match the rest of the room. He was much older than I'd expected, at least seventy. He wears an old-fashioned wig the like of which I'd not seen on anyone's head since I was a boy.

We got off to a slow start because he thought I'd come to consult him. He asked me what was wrong with me and before I could answer, observed that I was a very unhealthy colour.

I replied that if I was a bit red in the face it was because I'd ridden there and added I wasn't ill.

'Not ill?' he replied. 'What do you want, then? Are you selling anything? I don't want anything.'

I managed to get him to look at my warrant card and persuade him what it was, as he seemed puzzled. I then asked if I could put a few questions to him, as we were investigating the death of the rat-catcher. After a bit of argument, he agreed. Unfortunately he's somewhat on the deaf side. I had to bellow out my questions. I dare say the whole household heard me. Even the boy holding the pony outside could have heard me.

I began by asking whether he had attended Mrs Craven in childbed. He said he had and it had been a very easy birth. (Just as well, thought I! I wouldn't have much confidence in this old fellow if there were to be a complication.)

'Mother and child well?' I asked.

'As well as could be expected,' says he.

'Yet two days later the infant was dead,' I pointed out.

He gave me a sharp look then, as if I had suggested some neglect on his part. 'These things happen,' he said. 'They sometimes die in their cradles for no known cause.'

'You examined the dead infant?' I asked.

'I certified death,' he said in a manner I'd call shifty.

'You did not examine the baby, then?' I repeated.

He looked huffy. 'There was no need. The child was dead. I detected no heartbeat and there were other signs of death. The body was cold and turning blue. I was more concerned for the mother.'

'Why was that, Doctor?' I asked, glad he had brought the conversation round to Mrs Craven without my prompting.

Dr Barton straightened his wig, which I took to mean he was gaining time to think out what he should say. At last he came out with, 'She took the barest glance at the dead infant, when it was shown to her, and would not look again. She screeched out that the nurse should take it away, it wasn't her child. I attempted to soothe her and persuade her of the true case, but she became distraught. I prescribed a sleeping draught.'

'What did you make of her reaction?' I asked. 'Have you seen that before?'

'Oh, well,' says he, 'it is a difficult moment. Of course the mother does not wish to believe it at first. But my suspicion was that her wild manner indicated the onset of childbed fever.

Indeed, it is my opinion that was the case and her incoherent statements following this tragic episode, and somewhat, ah, eccentric behaviour, were due to the lingering presence of the fever. Eventually she recovered. She's a healthy young woman and I expected no less.'

'What had the nurse to say? Was she a local woman?' I thought there must have been a nurse.

'She'd come from Hythe on my recommendation,' he puffed at me. 'She is a very experienced lying-in nurse. She told me the child appeared well when put down to sleep after its last feed. She, too, recognised the mother's state of mind as the result of a touch of childbed fever.'

The doctor then suddenly remembered discretion and declared he couldn't discuss his patient any further. Very hoity-toity, he was, when he said that.

'If you are here about the death of the rat-catcher,' he said, 'I can't see what all this has to do with it. I was not called upon to certify his death. There was, I understand, another medical man visiting the house at the time and he did that. I can't help you.'

So I left him. I wasn't best satisfied but I felt there was no more to be gained. If you ask me, he learned his medicine fifty years ago, hasn't learned a thing since, and wouldn't hold down a practice anywhere but in a rural backwater like this. I certainly wouldn't let him near my teeth or any other part of me. He is only interested that no one should blame him for the death of the infant Craven – or blame the lying-in nurse he recommended. I can seek her out, if you wish, sir, but I reckon she'll back him up and will only be afraid we'll say it was her fault.

I got back to the inn rather quicker as Comet knew he was on the way home. I had to give the boy his sixpence. I don't know if that will be covered by our expenses. What with that and the hiring of the pony it's been an expensive morning for me, sir. I can't say as it's been a very productive one, either.

Inspector Benjamin Ross

I was glad of Morris's account of Dr Barton's somewhat chaotic household. (It was one of the details he probably wouldn't have written down if I'd left him to compose the report himself on paper.) But from what he told me, I was inclined to agree that the doctor hardly sounded a man at the top of his profession. He wouldn't have held down a practice anywhere but here in the middle of nowhere. He also sounded like a man who would take great care not to offend his wealthier or more influential patients. If he'd thought there was anything irregular about the death of the infant Craven, he wouldn't have said so at the time and was extremely unlikely to say so now.

But he would know a dead baby from a live one. There was no doubt now the child had died. Lucy Craven had suffered from childbed fever. No wonder she'd raved. With better care after the birth she'd have recovered her senses (and probably not taken a fever in the first place). In Barton's hands she'd been left unwell and confused. Barton could pull teeth, set bones and do other routine doctoring. But by the sound of it afflictions of the mind were beyond his competence. That, I thought sadly, was why Lefebre had been sent for.

I thanked Morris for his efforts and promised him I would do my best in the matter of his out-of-pocket expenses. I then suggested that as it was noon, we take the opportunity to eat. Mrs Garvey offered thick slices of the ham boiled the day before, with fried eggs. There was a freshly baked fruit tart to follow. That sounded excellent to both of us and we proceeded to make a good luncheon.

We'd hardly finished it when we heard a commotion outside. It seemed from the clatter of hooves and rumble of wheels that someone was arriving. I got up and went to the window to see the very fly that had brought us to The Acorn and descending from it, with some effort and the help of the potboy, no other person than Charles Roche.

The sight of him was as unwished as unexpected, but there he was, puffing and panting. Though still city-smart in his black cutaway coat and brocade waistcoat, he grasped a stout country walking stick in his hand in lieu of a gentleman's cane. He clapped his silk hat on his head as I watched, and fell to paying off the driver and ordering the potboy to take his bag.

'Confound it!' I muttered. 'So he's decided to turn up at last. I don't know that I want him here just now.'

Morris had joined me and enquired who the stout gentleman was.

I explained and added, 'He will have come to protect his sisters from being unduly troubled by us, mark my words.'

But I was wrong, as we soon found out.

Mrs Garvey flung open the door of the snug and announced, 'Gennelman to see you, sir!'

She gave one of her bobbing curtsies and Charles Roche, sweating and patting his forehead with a large handkerchief, erupted into the room.

'Thank God you're here,' he gasped. 'I have dreadful news!'

The door was still open and Mrs Garvey goggling at us. I called out to her to bring us some tea and urged Charles Roche into a chair. Morris shut the door and took up position before it.

'Calm yourself, sir,' I told Roche. 'Have you come directly from London?'

'Yes, yes,' he wheezed, 'I came straight here, hoping to find you. I wanted you to have the news first and I'm still not sure how I'll break it to my sisters – and my niece, of course. I suppose my niece must be told straight away. It would be much better if she weren't. Yes, that's it . . . she mustn't be told yet. We'll wait for a better moment, as if there could be one . . . Oh dear . . .' He mopped his head again. 'My sisters will be so distressed. They lead quiet lives, you know. This will be all too much for them.'

It – whatever it was – was evidently all too much for Mr Roche; I hoped he wouldn't have a heart attack, since the only medical man on hand to attend him was Dr Barton. Although there was Lefebre: he must know more medicine than the inside workings of people's heads.

'Just tell me, sir,' I encouraged him, 'and we'll see what's best to be done.'

We were interrupted before he could begin by a knock at the door heralding the tea. Morris relieved Mrs Garvey of the tray and shut the door in her face before she could look past him.

'It's my nephew-in-law, James Craven.' Roche's fingers fumbled at the teacup and the liquid spilled.

'Not dead?' I asked sharply.

It wouldn't astonish me to hear that he was, the death rate among Europeans in the Far East being so high. I was a little surprised at Roche's extreme distress, if that were the case. He must have realised the possibility when he sent the young man to China. Perhaps, as I'd already conjectured, he'd even secretly hoped it. (Police work makes a man cynical.) Now that it had happened, he was suffering pangs of conscience. More likely, he was dreading the moment when he told the young widow.

But Roche was shaking his head. 'No, no . . .' he said despondently.

I must have raised my eyebrows at his tone, because he went on, 'I'll confess to you, Inspector Ross, it would be better for us all if he were. There! That's a cruel thing to say, a barbaric thing, and I'd say it of no other living soul. But that boy has never been anything but trouble. I really did think that sending him out East would at least get him out of the way. But no . . .'

He paused as if the recital were all too much for him and managed to drink a little of his tea.

I was by now in nearly as distraught a state as he was. If not dead, what? I wanted to shout, 'Get on with it, man!' I actually said, 'Take your time, sir.'

He set down the cup and made an effort to pull himself together. 'I've heard from our agent. James Craven disappeared from everyone's sight and knowledge more than twelve weeks ago. For three days our agent did not know. He hadn't returned to his bungalow for a couple of nights, but that had happened before. The manservant engaged to look after him thought nothing of it. But when Craven failed to return for a third night the fellow got alarmed and reported his master's absence.

'Our agent began enquiries. He didn't let me know at once, as he had no wish to cause unnecessary alarm. He was in a dilemma, you understand, since he didn't want to raise the possibility of scandal. He thought Craven might be with a woman. He made discreet enquiries among the Europeans there first but drew a blank. He asked more openly. No one knew a thing. Craven had not been seen, not had he given any indication he intended to absent himself for any reason. Our agent found himself obliged to visit some insalubrious places where Craven had been known to go, opium houses and – and other places of entertainment. But no amount of reward offered there drew the slightest response. So he was forced to involve the Chinese authorities and that proved a complicated business and wasted more time. They eventually instituted a search but again with no success. Then, when our man was in despair and about to write to me that Craven had almost certainly been murdered and his body disposed of, a shipping agent called at his office. He told him that a young Englishman of Craven's description, but using the name Harrison, had taken ship on a tea clipper bound for Bristol. It sailed just about the time he went missing.

'I made immediate enquiries here and discovered that ship, the *Lady Mary*, docked a week ago. The passenger known as Harrison disembarked and no one knew where he'd gone.'

'Craven's *here* in England!' I cried, jumping to my feet. No wonder Roche was so distressed. This was the worst possibility of all, from his point of view. The black sheep had returned.

'I'm afraid so, Inspector,' Roche confirmed. 'But *where* in England, well, that's another matter.'

'He'll very likely be looking for his wife,' observed Morris gloomily from the door.

Roche winced. 'I agree. He'll have gone first to London and finding my niece was not at the Chelsea house, set off to find her.'

'But he hasn't enquired at your London house openly, or quizzed the servants?' I pressed him.

'No, no, I should know of it if he had. The servants have all been with me some time and are utterly reliable. They would have reported it. But there are other means of finding out. Delivery boys, chimney sweeps, postmen and laundrywomen, all manner of people are in a position to mark the comings and goings at a house, and are able to tell if someone is in residence or not.'

'Indeed,' I agreed thoughtfully.

'So he could have guessed she's in the country and set off here, then?' asked Sergeant Morris.

Our visitor's distraught state rendered him temporarily dumb before he managed to croak, 'As you say, Sergeant. He knows my sisters live at Shore House. He could indeed be here and awaiting his opportunity to contact my niece. He knows he wouldn't be welcome at the door. He'll try to contact her secretly and spirit the poor child away, that's what he'll do! Craven could be hiding out somewhere a stone's throw from us and we don't know of it.'

Roche's despair echoed in his voice and had transformed his usually florid, self-confident features. He even forgot himself so far as to lean forward and grip the lapels of my coat. 'He must be found, Inspector! He must be found before he does more mischief!'

If he hasn't done some already, I was thinking, but didn't say.

Roche disengaged himself with apologies for taking hold of me. 'My dear sir . . .' he mumbled several times, 'so many troubles, and all at once. I hardly know what I'm doing. Nothing seems to be going right . . .'

I told him briskly to bear up and succeeded in drawing his attention back to the main matter. We had a long discussion as to what was best to be done. I pointed out to Roche that Mrs Craven must be told immediately. To delay would cruel. He was vehemently against this at first; but in the end I made him understand that if he didn't tell her, I would. My own brain was buzzing. The news introduced an entirely unforeseen element into the business. I'd have to ask the lady if she'd seen anything of her husband or if he'd contacted her.

I was also thinking I'd have to warn Lizzie to keep an eye open.

In the end, when Roche had got his breath and composure, we set off all three to walk to Shore House. The potboy had been directed to bring Roche's bag after us a little later.

When we got to the house, we left him to go in and tell his sisters and niece the news. I would dearly have liked to be there when he did but he turned down that suggestion flat. So Morris and I walked round to the back of the building. Our intention was to ask any member of the domestic or outdoor staff we encountered if they'd seen a strange young man of gentlemanly appearance, possibly travel stained. We had learned from Roche that Craven had not visited the house before, although he knew of it, so was not known to the staff by sight. It was unlikely they would guess who he was, even if they sighted a stranger. They all knew he was in China, or supposed to be.

'He'll have kept out of their way,' said Morris. 'A stranger hereabouts sticks out like a sore thumb. Look at the way they all turned out to see us!'

'Miss Martin saw someone hiding beneath the yew tree in the churchyard,' I reminded him. 'And someone put a posy on the infant's grave. There was also someone, she thinks, camping out on the shore. She saw a campfire. So he may well be here. But thanks to Lizzie's – I mean Miss Martin's – attendance on Mrs Craven, he hasn't been able to get his wife alone.'

Morris looked doubtful but at that moment, I heard my name called and saw the stable boy hurrying towards us. His expression suggested he had a message and was carrying it with all the urgency of the news of the imminent arrival of Blucher's Prussians on the field of Waterloo.

'It's in Fred's shed!' he announced in a hoarse whisper, with much jerking of his head in a vague direction behind him. 'Mr Greenaway has just this minute sent me to fetch you, sirs. "Be quick about it, Joe," he said to me. So I've come running. But here you are, anyway.'

'What's in the shed?' demanded Morris. 'Stop twitching, boy!'

'The cat,' retorted the stable boy indignantly. 'Fred dug it up, just like Inspector Ross wanted him to. It's nothing but bones,' he added, 'I seen it.'

'Take us to the shed,' I ordered him. 'And not a word about this, mind.'

It was only a very small potting shed and we all gathered in it: Morris and Greenaway, Callow the gardener and myself. The stable boy squeezed himself in despite being ordered to stay outside and knelt on the floor peering between Greenaway's legs. At our feet on a piece of sacking lay a sad little skeleton. It appeared to be complete and I thanked Callow for the care taken in disinterring it.

'What do you think?' I asked Morris.

'Head smashed in,' observed Morris lugubriously.

The damage to the skull was the more noticeable for the good state of the other bones. The spine had split, but Callow admitted that had happened when he lifted it out of the ground. The skull was quite crushed.

'Could two dogs fighting over their prey have done that?' I asked the two local men. 'What's your opinion?'

Greenaway and Callow exchanged glances. Callow cleared his throat and observed that the terriers had powerful jaws. 'Little beasts, but when they get a grip, they don't let go, sir.'

Greenaway mumbled assent.

From between his legs, the stable boy observed that he thought it pretty difficult for a small dog to do that sort of damage.

Greenaway moved his foot and contrived to give his underling a kick. 'You keep quiet and mind your manners, Joe Prentice. You don't know anything.'

'When you came upon the dogs tugging the cat's corpse between them,' I asked Greenaway, 'did one of them hold the cat's head in its jaws?'

'I don't rightly mind,' said Greenaway. 'It might have done. They were worrying at it, tugging it all ways.'

'But it was dead?'

'Oh yes, sir, it was dead. It hung limp and made no sound. I couldn't have rescued it.'

'Very well, then,' I said, 'that's all. Thank you again, Callow.'

'What shall I do with it now, sir?' he asked.

'Bury it once more,' I told him. 'And not a word to anyone about this, is that understood?'

The gardener and groom exchanged glances again and Greenaway shrugged.

'Right you are, then,' said Callow.

I stooped and called out to the stable boy in the dark corner, 'Do you understand, Joe?'

'Yessir, I won't tell no one!' came back a voice at knee level.

'He won't tell anyone,' growled Greenaway in confirmation. 'Or he answers to me, hear that, Joe?'

'I hear you, Mr Greenaway!'

Morris and I left the shed; when we were out of earshot, I asked him, 'What do you think?'

'Someone smashed it over the head with a blunt instrument,' returned Morris promptly. 'That's my opinion. Something like a spade or a brick, say, even a really big stone. Smashed it and kept on smashing it in a rage or a frenzy. The dogs may have found the body and had some sport with it. But I reckon that cat was dead when they did so.'

'Someone has a violent temper,' I observed.

Morris asked the question hovering in my mind. 'Could the little lady, Mrs Craven, have done that, sir? To her own pet?'

'She could have done it,' I replied. 'But why should she? Why should *anyone*? Why, to take it a step further, should some rational human being kill an itinerant rat-catcher of no importance to anyone – and with a knife taken from this house?'

'How about an irrational one, then, sir?' asked Morris, with a sideways glance at me.

'Lucy Craven, you mean?'

'Well, she doesn't seem quite right in the head, sir. I mean, the way she goes on insisting her baby isn't dead, though Dr Barton confirmed it and signed the death certificate. I'm not saying he's the best doctor ever walked this earth, but he'd know a dead baby from a living one. I'm sorry, though, that he didn't examine the child closer.'

There was a long and awkward silence, neither of us wanting to make the accusation that lingered unspoken in our minds. At length, Morris began to speak again.

'I remember, sir, when I was just a young constable. I hadn't been a year wearing the uniform. There I was in my smart new blue frockcoat and proper top hat like we wore then, no silly helmets. Well now, I was patrolling my beat when a woman came running from a house and declared a girl living there had murdered her baby. So I went to investigate and found a young female, very distressed, tearing of her dress and wailing, sitting on the staircase. The woman who had fetched me hurried me past her into a downstairs room. There lay a dead baby, not above two or three months old. The woman told me the girl on the stairs, who was the mother, had smothered the infant deliberately. She'd been found bending over the crib with a pillow in her hands. The other woman had snatched the child up and run downstairs with it to try and revive it but in vain.

'It was decided, sir, that matters were as the woman described, but the mother was unfit to plead, being not in her right mind. Doctors declared she had never recovered from the birth. It had been an uncommon difficult one. She had nearly died, taken the fever, never fully recovered and behaved strangely ever since. She had two or three times been prevented from doing the child harm, although at other times she seemed uncommon fond of it. The child being under one year of age, sir, the charge would've been infanticide. But they took her to the madhouse instead of to the prison and there, for all I know, she still is, although it'll be twenty years ago.'

I couldn't help but suppress a shiver. 'And you think, Sergeant, young Mrs Craven may have smothered her baby or otherwise done it harm? That the doctor, the nurse and the family have conspired to hide the fact? That the rector who conducted the funeral service was duped? As for the mother, her mind has refused to accept the horror of her action and she's persuaded herself the child is still alive somewhere?'

'I'm only saying, sir, that such things do happen from time to time and the law, in its wisdom, takes account of them.'

I shook my head firmly. 'It still doesn't explain why she should attack the rat-catcher. No, no, Morris, I can't believe it. We are trying to fit together pieces of some puzzle, but a vital one is missing. When we have it, we shall find all this is linked together.' I heaved a sigh born of frustration. 'But as yet I don't know how.'

'Think we shall find out, sir?'

'Believe me, Sergeant,' I told him sharply, 'we have not come all this way to be fobbed off by people who put reputation above justice.'

We walked on in silence for some minutes. 'However,' I said at last, 'I have ordered a cat to be dug up and, if it seems necessary, I'll request permission from the Home Office to open up that child's grave in the churchyard here, and ask a police surgeon to examine the remains.'

'Family won't like that, sir.'

'Nevertheless, if I think it necessary, I shall do it.'

Part Three

Chapter Nineteen

Elizabeth Martin

'LIZZIE, LIZZIE!' I heard my name called outside my door, followed by an urgent tapping at the panels.

After returning from the church and churchyard, Lucy and I had gone upstairs to our rooms to take off our hats and shawls and get ready for luncheon. Lucy had also declared herself exhausted after her talk with Ben and wanted to rest before joining any company.

'Of course I understand that,' I told her, 'but be of good cheer, Lucy. It was a difficult interview but it's done now. Doesn't that feel better than being in a panic and refusing to meet the inspector?'

'Oh, I suppose it is,' sighed Lucy, putting a hand to her brow, 'but I'm sure my poor head aches after all the fuss and bother. Still, he is a nice man, just as you said . . . and it's my opinion you should marry him, Lizzie.'

'What?' I exclaimed, thoroughly taken aback. So Lucy had not had her mind entirely on their conversation about the rat-catcher!

'He's so taken with you, Lizzie, anyone can see it. Now, I'm going to rest. Let's hope Williams doesn't sound the gong early.'

With that she left me gaping after her in the corridor outside her room. I stared at her closed door. The child was like quicksilver. Just when I thought I was beginning to know her character, she slipped through my carefully constructed understanding of her; and brought it tumbling down.

I made my way to my own room. I'd just about tidied myself, and was listening out for the gong, when I heard her voice again outside my door. It was clear from the tone that something unexpected had happened. I hurried to open it and find out what was amiss. As soon as she saw me, and before I could say a word, she grabbed me by the wrist and towed me along the corridor until we reached the first-floor landing.

'Down there!' Lucy pushed me forward with such force I tilted alarmingly over the banister and was glad she still gripped my arm. 'Do you see? It's Uncle Charles!' The last words were hissed right in my ear.

She was quite right. To my astonishment Charles Roche stood below us in the hall, handing his hat to Mrs Williams. The housekeeper, looking unusually flustered, was doing her best to welcome him and answer his questions as to where his sisters and his niece were.

'The ladies are in the drawing room, sir. They will be very pleased to see you. If we had known you'd be here, sir, Cook would have prepared something extra for lunch. Let me put your stick in the stand, sir.'

'How are they?' demanded Roche in a low, urgent tone, settling his coat lapels and adopting the stance of a man about to face some sort of ordeal.

'Bearing up, sir, very well, but it has been a very difficult time. The police are still about the place and it doesn't help, sir, even if it's necessary.'

'Yes, yes,' mumbled Roche. 'But there have been no further alarms?'

They exchanged a glance that seemed to me one of complicity.

'No, sir,' said Mrs Williams in a steadier voice. 'Nothing to worry about.'

Roche murmured, 'Good . . .' but didn't look much reassured.

He could hardly have been looking forward to facing his sisters, but his sudden arrival raised several questions. He hadn't come when the first news of Brennan's death on the premises reached him. He'd written to his sisters, I knew that. I'd wondered what excuse he'd given them for his absence at a time of crisis. I was certain they hadn't expected a visit today. There would have been some sign of it. Williams would certainly have been informed. There would be a bedroom to be prepared; a discussion about the day's menu; increased bustle on the part of the maids. Surely I'd have noticed some air of anticipation on the part of his sisters? Even if, for whatever reasons of their own, they hadn't wished to tell their niece of his impending arrival. What on earth could have happened to bring him down from London at this moment without a word of warning sent in advance? What about Lefebre? Had he known Roche was on his way?

The question was soon answered. At that moment, the door of the small parlour opened and the doctor himself came out. He'd adopted this neglected room as his private retreat, to read his newspapers, write his letters and perhaps just to be away from a house full of women.

'Charles!' he greeted the newcomer and it was clear he was as surprised as any of us. 'Good heavens! Where have you sprung from?'

'My dear fellow!' returned Roche, shaking hands with his

friend. 'This is a damnable business, damnable. And now it gets worse.'

Mrs Williams, who had been hovering, asked hesitantly, 'Shall I announce you, sir?'

'No, no, wait a moment . . .' Roche held up his hand in a gesture indicating she should wait. 'A word with you first, if you don't mind, Marius?'

'Yes, yes, of course, come in here.' Lefebre indicated the small parlour behind him.

'Give us ten minutes, Williams, if you would, then tell my sisters I'm here,' Roche ordered her.

The two gentlemen went into the parlour, leaving Mrs Williams standing alone in the hall looking very unhappy.

Lucy and I still hung over the banister like a pair of children crept from the nursery to spy on guests. I straightened up and pulled her away. She was about to object but I whispered, 'It would never do if we were seen to have been listening!'

We stood still and waited until we heard the housekeeper move away in the direction of the kitchen, probably to rouse the cook to extra effort.

'What are my uncle and that doctor saying? Oh, I wish I knew! We can't hear anything from up here!' wailed Lucy. 'Shall I go down? Perhaps I could hear them talking through the door? Men's voices carry very well.' Her face lit with enthusiasm.

I knew the circumstances that had led to Lucy becoming such an eavesdropper but I couldn't allow her to take this risk, curious though I was myself.

'We'll find out, Lucy, never fear. Of course you mustn't go downstairs. What if one of them opened the parlour door and found you crouching outside?'

Lucy looked sorry not to be able to demonstrate her spying skills but acquiesced. We moved away and by common consent returned to my room. Lucy began to turn up and down in a fever of excitement, twisting her hands nervously. I begged her to calm herself but she burst out,

'How can I be calm? What does he want? Why must he and that horrid doctor consult together privately? It's about me; I know it. Uncle Charles has come down to learn Dr Lefebre's opinion of my state of mind.'

She darted forward and gripped my hand. 'Oh, Lizzie, what will the doctor tell him?'

'We don't know that's why he's come, Lucy,' I soothed. 'It's far more likely he wants to know what progress Inspector Ross and the sergeant have made. It's quite normal that he wants to talk to Lefebre first. He's obviously worried about your aunts and how upset they must be.'

'He'll remember I threw stones at him, won't he?' said Lucy morosely, ignoring my entire speech. 'But I didn't stab the rat-catcher. Why should I go stabbing people?'

I couldn't resist the opening and asked, as coolly as I could, 'Have you never done such a thing, Lucy? I don't mean take a knife and made a murderous attack. But have you never used a smaller weapon to inflict a lesser injury on someone?'

Lucy head flew up and her blue eyes blazed at me. 'Oh, so they have told you about that, have they? When I was at school? I'm surprised my aunts revealed that little piece of my history. They were so very embarrassed at the time and *so* concerned for the name of Roche!'

'They didn't tell me,' I said. 'If you must know, and it's only fair you should, it was Higgins.'

'Higgins?' returned Lucy in surprise. She paused and thought it over before shrugging. 'Oh, well, she would, I dare say. She never liked me.'

'I didn't believe her at first,' I said. 'I couldn't imagine you doing such a thing, actually inflicting harm on anyone. Why did you?'

'I was eleven!' Lucy stamped her foot. 'And the girl was teasing me. Her name was Charlotte Porter, a hateful girl. She was clever at getting other people into trouble, generally by tormenting them until they retaliated, and then looking herself as if butter wouldn't melt in her mouth. Or she would pick on some girl who was easily led and urge her to some mischief. Charlotte herself was never there when it was found out. I didn't like her; no one did. But she was the teacher's little pet. She had such a simpering, namby-pamby way with her! I just lost my temper. She was pulling at my embroidery so I couldn't stitch properly. I only meant to ward her away, but I held the needle in my hand and, somehow, it went right into her arm.' Lucy smiled. 'She let out an awful screech. It was very satisfying.'

I found myself staring at her in something like despair. Lucy was so artless; she seemed to have no idea what sort of impression her words and actions made on others. Only now that her uncle had arrived was she regretting throwing stones at Dr Lefebre. At the time, I surmised, she found that action 'very satisfying'.

We had been unaware of any footsteps in the corridor outside but now came a sudden rap at the door that made us both jump.

'Open it, Lizzie!' urged Lucy, pushing me towards the door. 'It's your room. I'll hide behind the bed.'

'Don't—' I called out, but she was already scuttling away and by the time I opened the door, Lucy had sunk down on the further side of the bed out of sight.

Christina Roche stood in the corridor and, as might have been expected, was not fooled. She had probably heard us talking through the door panels. Doubtless this eavesdropping business, I thought grimly, runs in the family.

'Where is my niece?' she demanded. 'Lucy!' She walked past me into the room. 'Come out at once!'

Lucy rose sheepishly to her feet from behind the bed and shook her skirts straight.

Miss Roche watched her dispassionately. 'Come downstairs. Your uncle is here and wishes to speak to you.'

'Is it about James?' Lucy asked suddenly, fear in her voice. 'Has something happened to James? Don't tell me he's dead. If he's dead I shall throw myself out of the window!'

'Don't talk such nonsense!' was the brisk retort from her aunt. 'If you wish to persuade us you're sensible you have a very strange way of going about it. There will be no more such silly talk, do you hear? As for Mr Craven, he is not, to my knowledge, dead or sick.' She turned away and walked towards the door. 'Come along, Lucy.'

'Oh, Lizzie, come with me,' begged Lucy, catching at my hand.

Miss Roche paused and half turned back. 'No,' she said shortly. 'This is a family matter. Miss Martin is not involved. In fact, Miss Martin, I should prefer it if you would take yourself off for another walk.'

'*I* do not listen at doors!' I told her.

'One hopes not,' was the dour reply. 'However, it is possible that my niece may choose to indulge herself in one of her theatrical fits of hysteria for the benefit of her uncle; and I'd prefer it if you were not in the house at the time. Please take at least half an hour over your walk, Miss Martin.'

With that she walked out, erect as a guardsman, Lucy trailing miserably behind her.

I had just time to whisper, 'Lucy, do and say nothing!' But I had no way of knowing if she heard me. She gave no sign.

Worried and angry, I pulled on my boots, jammed on my hat, and set out on a second walk before lunch.

Miss Roche's high-handed way of dismissing me about my business had so ruffled me that I set out to walk as fast as I could to work off my bad mood. No one thinks clearly when in a temper and I had need of such wits as I possess. I marched along in a most unladylike fashion, and made such good speed that I'd reached the churchyard almost before I realised it. I peered over the wall to see if the sexton was still about but there was no sign of him and the church door was shut. Closer inspection and a good rattle of the iron ring handle confirmed it was locked. So Jarvis had gone home for his lunch . . . or down to The Acorn. I sighed in relief and turned back towards the lych-gate to sit there awhile.

Then my eye caught a movement over to my right. Someone bent almost double was scuttling away from the area where Lucy's child was buried. The figure brought to mind a crab on the seashore scurrying from rock to rock, as it weaved between the headstones, trying to get cover from them wherever possible. The furtive fleeing form would attract curiosity at any time, but it appeared to me to be making for the sanctuary of the shadows beneath the yew tree where I'd noticed a watcher before. This time I was determined whoever it was shouldn't escape.

'Wait, wait!' I called and ran full pelt between the hummocks, my skirts held high in both hands. I jumped disrespectfully over last resting places, stone kerbs and Grecian urns of wilting flowers, in a way that would have given poor old Jarvis a fit had he been able to see me.

I could now distinguish the figure as that of a woman in dark clothing and a familiar-looking tartan shawl. I took a gamble.

'Mrs Brennan!' I shouted.

At the name the woman stumbled, gripped a convenient headstone to steady her, and stopped. It allowed me to catch up and see that it was indeed the rat-catcher's widow. She was still hunched, her face averted from me and looking down at the earth, as if she wished to avoid my scrutiny.

'My dear Mrs Brennan,' I said, as steadily as I could between gasps, 'I am Miss Martin, companion to Mrs Craven at Shore House. On my journey here a few days ago, we passed you and your husband on the heath. Greenaway was driving me and a gentleman in the trap.'

She straightened up reluctantly but still avoided my gaze. 'Yes, miss,' she said in a low hoarse voice.

'I am sorry for your loss, and I'm so glad to see you. We have all been very worried about you,' I went on. 'No one has known where to find you or if you were in any need.'

'I don't need anything,' she replied in that husky tone.

She was of dark complexion with a weather-beaten skin and small elusive brown eyes. I was close enough now to smell a strong odour of burnt wood emanating from her clothing. She has been sitting at an open wood fire, I thought. Then it all came to me in a flash. Greenaway's claim that Brennan was of gypsy origin, the gypsy caravan with the piebald horse we had passed en route to Shore House, the gypsy woman selling pegs who had called at the house . . .

'You have been living with the gypsies,' I said. 'You were in trouble and you went to your husband's people.'

She looked up at me then with surprise. 'How do you know that, miss?'

'I worked it out,' I said awkwardly. 'Why did you run away? I don't mean from me just now, but from police enquiries?'

She shook her head and her long greasy locks fell about her face. The black hair was early streaked with grey. 'I weren't running away, miss. I had nowhere else to go but to the travellers' camp. The constable told me I must stay in the district so I stayed.'

'But you didn't tell the constable where!' I said in exasperation.

She cowered at the cross tone and I was instantly sorry. 'I mean you no harm, I promise you,' I said. 'But please, Mrs Brennan . . . I do believe you know so much that you must tell us – the police, me! I believe you were watching Mrs Craven and myself from over there, by that tree, when we came here the other day. Why were you—'

I broke off then because my mind was ahead of me, leaping from one conclusion to another by such leaps and bounds that I hardly had time to make sense of all the ideas crowding my brain. I turned my head and looked back at the child's grave. A fresh posy of wild flowers lay on it.

The woman had seen my glance; she gave a little moan and clutched at the neck of her shawl.

I reached out and took hold of her grimy but unresisting hand. 'My dear Mrs Brennan, it's *your* child buried there, isn't it? It's not Mrs Craven's baby.'

She gave another whimper of distress and shook her head.

'I believe it is,' I said as firmly but gently as I was able. 'And the moment has come to say what you know about it. Let's go and sit on the bench under the lych-gate and you can take as much time as you like. But you must tell me everything, don't you see? Above all, if you know what happened to Lucy Craven's baby, where she is or – or if she is alive or dead . . . Don't you see, poor Mrs

Craven has been half driven out of her mind by all this.'

She nodded and allowed me to lead her to the lych-gate where we took seats. I hoped no one, neither Jarvis nor any chance passer-by, disturbed us. Mrs Brennan sat silently beside me, twisting her workworn hands. It was difficult to guess how old she was. Probably not so very old but life hadn't been kind to her and her suffering was written in the lines on her skin and her defeated air. She opened her mouth, giving a glimpse of gappy discoloured teeth, and closed it again with a shake of her head. I sensed that she was not unwilling to speak but didn't know how to begin.

She needed help and it seemed easier to start with the most recent events and work backwards. 'Tell me,' I said, 'why you left your camp on the heath and went to the gypsies without telling the constable. The police were afraid you might have perished in the fire.'

At the word 'fire' her head shot up and she stared at me in terror.

'But I didn't mean it!' she burst out in a distraught wail, waving her hands. 'I didn't mean for the fire to catch and spread like it did. I'm no fire-raiser, miss, but they will put me in prison for it, I know they will.'

'No one is going to put you in prison for starting the fire if it wasn't your intention,' I replied, hoping I was right. 'Why did you light it? To cook your food?'

'No, miss, to burn Jed's things.'

I must have looked my incomprehension because she went on quickly, anxious now to explain her actions.

'It's the gypsy way, miss, when someone dies. Anything that's their personal things is burnt.'

'I see . . .' I said. 'So you piled up your husband's clothing and belongings and set them alight, because that's the gypsy custom, your husband was of gypsy origins, and you are also, I think.'

'The heather was dry,' she began again, almost gabbling out her tale now, 'there's been no rain. The fire caught and spread so fast I couldn't stamp it out. I just ran or I'd have been burned with it. Then I was so frightened, because they would say I was a fire-raiser and put me in gaol. I knew there were gypsies nearby because we met them, Jed and I, on our way here. So it's to them I went.'

She wasn't, I thought, the most intelligent of beings. But she had tried to do what she thought was right by her man. I had to trust that a sense of doing what was right would prompt her to tell me the whole wretched business now.

'When you came some months ago with your husband, on a previous visit,' I said carefully, 'you were with child yourself, is that not so?'

Brennan's wife always travelled with her husband, so Greenaway had told the doctor and myself that first day, even when she was 'carrying'.

She nodded. 'I gave birth up on the heath.'

'All alone?' I asked, aghast.

She stared at me as if unable to comprehend my shock.

'I done it before,' she said simply.

'What happened then?' I asked.

'The baby was sickly. After a couple of days, she died. So many of my babies have died, miss. I've buried six of them. I did hope, this time, this baby might live. But she died in my arms while Jed was away from our camp, and I sat there grieving all alone, as I thought. But then I realised someone was there and I looked up and saw one of the ladies from Shore House.'

'Which one?' I breathed, almost unable to get the words out.

'Miss Christina, it was. She had been walking out on the heath.

She'd heard me wailing and come to see what was amiss. I told her my child had died and I showed her.' The woman paused and her brow crinkled. 'I mind her words well. She said, "Your baby has died and my niece's is thriving. I wish it had been the other way about!" That did seem a strange, unnatural thing for anyone to say, miss.'

'It is,' I said bleakly. 'Go on.'

But I knew what was coming.

'My husband came back just then. He and Miss Roche fell to talking together. They agreed . . .'

She paused again and wrapped her own arms about her body, beginning to sway back and forth. ''Twas a terrible thing to do, miss. But my man said, Miss Roche was rich and was willing to pay well for our dead baby. She meant to exchange it with the child her niece had been delivered of. Jed – we – should take little Mrs Craven's baby to London. It could be done, she said. My milk had come in and I could feed her. When we got to London, we should give the baby into the care of a workhouse under a false name. She didn't care which one. She only wanted it made sure no one should trace the child back to this place. And Jed, he said we would do it.

'After Miss Roche had left, I told Jed it was a bad business and we would suffer for it. It was mortal wrong. Nor did I want to give up my dead child, just like that. But Jed, well, he just gave me a clip round the ear and said I shouldn't be fussing. Our baby would get a decent burial and it not cost us a penny. He was a – a strong man, strong in his body and strong in his mind. There was never any arguing with him. He took our baby away that night late and came back, while it was still dark, with the other baby. He had told me to pack up and be ready to leave as soon as he got back, so I'd done that. We moved out straight away, even though it was still night. There was a moon, luckily, and we could see our way.'

She hesitated and gave me a shy, sideways look. 'It were a nice little baby and smelled so fresh of good soap. I did ask Jed, when we were nearing London, if perhaps we couldn't keep it, since ours had been taken. But Jed said he always did a good job, whether it was clearing rats or delivering a baby to the workhouse. He did what he was paid for. It was a kind of . . .'

She tailed off, her vocabulary lacking a suitable word.

'A matter of principle,' I supplied bitterly, as if that scoundrel could have been said to have had any principles.

But the phrase appealed to his widow. She brightened. 'Yes, miss, that's it! He always did what he'd said he'd do.'

'And you took the baby to a workhouse?'

But she looked vague. 'Not I, miss. We got to our place, where we lodge when we're in London, Jed took the baby and went out. When he come back he didn't have her any more.'

'And you didn't ask what he'd done with her?'

'I daren't ask, miss.' She leaned forward earnestly. 'But he set off to go to the workhouse and that was what he'd told Miss Roche he'd do and like I was saying, he was a man who kept a bargain. I did take good care of that little 'un while she was in my keeping, miss. I would've kept her if I could.'

I sighed but did my best to sound brisk and encouraging. 'I'll take you to Inspector Ross at The Acorn. Let's hope he's there. You must tell him everything you've told me. Don't be afraid. Just tell the truth so that justice may be done.'

Unfortunately, when we reached The Acorn, neither Ben nor Sergeant Morris was there. Mrs Garvey told me she believed the police officers had gone to Shore House with Mr Roche; she had seen them all set out together.

I knew Ben and the sergeant hadn't entered the house with Charles Roche, so somewhere along the way they had parted company. I thought that if I went back to the house I might meet them, so I gave Mrs Brennan into the care of Mrs Garvey. We arranged that the woman should wait in the snug, since that was given over to 'police business' as the landlady put it. Mrs Garvey would provide the woman with tea and something to eat and make sure she didn't slip out.

I elicited a promise from Mrs Brennan that she would stay at the inn. She seemed to be exhausted, just nodded and whispered, 'Yes.' I thought she would do as bid. Like her late husband, she probably believed, in warped fashion, in keeping her word. Moreover, there was nowhere now that she could run. But as a precaution I murmured to Mrs Garvey as I left the inn, that perhaps William the potboy could be sent to find Constable Gosling and bring him to the inn as quickly as possible. With that arranged, I set off back to Shore House.

I wasn't sure how long I had been absent, probably a good half-hour, as requested by Miss Roche. But I walked back far more slowly than I had done earlier. I wanted to find Ross and give him the news, but I needed to sort out what must have happened. I felt sick to the stomach when I thought of what might have befallen the baby, but I could not be worrying about that immediately. I had to have everything clear in my head before I could tell Ben what I had concluded.

The two figures talking together in the garden the first night must have been Brennan and Miss Roche. It had after all been Brennan's terrier I saw. Brennan had come to report success in disposing of the infant, however he'd done it.

I had no intention of announcing my return and being sent out again. I walked round to the dining room where the French windows stood ajar and let myself in. At the foot of the stairs I paused to listen. Voices murmured behind the drawing-room door. I identified Lefebre's, another male voice I fancied belonged to Charles Roche, and a decided female voice I attributed to Miss Roche. A fainter murmur must be Miss Phoebe. A young childish voice giving a sudden cry of alarm meant Lucy was there, too. They were all gathered. I had something to do and I would never get such a good opportunity again.

I hurried upstairs and along the corridor to the sisters' rooms. My one fear was that Higgins would be in one of them, engaged in some sewing. But the upper floor was very quiet. Probably Higgins had joined Mrs Williams to discuss Charles Roche's arrival. Gently I turned the knob of Miss Phoebe's door. The room was in the front of the house. It didn't receive the afternoon sun and appeared gloomy. I hastened to the massive wardrobe of polished walnut, its doors decorated with curls and swags very much in the French style, and opened it. An overpowering scent of lavender thus released made me stifle a sneeze. As quickly as I could, I worked my way along the gowns hanging there, listing the patterns in my head as the soft silk fabrics rustled between my fingers.

When I thought I had the patterns fixed in my memory, I shut the door and let myself out of the room. The corridor was still empty and quiet. I made my way to Miss Roche's room, overlooking the garden and the sea view, and bathed now in afternoon sunshine. Through the window I could see how the sea rippled and hear how it slapped on the stones of the beach. A fresh wind had sprung up and sent the yachts scurrying across the Solent towards the harbours of the Isle of Wight.

I opened a wardrobe pair to the one in Miss Phoebe's room,

and began to search feverishly. The tartan gown was missing. The sisters had worn those gowns the day I had arrived and Miss Phoebe's hung in her wardrobe.

My head swam and I leant my head against the wardrobe door. The flickering glow I'd seen on the beach on the night of the murder had come from the tartan gown as Miss Roche committed it to the flames.

There was the faintest creak behind me and a prickle of alarm ran up my spine. I was no longer alone. I turned slowly and saw Christina Roche standing in the open doorway of her room.

Chapter Twenty

Elizabeth Martin

THERE WAS no excuse I could give for my presence there. It was obvious what I'd been doing . . . and one look at her face told me that she knew only too well the reason why.

During my stay at Shore House I'd avoided Christina Roche's disapproving stare. Now I couldn't take my eyes from her face. My first impression of her on my arrival had been of a ship's figurehead; this now returned even more strongly. Her jutting nose seemed carved from some hard substance, teak or marble, rather than fragile bone. Beneath it her mouth was pursed in disapproval not just for the present circumstances but permanently, the lips pressed to a thin line. The gleam I had observed in her eyes when they first set their gaze on me was now a glitter of hostility and contempt. As I watched, the expression cleared, and her eyes became flat opaque chips of dark grey, like fragments of slate. They were the closed portals not only of an unreasonable mind but also of unreason itself.

I had to say something. What came out when I opened my mouth (I wonder at it now) was, 'I trust Mr Roche had a comfortable journey from London?'

Thinking back, those bland words seem the height of foolishness. But in fact, I couldn't have chosen better. The sheer normality of my enquiry, its unexpectedness, and its total irrelevance to what I was doing in her room, took the woman momentarily aback.

'Yes,' she said curtly. 'But you have not explained your presence, Miss Martin, or why you appear to be searching my closet.'

I had no intention of trying to make any excuse. I'd only end up stammering and appearing weak. Since battle couldn't be avoided, I went on to the attack.

'Does Mr Roche know,' I asked, 'what you did with Lucy's baby? Does he know that Brennan took her to London and left her in a workhouse or, for all we know, in some back alley for anyone to find, or not to be found alive at all?'

'This is nonsense,' she said coldly, 'a fiction. From where do you come by such an idea?'

'From Mrs Brennan, who's confessed everything. Sadly even she doesn't know for certain where her husband took the child after reaching London.'

'So,' Miss Roche murmured, 'you've found his wife. That's a pity. If I had found her first, I should have closed her mouth.' This was said without any threat in it, just as a simple statement of fact. The words were the more chilling for it.

I found myself blessing the fire Mrs Brennan had so clumsily started. It had forced her to leave her tent and flee to the gypsy camp. If she had remained in her original place, Miss Roche might have discovered her there, as she'd discovered her once before cradling a dead infant. Fate had led me to find the rat-catcher's wife first, and I'd be forever grateful.

Unexpectedly, Christina Roche started forward. I couldn't help but jump back in alarm. Her features worked uncontrollably and when she spoke the words were spat out at me.

'How dare you criticise my actions! I did what was *right*! Should I allow that squalling brat to grow up and have a part in the Roche fortune? Should the scandalous circumstances of Lucy's marriage be called to mind every time anyone set eyes on the child and remembered she's James Craven's daughter, conceived out of wedlock, and sired by a conniving, useless trickster? Is my niece even capable of raising that or any child? She is but a child herself and a silly one, full of moods and fancies, easily seduced by a wretch like Craven, unable to uphold the honour either of herself or her family name.'

'It was an unspeakably cruel act to part mother and baby!' I shouted at her. 'Honour? *Honour*? Where's the honour in any of that? To lie and pretend the infant was dead, to ignore the mother's distress, to take advantage of a girl who, yes, is little more than a child and should, for that reason, be treated all the more sympathetically . . . none of these things can ever be forgiven or justified. You were driving her out of her mind! How could you even think of doing such a thing?'

Christina, taken aback at the vehemence with which I spoke, something she was little accustomed to hear when others spoke to her, blinked at me and looked momentarily nonplussed.

'How did you manage it?' I asked as calmly as I was able.

'It was Providence,' she said and her air of conviction returned. 'Yes, *Providence*, Miss Martin! Neither you nor any other person can deny it. What else could have put me in the way of the rat-catcher's wife that day on the heath? I was shown the way by some higher power and I merely followed the signs so clearly given. I'd sought out the isolation of the heath, space to think, to plan. My mind was spinning. I tried to imagine what on earth could be done, now that Lucy had been safely delivered of Craven's child. How could I remove this blight upon our name? How could I protect the house of Roche from this interloper? Can you imagine how it felt when I found Brennan's woman lamenting and cradling a dead infant? It was as if the clouds had parted and allowed the sun to shine. A solution, there at my feet! It was meant, I tell you! You cannot deny it.'

She was speaking ever faster, the words tumbling eagerly from her lips. Her eyes glowed with triumph. 'Brennan was perfectly willing to aid me to exchange the babies. He assured me there would be no problem in leaving the infant at a workhouse in London. Why, unwanted infants were handed in at institutions of all kinds, public and private, all the time. He would declare he had found the child abandoned. Who would prove otherwise?

'I arranged he should come at midnight, bringing his dead child. My niece was restless following the birth. Dr Barton feared the onset of childbed fever. He'd left laudanum for her. I gave her some that night and she soon fell asleep. As for the nurse.' Christina Roche smiled. 'Believe me, I know how such women are. I took her a bottle of brandy, laced with a little laudanum, and said she should keep it by for medicinal purposes. Her eyes lit up when she saw it. I knew she'd drink herself senseless as soon as my back was turned.

'Sure enough, I went up to the nursery at midnight and found the woman snoring in a chair and the bottle half empty. I took the infant, undressed it and wrapped it in a shawl. Then I went downstairs and met with Brennan, as arranged, in the garden. I handed over Lucy's baby and he gave me his dead child. I took the dead one back upstairs and dressed her in the nightgown and cap I'd taken off Lucy's child. To my eye they looked exactly the same.'

'But not to a mother's!' I exclaimed. 'Lucy knew at one glance that wasn't her baby.'

'That was annoying,' Miss Roche agreed. 'But Dr Barton, who is an old fool, only took one look at the dead infant and was happy to sign a death certificate. He declared Lucy to be raving as a result of fever; her insistence the dead infant wasn't hers a delusion. If the nurse noticed anything she was not such a fool as to speak up. She knew she had been drunk.'

She made an impatient gesture. 'I hoped, we all hoped, that Craven would never return from the East. If some fever took him off, and the baby had been disposed of, then it would be as if this foolish, ill-advised marriage had never taken place. But no, you had to meddle and seek out the rat-catcher's wife, after bringing your policeman friend here to ask his impertinent questions. And now my brother is here and tells us James Craven has vanished from Canton and might well be in this country!'

She fell silent, glaring at me.

'James Craven is in England?' I exclaimed. 'Has Lucy been told?'

'Oh yes,' said Miss Roche bitterly. '*I* should not have told her . . . nor would my brother. We should have sought out Craven and bundled him off East again. My niece would have been none the wiser. But your Inspector Ross would have it that my niece must hear the news! What good has that done? Lucy is weeping one minute with joy and the next with despair because he hasn't shown his face and she's imagining all sorts of accidents. Suppose Craven arrives on the doorstep and Lucy leaves us and sets up a home with him? They may have more children. Everything generations of Roches have worked for and achieved will pass into the hands of an unworthy, gambling idler and any children he may spawn. Once Craven had been sent off to China, and Brennan had taken away the child, I believed we'd settled everything. Now everything is as bad as before, if not worse.'

'And as part of settling everything, you killed the rat-catcher,' I said. 'I doubt even you can claim a higher power directed your arm.'

'Nonsense,' said Miss Roche simply. 'I don't deny I arranged for him to take the child. Why should I kill him? He had done excellently.'

We had both of us been so intent on one another that we had remained unaware of anything else. Now, suddenly, the door was flung open and Lucy Craven erupted into the room. Her face was red with rage and her eyes blazed. Her fair hair had tumbled free of the plaited twist at the back of her head, and fell in disarray on her shoulders.

'I heard!' she shrieked. 'I heard you tell Lizzie all of it! I came upstairs to tell Lizzie that James was back in England, and I heard you both talking in here. I listened and I heard it ALL! You lied to me! You took my baby and you gave her to that dreadful man! You gave her to *him*!'

She rushed forward and scooped up a pair of scissors lying on a worktable. With the blades held like a weapon in her hand, she flung herself on her aunt.

Miss Roche was so surprised that she stumbled back. I leapt at Lucy, seized her arm, and cried, 'No, Lucy, don't!'

I wouldn't have believed that child-like frame now in frenzy could be so strong. We wrestled for what could only have been seconds, but seemed much longer. More than once the open blades flashed dangerously close to my face. Then, without warning, hands appeared to grasp Lucy's shoulders and jerk her backwards.

Lucy squealed. The scissors clattered to the floor and I grabbed them before she could seize them again. I saw that the person, who held Lucy tightly and in a most professional way, was Lefebre. The others had followed him into the room and all crowded by the door: Charles Roche, his face foolish with dismay and surprise. Phoebe, white-faced, her hand clasped over her mouth. As before, Williams had come running and Higgins, too.

Faced with the new arrivals, Christina Roche regained her self-control. 'Well, Miss Martin,' she said. 'Now perhaps you are satisfied and see for yourself who stabbed Brennan.'

And she pointed at her niece.

Lucy sagged in Lefebre's grip and began to sob softly, shaking her head. He led her to a chair and she sank down on to it. 'No . . .' she repeated between gasps, '*No, no . . .*'

Before anyone else could reply I spoke as loudly as I could. I wanted them all to hear me. 'No,' I said. 'Lucy didn't kill the man. But you did. To try and blame an innocent girl is cowardly as well as wicked.'

I turned to Charles Roche. 'Your sister arranged to exchange Brennan's own dead child for Lucy's living baby and to take Lucy's child to a workhouse is London. Lucy heard your sister confess to it. No wonder she flew into a rage!'

I turned back to Christina Roche. 'You asked me why you should kill the rat-catcher. My guess is that he asked for more money. Or you felt you could not trust him to be silent forever. He knew the whereabouts of the child. At some later date he might seek out the infant and produce her. You had to silence him. What I don't understand is, why didn't you kill him that first night I was here, when you met him in the garden? Because you did meet him, didn't you? I saw you from my window, and his little white dog.'

Her eyes glittered with hatred. 'Well, Miss Martin, is there nothing you don't know? As soon as I heard Brennan had returned to the district, I did indeed send Greenaway to him with a request to come and destroy a rat. It was an agreed message between Brennan and myself. I went out into the garden after everyone, as I thought, would be asleep, and there he was. He was a curious fellow but reliable in his rough fashion. I met him only so that he might confirm he had taken the child to a workhouse, as arranged. I did not, for all your impudent theorising, have it in my mind to kill him.'

'Not at that moment,' I retorted. 'You hadn't come armed because you only came to hear if he'd carried out your horrible plan. But when he asked for more money, you told him you would meet him secretly in the garden the next day and pay him more.'

'Pay him more . . .' murmured Miss Roche thoughtfully. 'The man was out of his head. Did he think I was so stupid that I could be blackmailed by a *rat-catcher*? That he could threaten me with impunity? I am a *Roche*!'

Lucy was crying softly, hugging herself and rocking to and fro. As before, Williams came forward to put an arm round her and lead her away.

I took up my accusation. 'You lay in wait with a knife taken from the hall table and you stabbed him! But your clothes were blood-stained. You ran upstairs and changed into another gown so that when you appeared in the garden after Lucy had found the body no one should see the telltale bloodstains that showed you'd already been near the body. When you went to tell your sister of the murder, she was so upset she probably didn't notice you didn't wear a gown of the material she and you had agreed for the day. But later she might have done. Dr Lefebre and I should certainly have observed you wore different gowns, when we next saw you. So you persuaded Phoebe that you should both wear mourning black for the rest of that day. I thought it was excess of formality that had made you do it. But you wouldn't have done that for a casual labourer, of course you wouldn't. I should have realised at once the black gowns were meant to mislead. That night you – or perhaps Higgins who is your creature – took the stained gown to the foreshore and burned it. I saw the fire.'

'Do you, I wonder, ever sleep, Miss Martin?' asked Christina Roche with what sounded like genuine curiosity. 'Or are you like the dog guarding Hades, one of whose three heads is always awake? I thought my brother had sent Lefebre to spy on us but it seems he also sent you.'

'No,' I denied. 'I don't know the reason for Dr Lefebre being here, but I only came to be companion to Lucy.'

'Then you have far exceeded a companion's duties!' she replied coldly.

I ignored the jibe. 'When you came in just now and found me searching in your wardrobe, you knew at once I'd worked it all out, that I'd probably already checked your sister's wardrobe, and was now looking to see if any corresponding gown was missing from yours. There is one gone, the tartan one. Where is it, Miss Roche? If I'm wrong, then produce it.'

Christina Roche was silent, her cold slate eyes expressionless.

Lefebre spoke up. 'I suggest we go downstairs, with the exception of Miss Roche. You will not object, ma'am, if we lock you in your room for the next half-hour or so? Just while we discuss all this.'

'How good of you to ask,' remarked Christina Roche drily. 'Are you, I wonder, Doctor, as polite with the unfortunates incarcerated in your clinic?'

Higgins's harsh voice broke in. 'I'll sit here with madam. You can lock me in too. Miss Christina shouldn't be left alone. It's not decent.'

'It might not be a bad idea to secure Higgins,' I said. 'Or she might let Miss Roche out.'

Miss Roche sat down on a small stool and folded her hands composedly. 'Do as you wish!'

The two women were duly locked in after some demur on Charles Roche's part. We then all traipsed back downstairs to the drawing room. A maid was sent to find Ben and Sergeant Morris who were, with luck, still on the premises.

Charles Roche spoke. 'Do you know anything of this, Phoebe?'

Phoebe shook her head so hard that her false ringlets bounced around and threatened to detach themselves.

'I didn't know Christina had, had killed Brennan . . .' she whispered. 'I knew she'd killed the cat Mr Beresford gave Lucy. She believed it wrong that a married lady should receive a gift from an unrelated gentleman.' Phoebe moved forward, wringing her hands. 'She did tell me what she'd done with the baby, but only after she'd done it and Brennan had left the district. What could I do? She was proud of having arranged things so well . . . Christina said we are a respectable family and James Craven's child must be . . . got out of the way. I thought it wrong but Christina was so sure . . . I was so afraid of the scandal if I told anyone. But as for killing Brennan, I swear . . . I knew nothing . . . I can't believe that's it's true!'

'Respectability . . .' Roche said heavily and followed it with a disgusted snort. 'What my sister *calls* respectability has always been her guide . . . her master! She . . . she was always difficult, obsessive about the good name of our family and our family business. She has always held strong views and can become violently agitated if crossed. She made my life in London quite intolerable so I arranged for her – and for you, Phoebe – to live here quietly.'

He looked at me in a way that was almost comical in its attempt to make all he said seem reasonable. 'I thought it best, and Dr Lefebre here knew of a suitable housekeeper. Williams had worked for him in his private clinic for the insane as a nurse before she married. Now she was widowed and seeking a position. She seemed ideal. Not of course that my poor sister is mad. At least, not as it's normally understood.'

'What you are telling me,' I said quietly, 'is that you – and you, too, Dr Lefebre – knew Miss Roche to be unstable. You sent her here with Miss Phoebe for company and Williams to be her keeper. Before Williams came, Higgins probably filled that role. And then you sent poor little Lucy Craven here for her lying-in. How *could* you?'

Roche stared at me, still bewildered, and spread out his hands in a hopeless gesture. 'But what else could I do? I'm unmarried. I couldn't have my niece giving birth in my house! My household was not adapted for – for newborn infants and women lying-in. I had no idea that my poor sister's obsession would lead her to commit such dreadful acts. I swear this to you.'

'Lucy should have been in her own home with her husband!' I informed him.

'But I had sent him to China,' said Roche and gazed at me pleadingly as if I really could be made to accept his explanation. 'He was so unsuitable. The whole marriage was unsuitable. I had been forced to allow it. The scandal of my niece's condition, her being with child . . . She had to be married but . . .' His voice tailed away. 'We have always been a *respectable* family,' he finished, but he sounded like a man lost in some desolate wilderness with no idea which way to turn.

'Well, this is where your respectability has got you!' I said unkindly. I had no more time for him or for any of them and certainly no sympathy.

He drew in a deep breath and straightened up, attempting something of his former dignity and authority. 'You are right, of course, Miss Martin. Respectability made a kidnapper and, you say, a murderer of my poor sister. Long before that it had confused and distorted her view of life. I feel responsible, of course I do. I shall make every effort to see that – that Inspector Ross understands, and the law understands that my sister is not fully responsible for any of her actions.'

'What actions might those be?' demanded Ben loudly from the doorway.

Sergeant Morris loomed up behind him. Before Roche could answer, I burst out impatiently, 'Your sister, your sister! The law must deal with her as it sees fit. Your concern should be for that hapless baby!'

Chapter Twenty-one

Inspector Benjamin Ross

I RETURNED to London with Sergeant Morris after we had seen Miss Roche taken into custody. As you can imagine, this wasn't achieved without some vigorous opposition on the part of Charles Roche who refused to accept his sister be treated as a common murderer . . . as if there were an uncommon kind. But Mr Roche was finding it difficult to accept that his sister could be any kind of murderer. There had been some mistake, he kept insisting. His sister's mind had given way under all the stress and she was the victim of her own derangement. His good friend Lefebre the mad-doctor, an acknowledged expert, agreed people suffering from mental illness often made extraordinary and untrue claims, or related wild stories sprung from their diseased fantasy.

When he saw his protests weren't accepted, Roche proposed that instead of gaoling her until she came to trial, he should stand surety for her, so avoiding incarceration.

This suggestion was turned down on practical grounds. She couldn't be left at Shore House with only Miss Phoebe to watch over her. Roche himself couldn't remain at Shore House because of his business commitments. Nor could she be taken to London and lodged with him in Chelsea, because Lucy was there now. To force Lucy, who had been so wronged by Christina Roche, to live under the same roof was out of the question. The chief constable intervened. It was agreed that until her trial Miss Roche would be lodged with the senior warder in his home within the grounds of the prison. Thus she would be kept apart from common criminals of the female variety. There would be costs involved, of course, but Charles Roche would meet those.

He had to be satisfied with this arrangement, and the chief warder and his wife were no doubt very satisified indeed. For Miss Roche's three badly cooked meals a day and bed with grubby linen they would be well recompensed.

Lizzie had already escorted Lucy Craven back to London. Dr Lefebre had also returned, to his private madhouse and medical practice, and was keeping well out of our way. To my mind, he had some explaining to do.

With Dunn's support, I laid the details of the affair before the chief commissioner of police. With his approval, we now took ourselves off to a magistrate to obtain a warrant allowing Mr Charles Roche to take custody of a female infant, legally called Louisa Craven but present name unknown, who had probably been delivered into the care of the parish of Whitechapel in April that year by a man named Jethro Brennan. As for Roche, he was so anxious to make amends in some way for his responsibility for setting in train the whole wretched business that he was now in a fever of impatience to find the child.

I thought it well to take Sergeant Morris along before setting off to tackle parish officials. Although I was about my duty, and Mr Roche had his warrant, to say nothing of having moral right on our side (as if that and the law always went together), a force of three carries its own argument.

The Whitechapel workhouse was then situated in the heart of Spitalfields in Vallance Road. We had sent word ahead that we were on our way, but to reach the place took a perilous journey by cab. I saw that for Charles Roche, plunging into the crowded streets of Whitechapel proved an alarming experience. Quite apart from the pressing concern that occupied him regarding the recovery of his niece's child, he seemed at a loss to comprehend his surroundings, although not far from here his own ancestors had first set up in the silk business. I knew that there were still silk weavers here among the crowded tenements, but their output was a mere fraction of what it had been now that manufacture had moved to the great factories of the north.

In the days of John Roche, whose portrait hung at Shore House in a place of pride, Whitechapel had been respectable and prosperous, full of those industrious Huguenots. Now I think there can be few districts in London more crowded and insalubrious and certainly none so motley. Whitechapel is a receptacle into which pour people from all corners of Europe and, indeed, beyond. The houses are crammed with as many families as can draw breath in their fetid interiors. During our visit we heard a veritable Babel of tongues spoken around us. The shops offered unfamiliar foodstuffs for sale, much to the horror of Sergeant Morris whose own tastes run to nothing more exotic than jellied eels. Pawnbrokers' establishments abounded. Careful fingers picked over second-hand clothing and oddments of pots and pans spread out on barrows in the street.

We saw several of the area's sizeable Jewish population, many of the men easily identifiable in their kaftans and with their ringlets dangling from beneath their black hats. I knew this community to be for the greater part industrious and law abiding, 'keeping themselves to themselves' as the saying goes. Not so many of the others we encountered or who brushed against us accidentally or on purpose. Whitechapel is a notorious haunt of petty criminals and prostitutes. All spilled out into the streets dodging between handcarts and drays and generally impeding the traffic; or thronged the pavements pushing and shoving. We could hear our cabbie shouting and swearing.

We were received by the poor law officer and a gentleman who represented the board of guardians of the workhouse. The last named had been hastily brought from his place of business and was none too pleased about the fact. He begged us to be brisk about our errand. Time, he informed us, was money.

To discuss that business we were led to a room where we established ourselves, once the poor law officer had evicted the slovenly female who had been mopping the floor. She departed with her bucket of dirty water leaving behind an unpleasant odour and air of dampness and depression.

'I understand the board has responsibility for orphaned or abandoned children who have come upon the parish,' I began as we seated ourselves in a row on one side of the long table. The two parish representatives took seats on the other side facing us.

'They do, sir, or Mr Stoner should not be here!' snapped the poor law officer. 'In the first place the matter comes before me, and I decide what should be done. I declare it a pauper. In the matter of a very small parentless infant, naturally it cannot be taken into the workhouse itself. Other arrangements have to be made for it but it is still on the list of paupers and the board of governors count it among their charges. May I ask the reason for your interest?'

The speaker went by the name of Potter. He was a spindly fellow who might have been any age but I judged about fifty. His high bulging forehead was crowned by a scattering of faded red hair and his complexion was of that whiteness which sometimes accompanies such hair colour. His pinched expression suggested a man who lived by the rule book. His colleague, Mr Stoner, was in contrast plump and hoarse of breath with a red complexion and untidy linen. Clearly neither was pleased to see us. They shared an air of wariness.

There was, in addition, a faint odour of brandy about Potter, which he endeavoured to disguise by constantly popping into his mouth some pastilles giving off a smell of violets. His linen was grubby. Brandy, violets and sweat-stained clothing do not make for good company. Stoner had taken out his snuffbox and was tapping out a pinch on the back of his hand. I hoped we would not need to spend longer with them than we needed to complete our business with all speed.

'I suffer from a weak stomach,' Potter informed us, indicating his box of violet cachous.

'Indeed?' I replied.

Charles Roche, who had been looking around him with increasing dismay, asked, 'Can't we get to the matter swiftly?'

Potter agreed. He made a steeple of his fingers with his dirty nails at the tip. 'Well, gentlemen, what is this matter that brings the Metropolitan Police to see me?' (I had shown him my warrant card on our first arriving.) 'And plain clothes, too?' he went on. His mouth twisted in what might have been intended to be a smile but only succeeded in giving the impression of a nervous tic. 'All is in order here,' he added with a certain belligerence creeping into his voice.

'Good,' I told him briskly. 'Then there should be no particular problem presented by our errand. We're seeking a female infant who was given into parish keeping last April. The child was then very young, practically a newborn.'

Stoner sniffed up his pinch of snuff and sneezed into a large red-spotted handkerchief. His small eyes, fragments of granite sunken in his puffed face, fixed their gaze on us without expression.

Mr Potter pursed his thin lips and looked at us more speculatively. 'May I ask your interest in this child?'

'Certainly,' I said. 'We have reason to believe the infant was abducted from her mother, her death falsely recorded, and that she was brought by her abductor to London and handed over to you by a man named Jethro or Jed Brennan, a rat-catcher by trade, who was normally resident in Whitechapel when not tramping about the countryside.'

The officials exchanged glances and took their time thinking about my words, both frowning all the while.

'You are certain of this?' Potter asked at last. 'The story seems, if you will excuse me, extraordinary.'

'It is, but it is true.'

Stoner cleared his throat. 'And if you should discover this child, with our help, what do you propose to do?'

'Remove her from parish care and return her to her family. This gentleman is Mr Charles Roche and the child's great-uncle. The whereabouts of the infant's father is not currently known. He went away on some family business to China and to all intents and purposes became a resident of that country for the time being. There has since been reason to believe he has left the Far East, but no proof he is in this country. The mother, who is but seventeen years of age, is at present in London and resident in Mr Roche's house. A magistrate has recognised Mr Charles Roche to be acting head of the family in these circumstances. I have here his warrant requiring you to surrender the infant into Charles Roche's custody. Sergeant Morris and I are here to see all is done properly.'

Mr Roche, on cue, produced his magistrate's letter and laid it with some ceremony on the rickety table serving as the official's desk. Mr Potter unfolded the letter and slowly and carefully read it at least twice. He passed it to his colleague Stoner who did the same and passed it back again. Potter then spread it out flat on the surface of the table and placed his clasped hands on it. Perhaps he thought we might snatch it away again.

'There can be no question that any official of this parish will be charged with any wrongdoing?' His voice was pitched between a question and a statement and veered almost comically between defensiveness and truculence. 'The parish can only accept an infant in good faith. We try to make sure, of course, that there is no one else who can take financial responsibility for the child. We have to be aware that we are answerable to the ratepayers. Indeed, in this matter, there will have to be an inquiry as to why a child with family willing and able to care for it ever came upon parish resources in the first place.'

'That matter,' I interrupted, 'forms part of criminal investigations taking place as we speak.'

Whatever these gentlemen from the parish board wanted, it was not to be drawn into any investigation into criminal matters.

Mr Stoner spoke up, scattering snuff upon his waistcoat as he did and brushing it away in an automatic gesture. 'As my colleague was saying, we always try to establish if there is any relative who can contribute financially to the support of orphaned children. But it is very difficult to get them to pay up, even if we find anyone. The matter is awkward. If we were to ask too many questions . . .' He wheezed and coughed into his handkerchief. 'The babies would simply be abandoned on our doorstep. That happens from time to time, does it not, Mr Potter?'

'It does,' agreed his colleague. 'The taking in of such

abandoned infants causes endless trouble for the board of guardians. There is nothing with them to give us any help, no birth or baptismal certificate, nothing. Mostly such infants are born out of wedlock. If names are given, we know full well that they are likely to be false. The officer receiving the child must make an instant judgement. He cannot be held responsible for any – any mishap. Do you have any idea how many cases come before the board in a parish like Whitechapel? We are overwhelmed, gentlemen, overwhelmed! We do our very best.'

'Yes, yes,' said Charles Roche impatiently. 'We just want to trace the child!'

But Mr Potter still made no move. 'I can look the child up in our records. We keep full written records of the destitute poor who come upon our charge. The system is a model of efficiency. I should, however, warn you that newborn infants who come into our keeping do not always, despite all possible good care being taken and their wanting for no necessity, survive.'

My heart sank and I saw consternation on Charles Roche's face. Were we to discover that Lucy's baby had, after all this, died?

Potter rose and went to the far wall where a shelf was stacked with ledgers under a coating of grey powder. The skivvy with the mop and pail apparently did not include dusting in her duties. Potter, muttering, '*April* . . .' to himself, ran his finger along a row and finally selected a thick tome. He brought it back to the table and opened it, turning the pages with the agonising slowness with which he seemed determined to do everything.

'Ah . . .' The forefinger he had been running down the page came to a rest. I had been watching its progress in a fever of impatience, and found myself irritated anew by the dirt accrued beneath his fingernail. 'The infant you speak of would seem to be one entered as an orphan pauper, number twenty-seven taken in during this present *annum*. She was handed over by a man giving his name as Brennan and occupation as itinerant rat-catcher who claimed she had been found abandoned in the stairwell of the house where he lodged. Questioned closely he stuck to this story. The house was located in Flynn Court. Lacking any other identity, the official who took her in marked her name down as Flynn, therefore, and she was given the first name of Mary. Her age at that time was put by a medical man, employed by the parish to attend sick paupers in the workhouse, as about three weeks. His opinion was that the birth had been attended by a competent midwife or professional doctor. Her health was sound with no sign of malformation or disease. "Deceased" has not since been added to the record.'

All three of his audience heaved sighs of relief. Morris muttered, 'Thank Gawd for that!'

'Where is the baby now?' I demanded.

'The procedure with unweaned infants is that they are given into the care of one of the excellent women on our approved list who make a business of taking in such infants and caring for them on behalf of the parish, and at a suitable remuneration, until they are old enough to be returned to us. The babies are taken into the women's own homes and hand-reared.'

This did not sound promising. Hand-reared babies generally didn't thrive, even I knew that. The fact that 'deceased' was not entered in the record might turn out to be a clerical oversight, despite the vaunted efficiency of the system. My spirits, which had risen, plummeted again.

Beside me Morris fidgeted. I knew he was worried, too.

'Where might we find this woman, sir?' growled Mr Roche whose patience was fast running out.

'Number twenty-seven,' said Mr Potter 'was given into the care of Mrs Dawson of Scuttle Lane. I know Mrs Dawson. She's carried out this work for many years and has great experience.'

'Just so,' wheezed Stoner in corroboration.

'Then may I ask one or both of you to accompany us to the place?' I asked.

Both hesitated. Potter's gaze slid towards the magistrate's letter. 'It would be better, perhaps, if we sent to Mrs Dawson and asked her to bring the child here.'

'I think not,' I said firmly. 'Since it appears you identify the children only by number then Mrs Dawson might simply send us the healthiest at present in her charge.'

Stoner pursed his lips, gave us an angry look, but left any reply to his colleague.

Potter swelled up like an indignant rooster and his domed head turned bright red. 'What are you suggesting, sir? I'll have you know that Mrs Dawson is an excellent woman of high moral principles. She has done this work for the parish for a number of years without any complaint from anyone and we have every confidence in her.'

'I'm pleased to hear it,' I informed him. 'Then you shouldn't object to us paying her a surprise visit. For myself, I would prefer not to give the excellent Mrs Dawson time to think about it. Let's go right now to Scuttle Lane.'

Potter snatched up the magistrate's letter and thrust it into his pocket.

'As you wish.'

'You don't need me,' said Stoner, rising to his feet with an effort. 'And I have a business to attend to. Good day to you, gentlemen.'

We found, when we left the building, that our cabbie had not waited for us, despite being requested to do so. He had insisted on being paid immediately on arrival for the journey to the workhouse so perhaps it was not surprising that he had abandoned us. Cabs rarely waited here and were the object of some curiosity, to say nothing of the attention of grubby urchins. One of their favourite pastimes was well known to be throwing stones and lumps of brick at the cab and its driver; or at the stationary horse in an attempt to score a hit on its legs. We could not blame our cabman for his desertion. There was no hope of finding another cab in this vicinity; we set out on foot, plunging into the crowd.

The crush became easier as we progressed. Gradually the word had spread that 'the law' was visiting them. These people know a police officer instantly, plain clothes or no. A way began to open up before us, 'Much like the parting of the Red Sea,' I observed to poor Mr Roche who clutched his cane with one hand and held on to his hat with the other.

'I would not have walked here without police protection,' he said frankly.

'Have a care to your valuables, even so, sir,' advised Morris. 'There are any number of dips about, pickpockets, sir. You wouldn't believe the artfulness of some of them. They ought to be in the music hall doing a turn on stage, they're that clever at relieving you of your watch or pocketbook and you none the wiser.'

At last Potter led us to Scuttle Lane – if the title 'lane' or street of any kind rightly belonged to it. It was no more than a gap between buildings. The one on the left of the entry was a public house and the one on the right an establishment from which emanated such a foul stench that the business conducted there must involve boiling bones. Scuttle Lane itself was a dark malodorous alley with an open gully running down the middle of it carrying away filthy water the origin of which did not invite speculation.

Our arrival was noticed. Before the public house the regulars propped, pint pot in hand, on benches, turned their befuddled curiosity in our direction.

'It's the law . . .' observed one of these gentry inevitably.

'No, it ain't, it's old Potter from the parish,' argued another. 'Mean old skinflint what he is.'

'I know it's 'im, I seen his miserable face enough times, ain't I? But the two coves with him are peelers, the sort what dresses like lawyers' clerks and reckons no one will recognise 'em fer what they are!' The speaker spat, not exactly in our direction, but not a long way off.

'Here, Mr Potter!' yelled someone else. 'You remember me? Jones is the name. You refused to bury my old mother! My wife had to sell her winter gown to pay fer it.'

'Let us make haste!' Potter ordered us testily.

'Tell 'em anywhere,' said the drinker who had first identified us as policemen, sticking to his guns. 'I dunno who the cove what looks like a gent is. Proper swell, ain't he?'

'So much for plain clothes,' I observed to Morris *sotto voce*. 'I wonder we bother.'

'I did suggest,' Potter told me with some smugness, 'that it would be better to send to Mrs Dawson to bring the child to us. But you would come yourselves.'

He had stopped before an archway and ducked into it. We followed. He led us into an interior court crammed with rubbish, children and mangy dogs. An old woman sat before her door sorting a pile of rags. She didn't so much as glance up but she was well aware of us. Her foot knocked against a bucket, as if by chance, and the clang was certainly a warning to anyone in the sordid den behind her. In similar fashion the children scattered, no doubt running to warn their families of the approach of officialdom. Potter knocked at a door.

It was opened by a brawny woman in a tartan gown and grimy apron whose hair was twisted up into a wired 'Apollo knot' on top of her head. It was a fashion I believe was popular in old King William IV's time and little seen nowadays. But Whitechapel is a place where if they like a thing they stick to it. To my eye it looked like a knob on a biscuit barrel lid. Her expression on opening the door had been aggressive but on seeing Potter she melted into smiles.

'La, Mr Potter, I wasn't expecting you!' She put a hand to the loop of the Apollo knot and simpered.

'Good day to you, Mrs Dawson,' said Potter. 'I apologise for disturbing you. I bring these gentlemen with me. May we come in?'

Her eyes darted past him to us. 'The law?' she demanded, the simpers and smiles disappearing. 'I've no reason to be visited by the law.' She placed her hands upon her hips and took up a stance denying us entry.

I spoke up before Potter could. 'We are accompanying this gentleman, Mr Roche, who has some business to conduct with you.'

The virago's eyes took in Charles Roche. With great presence of mind, he took off his top hat and bowed.

'Oh well, a gent . . .' said Mrs Dawson, smile returning. She took her hands from her hips and dropped a curtsy. 'Come in, gentlemen all, come in. *Here, Dotty!*'

She turned her head and the sudden increased pitch of her voice caused us all to jump.

'Dotty! Stop stirring that porridge and put on the kettle for some tea. I got company!'

She led us indoors, untying the grimy apron as she did and casting it from her out of sight behind a rickety armchair.

The room we were in served both as parlour and kitchen. On the far side was a small range at which stood a slatternly girl of about fourteen struggling with a dented tea kettle. Dotty, I presumed. The abandoned porridge pot slurped and glooped away by itself. The smell of it suggested it had already burned. A rope tied across the room above the level of the range was festooned with drying rags I guessed served as swaddling cloths.

I remembered little Peter Harris abandoned at King's Cross station. He'd also been given into parish care before ending up in a place, Spartan enough, but marginally better this. The unfortunates present in this room had drawn the short straw.

'Sit down, gentlemen,' invited our hostess.

Potter seated himself but as for the rest of us, we were too fascinated by the other occupants of the room to do anything but stand rooted to the spot. There must have been a dozen infants of all ages in the one place. Some crawled, some toddled, others lay in cradles made of orange boxes. One or two slightly older ones had been put to work washing plates in a bowl of greasy water. It was probably the only water their hands were likely to see that day for none of the children appeared to have been bathed recently. Their clothes were equally grubby. All were thin and rickety and kept an unchildlike silence. Their large apprehensive eyes were fixed on us. One or two had their heads shaved, probably in an attempt to remove some infestation, and the shaven skin was daubed with patches of bright violet colour.

'Gentian Violet, that,' observed Morris to me. 'My wife keeps a bottle by in her medicine cabinet. Very good for skin troubles.'

I pulled myself together and sank down on the chair offered me. Roche took the rickety armchair. Morris stationed himself standing by the door.

Potter briefly explained our purpose and showed her the letter. She made no attempt to read it and I suspected she might be illiterate.

'Come to take one of 'em away, have you?' she enquired, cutting immediately to the heart of the matter. 'I'll be paid for one less, then, Mr Potter, I take it?'

'No doubt there will be another to take its place soon, ma'am,' Potter assured her.

'Which one do you want?' she asked carelessly, waving a hand around the room to indicate its infant occupants in general.

The girl, Dotty, appeared at my side and thrust into my hand a chipped enamel mug of black tea.

'Like a drop of rum in that, dear?' enquired Mrs Dawson politely.

'Thank you, no,' I replied.

'You'll be on duty,' she observed. 'Will the gentleman take a drop? Or you, Mr Potter? You usually do.'

Potter was not best pleased at this remark and said quickly, 'Only when my chest is affected by the fog.'

'Number twenty-seven!' I said loudly. 'Name of Flynn.'

She put a hand to the Apollo knot again and looked vaguely round her charges. 'Oh, well, let's see. I don't know I can rightly remember which one that is.'

'It's that one, Ma,' said Dotty, pointing at an orange box.

She took it upon herself to go to the cradle. We watched, hardly daring to breathe, as she stooped over it and plucked an infant from it. Dotty turned to us with a smile of satisfaction. ''Ere you are, then,' she announced. 'Number twenty-seven, like I said.'

The baby lay quietly in her arms. That she was awake was only indicated when she gave a sudden twitch and waved her tiny fist feebly in the air as if seeking to grasp something, but with little expectation of finding it.

'Are you sure?' asked Roche in a hoarse voice.

'Yes, of course I am. See here . . .' Dotty dragged up the little soul's grimy gown and indicated a piece of card that was secured to the baby by a piece of string round its ankle. 'I wrote on it like I write on 'em all when they come in.'

'Dotty's a great one for her letters,' said Mrs Dawson with maternal pride. 'She learned 'em at the Sunday School.'

I set aside the tea and went to inspect the child. She had her mother's beautiful blue eyes but they stared up at me incuriously. I had seen that lack of expression before on the faces of neglected children who had never been cuddled or had baby talk lavished on them. Here the babies would be ignored for twenty-three hours out of the twenty-four. Such babies do not cry. They have learned it serves no purpose. I was angry but knew I mustn't show it. I turned the label and read *27 Flynn* written in ill-formed characters.

'This is the one,' I said to Potter.

Charles Roche rose to his feet. He was an impressive-looking man with his silvery side whiskers, brocade waistcoat and gold watch chain, and just now he appeared in that grubby crowded little baby farm like Jove about to give judgement. Mrs Dawson got up and smoothed her gown nervously.

'We shall take my great-niece and leave at once,' he said.

'How?' enquired the practical Dotty.

It was a good question. We should have to carry the child until we reached a cab stand; and since cab stands didn't abound in Whitechapel that might be for some distance. That we should board a public omnibus carrying an infant would make us such objects of surprised curiosity that it was out of the question.

'If you can spare Dotty for a short while,' I said to Mrs Dawson. 'Perhaps she could carry the infant with us as far as needed. It will be worth her while.'

Dotty's eyes sparkled but her mother observed waspishly, 'We'll all be out of pocket. It costs me far more to feed 'em and clothe 'em than the parish pays me.'

Mr Roche knew his cue. He put his hand to his inside pocket. 'Allow me, madam, to recompense you for your trouble.'

His tone was sarcastic but Mrs Dawson was untroubled by that. Her hand shot out with the rapidity of a snake's tongue and grasped the bank note he held out.

'There,' she said, tucking it into the bosom of her grimy gown, 'I could see you were a gent.'

We quitted the wretched place, triumphant. But what a strange procession we formed for any onlooker! Potter led the way, trying his very best to look as if he were not part of our party at all. Dotty came next carrying the child and Roche, Morris and myself brought up the rear.

Roche, who was silent for some distance, found his voice. It shook with rage. 'Such a business should not be allowed! That – that harridan no more took care of those unfortunate children than—' His voice spluttered to a halt.

'It's all that's on offer, sir,' said Sergeant Morris unexpectedly. 'The parish won't pay her much. She has to take in so many kids to make a living at it. I'm not defending her, sir. I'm only saying that's the way of it.'

'Then I shall not rest until that is no longer "the way of it"!' Roche snapped.

I didn't doubt his sincerity but I did doubt his ability to change very much. The policy of the parish was to do as little as possible, to discourage application for relief. An orphan pauper was a burden upon the respectable ratepayer and unwelcome. However little the money spent, it was begrudged.

As for Potter, he made as if he hadn't heard Roche's outburst. He increased his pace and widened the distance between us even more. We were lucky enough to find a growler, a closed four-wheeled cab, before too long and hailed it.

'Who do I give the baby to?' asked Dotty.

'Here, Morris!' I ordered. 'You're a family man, I believe.'

Morris obligingly held out his arms and number twenty-seven was placed in them.

'Are you taking that little 'un in my cab?' demanded the driver. 'I don't want it being sick or worse on my cushions.'

'You'll be paid for the inconvenience,' Charles Roche said loudly.

The cabbie, like Mrs Dawson, recognised a well-to-do citizen. 'Right you are, sir.'

'I've a suggestion, gentlemen,' said Morris as we set off, our conveyance rumbling across the cobblestones. 'I was thinking that it would be better if the little lady, Mrs Craven, were to see her baby for the first time looking a bit tidier than she does now. If we could drive first to my house, my wife will bath the little one and find her a nice clean gown. I know she's got baby clothes laid by. Both our girls are married now and Mrs Morris is just waiting for one of 'em to produce!'

So that is what we did. Mrs Morris and her sister expressed vociferous dismay at the plight of the child. Snatching her away from the good sergeant, the two women whisked her off to be returned to us some short time later, washed and in a crisp white lawn gown, quite transformed although it would be a good while before some liveliness entered those blue eyes.

Back to Chelsea we carried her. When the maid opened the front door of the Roche house, my own dear Lizzie came running out into the hall, crying out, 'Have you got her? Oh, please God, do say you've got her!'

'We have her,' I said.

Lizzie burst into tears, something I'd never seen her do however extreme the circumstances. I cleared my throat loudly and spent some moments staring down the empty street. It would never do if an inspector of the Metropolitan Police engaged in the performance of his duty were to give way to emotion.

Later, of course, it was a different matter. 'I swear to you, Lizzie,' I said fervently when we stood alone on the front doorstep of the Chelsea house and I took my leave of her for the time being. 'When I saw that baby alive and well – or as well as the poor mite could be in the care of Mrs Dawson – I felt like shouting out "Hallelujah"!'

'I am so happy for Lucy,' Lizzie said. 'Although, Ben, to be honest, what will become of her now? She'll stay here, I suppose, at her Uncle Charles's home. Yet she's so inexperienced and there's no one to help her. They'll hire a nurse, I dare say. But Lucy needs someone at her side to look after her.'

'Not *you*, though, Lizzie,' I said gently.

'I understand it can't be me. It would only end in some disagreeable scene. I mean between Charles Roche and me. I couldn't keep silent indefinitely.' She sighed.

'Her Uncle Charles has a great deal on his conscience,' I told her, 'and will no doubt seek to do what he can—'

But here we were interrupted. Nearby a throat was cleared and a male voice asked diffidently, 'Excuse me. May I ask if you know whether Mr Charles Roche is at home?'

We both turned to see the speaker, a thin, pale, rather dishevelled young man. He stood on the pavement at the foot of the scrubbed stone steps to the front door, his hat in his hand.

'Who wants him?' I asked, before Lizzie could answer.

He flushed. 'My name is Craven,' he said. 'I recently arrived from China. I took a fever on board ship and I have been lying sick at a rooming house in Bristol for the past week or more. I – I am married to Mr Roche's niece and seeking to know her whereabouts.'

I turned back to Lizzie and raised my eyebrows. 'Shall I take him inside, Lizzie?'

'No,' she replied firmly, 'I'd like to do that, if you don't mind. Come along, Mr Craven, you've arrived at a very good moment.'

Chapter Twenty-two

Elizabeth Martin

'THOSE TWO women shouldn't have been locked in together,' grumbled Ben. 'If I'd been there, I'd have prevented it. If I'd known they were together upstairs when I arrived, I'd have sent Morris up immediately to separate them. But by the time I did find out, and we did separate them, they'd had plenty of time to concoct a story.'

'I'm sorry,' I said for the umpteenth time, 'I really am. I did not foresee that.'

'Why should you? No, no, it's not your fault, Lizzie. Don't think I mean that. You don't deal with criminals every day. I do. I know their tricks and ability to invent an alibi out of thin air.'

He referred, of course, to that precious half-hour when Christina Roche and Higgins the maid had been locked in the bedroom at Shore House and the rest of us had been arguing downstairs. I should have suspected Higgins's eagerness to be shut away with her mistress, and not been surprised that the two had used the time profitably to frustrate the law.

The fact was that Miss Roche was never charged with the murder of Jethro Brennan. We should have realised, from the fuss made by Charles Roche right at the beginning when he realised his sister had been arrested, and the excuses he at once began to concoct for her, that it might well turn out so. Miss Roche vehemently denied murder when questioned by Ben. Nothing she had said before his arrival on the scene, suggesting she admitted it, had been said before an officer of the law. Now it was agreed she had been confused by the horrific events and 'didn't know what she had been saying'. Dr Lefebre had obligingly confirmed that derangement of mind occasionally led sufferers to make false statements, sometimes of an incriminating nature. With such an authority to back up the story, I ought to have expected this version of events would be generally accepted.

I wasn't one of those happy to go along with this whitewash. But who listens to a companion? Ben listened, of course, but pointed out I was a lone dissenter and, on my own, I couldn't persuade a jury there was a case against the lady.

'There is no charge against her that will stand up in a court of law, Lizzie,' Ben had declared ruefully.

Nor would it. No witness had seen her kill Brennan. My arguments were circumstantial. As for the destruction of the gown, up stepped the loyal Higgins to swear that she was responsible for destroying the article, after it had been spoiled by an over-hot smoothing iron. Miss Roche had told her to dispose of it, and that was what she'd done. This was the story no doubt so cleverly thought up during that half-hour the women spent together.

So the death of Brennan was put down to an unknown quarrel with some unknown fellow ruffian. He was, after all, only a rat-catcher.

Christina had organised the kidnapping of the baby, that

couldn't be denied. But the child had been found and returned. No one was now anxious to press charges. All agreed Miss Roche had acted wrongly; but her judgement had been influenced by her state of mind. A highly strung lady, the worry about her niece had deeply affected her. The 'Providence' she had spoken of to me as placing Mrs Brennan and her dead infant in her path that day on the heath, she now called 'a higher power' which had directed her. It was decided that she was insane and directed she take up residence for some suitable period in Dr Lefebre's private establishment for the mentally ill.

Incidentally, it turned out little Louisa Craven had not been the first baby Brennan had carried, for a fee, to the workhouse. It had been quite a profitable sideline of his.

Now even the young parents, under pressure, fell into line with the rest of the family. There is truly, as I observed to Ben, no limit to the measures the respectable classes will take to protect their precious reputations.

'I could have told you that,' was his grim reply. 'But I shan't forget. The murder of Brennan lies unsolved on our files. Who knows, perhaps one day in the future Higgins may change her testimony. She certainly has a hold over the family they'll already be regretting. There may be a falling-out. We'll see. Higgins may be loyal, but I'm sure she can also be vindictive.'

It would have been nice to believe that Lucy and James Craven might settle down and establish themselves as a model family. Her Uncle Charles, it seemed, was now prepared to relinquish some of the grip he had on her fortune until her twenty-first birthday. The couple and their child would be comfortably established. I did wonder if this change of heart was due in any part to an agreement that they, in return, would 'forget' the abominable behaviour of Christina Roche. I hoped James wouldn't gamble or drink away Lucy's money. Perhaps his experiences in China had taught him a lesson.

So I tried to be optimistic. But my experience of Lucy was that she was so volatile, her reactions to anything could never be judged. James appeared equally unpredictable in his actions. Between the pair of them, there was no knowing what they might do.

As for me, there was nothing more I could contribute. I found myself back in Dorset Square with Aunt Parry. This was strictly on a temporary basis, it was understood, until a suitable new situation might arise for me.

Charles Roche had offered me a new position, that of companion to his sister Phoebe. As his other sister Christina was 'for the present elsewhere', as he put it, and Phoebe was unused to being without female companionship, perhaps I would consider . . .? I declined his offer. It was made, I suspected, in order to have me under his eye. I knew the truth of what had happened at Shore House. He was afraid I'd gossip. I don't gossip, but it would do Charles Roche no harm to worry that I might.

Aunt Parry was a little embarrassed at having suggested the post at Shore House in the first place. I fancy she felt some obligation to me. Also she hadn't managed to find a replacement companion during my absence, so I was more or less welcomed back.

I hadn't, however, seen the last of Dr Lefebre. One afternoon he called on me unexpectedly in Dorset Square.

'I feel I owe you some explanation, Miss Martin,' he said.

He sat on a chair in Aunt Parry's drawing room, just as neat and debonair as ever. Aunt Parry wasn't present; she'd gone to a whist party with some friends. It was just as well. I was sure Lefebre was precisely the sort of man to make a great impression on her.

'You owe me none whatsoever, Doctor,' I replied.

'But I see you disapprove of me and my actions.' He said this with a slight smile.

I was annoyed to feel my cheeks burn. 'I don't think you've behaved entirely well, Doctor. But my views are of no matter to you.'

'On the contrary, it distresses me to think you have such a poor opinion of me. In the short time of our acquaintance, my opinion of you has been more than favourable. I've formed a great admiration for you, Miss Martin.'

Oh, good grief! Thank goodness Aunt Parry wasn't here to listen to this; and I certainly wouldn't be telling Ben of it.

'But I see you're not impressed by my admiration,' he went on.

My face has always betrayed me. 'I'd rather you didn't express it,' I admitted.

'I never lied to you,' he assured me. 'I didn't go down to Hampshire to observe Lucy Craven. I went to observe Christina Roche and report to her brother how she was coping with a stressful situation.'

'You didn't lie to me, Doctor. I know that. But you were far from frank. You did nothing to correct the false impression Lucy had that you'd come to make a judgement on her state of mind. You concealed important knowledge from me. Yours was a sin of omission, if you like, rather than of commission. You could have spoken one sentence concerning Christina Roche's temperament, given one warning, but you didn't. That one sentence might have changed everything. Even before that, you allowed a vulnerable girl about to be delivered of her first child, to be put in the care of a woman of unstable emotions and warped sentiments!'

He had paled. 'You're harsh in your condemnation of me. I knew Christina Roche to be unpredictable, even eccentric, but I swear to you, I never thought she'd behave in such an extreme way.' He leaned forward earnestly. 'It's humiliating for me to have to admit this to you, but I misjudged the situation. I should have been more aware of the possibility that things might deteriorate. I underestimated the degree of her mania, for mania it is, this obsession with respectability. I hope you don't think I conspired to pervert the course of justice. I gave my opinion before a judge that she is insane, and I stand by it. I told you once before, not every mad person is a gibbering idiot. Many do appear as sane as you and I. Christina Roche is one of those. But her mind is beyond reasonable awareness of her actions.'

'Believe me,' I hastened to say. 'I have no wish to see Miss Roche or any other woman hang. Nor am I arguing that she's sane. I'm quite sure she isn't. I'll never forget the look in her eyes when she found me in her room . . .'

'You were in danger then,' he said quietly. 'And for that I'll never forgive myself.'

'Well, she's in your care now and you can observe her as much as you need. Please, Dr Lefebre, I don't wish to discuss this with you any further.'

He looked at me for a moment and then rose to his feet. 'Then I'll take my leave. I apologise for imposing my presence on you.'

I moved to tug at the bell pull and summons Simms, the butler, to escort my visitor out.

As we stood awkwardly awaiting his arrival, Lefebre suddenly said, 'I shall always remember you, Miss Martin, sitting on the ferryboat, with the wind catching at your hair and the breeze making your cheeks glow like cherries. I thought you beautiful and later I decided you were also intelligent, such a rare combination.'

Fortunately at that moment Simms arrived and I was spared

having to reply. I don't know quite what I should have said. Lefebre bowed and left briskly.

That was the last I saw of him. Yet I have an indelible memory of him, even as he claimed to have one of me. If I see someone waving a handkerchief in a farewell gesture, or even washing pegged out on a line and undulating in a gentle breeze, I see Dr Lefebre sitting across from me in the railway carriage, a silk veil draping his hat. Then it is as though someone has lit a candle in a strange and darkened room. There is a rasp of the match catching, the flame flickers and leaps into life; and things are revealed of which one had not the slightest indication beforehand.

I was perhaps too harsh on Lefebre. His situation had been a difficult one. Who doesn't hide some awkward fact, perhaps to oblige a friend? Who doesn't hesitate to make a statement that will 'set the cat among the pigeons'? What medical man is not cautious in his diagnosis? How can he discuss someone who may be his patient with an outsider? But I still felt that Lefebre had somehow misled me at Shore House.

Ben would say, of course, that half of London flies under false colours, if not all of the time, then at least some of it. It is the way of the world. Perhaps he's right. He told me that just before he came down to Hampshire, he had charged a dreadful man with deliberately abandoning a baby of eighteen months on King's Cross station. The plight of all the unwanted children up and down the country distressed me greatly. My own upbringing had been haphazard, but I'd always been loved.

Not all unwanted children lived in poor families. In well-to-do families, too, a child might become an 'inconvenience', due perhaps to remarriage, or being a girl when a boy was desired, or plain and awkward when pretty and charming was wanted. Or even, like Lucy, be the hapless orphaned baby with a quarter stake in the family firm, an object of fear and resentment.

The fate of these wealthy unloved children varied. They might be left alone with only servants to care for them; be bundled off to boarding schools, some of them with harsh regimes; or physically well cared for but emotionally neglected. 'A half-finished piece of embroidery left on a chair', was how young Lucy Roche had heartbreakingly described herself before her marriage. No wonder she clung to the man who had said he loved her!

I didn't tell Ben about Lefebre's visit, any more than I told him of Charles Roche's suggestion I become companion to his sister Phoebe. I could well imagine his reaction to either piece of news.

Ben seemed content that I was living in Dorset Square again, for the time being, at any rate.

'At least I know where you are,' he said. 'Let this be a warning to you, Lizzie!'

'Very well! Don't preach at me, Ben.'

'I'm not preaching and I don't want us to argue. But I do want you to be . . .'

'Yes?' I asked when he fell silent.

He shook his head. 'In truth I don't want you any other way than you are.'

This was straying into territory I wanted to avoid. I sought to change the direction of this conversation by saying, 'I can't help thinking of Andrew Beresford. What will he do? He would have looked after Lucy and made her happy, given half a chance.'

'Given a chance, we'd all like to make the woman we love happy,' said Ben simply.

'Thank you,' I said after a long silence. 'But we always seem thrown together in such violent circumstances. How can we forget all these things and just concentrate on ourselves?'

'Or how can you be married to an inspector of police who will

come home to his dinner from a scene of indescribable wicked-
ness and horror?'

'Don't!' I said quickly. 'I only need some time.'

'Of course.' After a moment he went on awkwardly: 'We are still
walking out, aren't we, Lizzie?'

'Yes, Ben,' I told him. 'We are still walking out.'

Although the inscription below is found on a gravestone in Oxfordshire, in Chipping Norton parish churchyard, and not in Hampshire, (and is one hundred years earlier than the date of Lizzie's journey to the south coast), nevertheless it provided the spark from which this story grew.

Here
Lieth the Body of
PHILLIS wife of
JOHN HUMPHREYS
Rat Catcher
Who has lodged
In many a Town
And Traveled [sic] far and near
By Age and death
Shee [sic] is struck down
To her last lodging here
Who died June Yar [sic] 1763
Aged 58